EDELAINE'S FOLLY

BOOK ONE OF THE IDORAMIN CHRONICLES

MORIGAN SHAW

Dedication

To my son, Deven — this book simply would not exist without you and your huge imagination. You cheered me on and gave the green-light to ideas, and your art and maps are incredible. (yes, I may be biased… but you are awesome!)

Love you to Idoramin and back!

Acknowledgements

To Kim at Atlantis Book Design (http://www.atlantisbookdesign.com)
You are brilliant! I can't thank you enough for all your hard work and talent!

CONTENTS

EXPLORE DEEPER INTO THE WORLD OF IDORAMIN

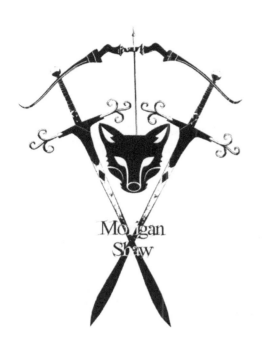

Register for behind-the-scenes access to Edelaine's Folly and the world of Idoramin

- Director's cut – deleted scenes from the book
- Exclusive maps, available nowhere else
- Early-bird pricing and access to upcoming Idoramin Chronicles
- Peek into the lives of your favorite characters like never before

"Yes, but what form would you have Time take in this mortal realm, young Cali? Time is a precious and precarious thing, it creeps along, there one moment and gone the next."

~ EAPARIUS

CHAPTER I

The metallic clank of swords and dull thuds of shields echoed in Cali's head.

As the fiery rage of battle closed in, a distracting bead of sweat tickled down the back of her neck. The long line of archers in their leathers stepped forward, loosing a volley of arrows, and with that, the tide of battle began to –

"Cali! Cal!" Her mom yelled. "Get your nose out of that book and get down here. You'll need some lunch before heading off to the west field."

"Yes, Mum, on my way," Cali yelled back.

Placing the braided ribbon in the book, she stood, stretching as the warm summer breeze rustled the tree leaves overhead. She'd have to wait until tomorrow to find out if the battle turned.

Walking down the hill she could smell the fresh-baked bread and something else… the faint whiff of cinnamon. She picked up the pace to the back-kitchen door.

The table was almost full, with some of the farmhands standing around eating before heading back out for the afternoon's work.

Cali was heading to the west fields today with her father and some workers to check the fences and animals. They had lost some livestock over the last month and needed to check the traps they'd set out.

Cali grabbed a bowl of her mom's famous sausage and wild rice, and added gravy over the top, sitting down to eat.

"Callera Flynn, why on earth do you cover up your food with gravy like that?" her mom laughed.

But of course, her mom reveled in the fact that everyone from family to farmhands loved her cooking. And even though she poked fun at Cali for putting gravy on everything, there always seemed to be fresh gravy made.

"Hey Cali girl, what're you reading on today?" Bodric asked.

Bodric was a dear friend of their family, and had been on the farm since before Cali was born. He helped teach her to ride and shoot and loved to hear her talk about the stories she was always reading.

"Oh, you know, Bodric, still the same one as last time," Cali replied between bites.

"Bodric, you know her, she fills her head with those fae-tales, of far-off lands and battles between good and evil. Silly stuff," her mom laughed again.

"Yes, Mum, and I was just getting to the battle when you called for me," Cali complained.

Her mom rolled her eyes, laughing and turned back to the stove.

They ate and brought their plates over to the large sink before heading out to the fields for work. Cali, Bodric, and her dad, Erwin, gathered supplies and headed out to the west fields.

Cali brought her large skinning knife and the short bow that Bodric hand-carved for her. They were hoping to catch what had attacked their animals, thinking it was maybe a wolf or a small bear. Cali, who was quickly turning into the best skinner and leatherworker of the lot, hoped to skin the beast.

It took some time, but they made it to the west fields. The animals were all accounted for, so they split up to check the fences. Nothing out of the ordinary, only normal needed fence repairs.

As Cali turned the last bend of her section of the fence she heard a quiet mewling coming from the woods. It sounded like a baby animal, a kitten perhaps.

Always careful, she readied her bow and stepped toward the tree line. The sound was close, and she searched the area to see if there were any large animals about. She saw a large fox laying near a tree, killed by the same animal that was terrorizing their flock it seemed. The silence under the heavy canopy of trees made the cries seem louder.

Keeping her arrow nocked and ready she continued to look around and found the source of the crying. A baby fox! Making sure there were no other animals around, she turned back to the baby fox. The dead fox must have been its mother. Putting her bow on her back, she took out her knife and knelt near the baby fox.

It was tiny, with a reddish-brown coat and some white around its muzzle. It had a large bushy tail, and its ears seemed twice as large as its head. Cali knew she couldn't leave it here to the same fate of its mom.

She pulled an apple out of her knapsack and cut off a small

piece with her knife. She sat near the fox and held the slice of apple close to it. The baby fox was still crying, but after a bit, its hunger ruled out and it inched toward Cali.

Sitting very still, she kept the apple slice in her hand and let the fox come to her. It grabbed the apple slice and backed away, eating quickly. Moving slowly, she cut another small piece of the apple and laid her hand on the ground again. The baby was quicker to come take the apple slice this time and didn't move so far away.

Cali was getting ready to cut another piece of the apple when she heard something moving in the underbrush nearby. Something definitely bigger than a fox. A shiver ran up her spine as her hair stood on end. She quickly grabbed the baby fox, and with the knife in hand backed slowly out of the tree line and to the fence. Whatever the animal was, it didn't follow her, but she could feel it was near.

As she reached the fence, Bodric and her dad were walking in her direction. Seeing her backing up brandishing her knife they ran to her side, then went into the trees after the larger animal.

She knew her dad and Bodric would be fine, they were both experienced hunters. The fox had started mewling again. She held him close while she pulled her other apple from her knapsack. She took a small bite of the apple and put it in her hand for the fox to eat.

Sometime later her dad and Bodric came out of the trees carrying between them what looked to be a large boar. Not an animal you would want to run into without a weapon. The large protruding tusks were longer than Cali's hand, and it still had blood on its muzzle from its latest kill.

"Hey looky at this beastie, Cali girl!" Bodric said with a huge grin. "We'll have to roast this one up!"

The thought of roasting a boar over the pit near the back garden made Cali's mouth water. She hadn't realized how long they had been gone to the west fields, but the sun had started sinking behind the trees.

"I have a beastie of my own! Da, Bodric, come look," Cali said.

The baby fox had decided it trusted Cali enough after stuffing itself full of apple, and it fell asleep curled in the crook of her arm.

"Cali. Sweetie, you know how much work that little guy will be, right?" her dad asked.

"Yes, Da. But I won't leave him out here to fend for himself, he's too little," Cali said, ready to argue her side.

"Okay, but he's yours, and yours alone."

And with that, they turned to head home with a fresh boar and a new baby fox in tow.

CHAPTER
2

It took much longer to return from the west fields with the weight of the large boar. The sun slid behind the mountains and darkness settled in.

Bodric talked about how he was looking forward to the smell of roasting boar. Erwin thought they should invite all the farmhands and their families over and make a gathering of it. Cali was most looking forward to working the hide into a new quiver or belts, or even a coat.

When they finally came into view of the house, Bethal, Cali's mom, came out to meet them.

"Well, that certainly does explain a lot!" She said, seeing the boar swinging between them as they walked.

"Beth, honey, our daughter has something to show you. I told her she could keep it, but that it was her responsibility," Erwin said, with a half-smile.

"Cali, what did you drag home now?" Her mom demanded.

"Mum! Look, isn't he just adorable? He's sweet as he can be, and he really likes me."

Rolling her eyes, her mom looked at the little furry bundle as he yawned and stretched in Cali's arms.

"A fox! Really, Cali?"

"Mum, I couldn't leave him there, I just couldn't. That boar got his mother, he was all by himself!"

Bethal knew better than to try to argue with her daughter about it. Cali had a big heart and animals just seemed to love her.

"Okay, honey. But he is yours. You have to train him and take care of him. I won't have some wild fox running around here stealing food and trying to eat the chickens!" Bethal sighed. "Now, there's food in the kitchen, you all go in and help yourself, everyone else already ate."

"We'll go get this boar handled, and we'll be in," Erwin said as they turned toward the small barn.

Bodric and Cali made quick work of the boar. Pleased with the hide they put it on the rack. She saved the coarse, quill-like hair to see if one of the farmhands knew how to make brushes. Her dad and Bodric hung and salted the beast, and decided tomorrow morning they'd invite everyone for the roast.

Famished and tired, they headed to the house to eat and rest. They sat at the table, talking about how the others would be happy to know the culprit behind their livestock deaths was no more.

Bodric said he and some hands would ride to the neighboring farms the following morning and invite them to the feast, and spread the good news.

Cali took an extra blanket and made a small bed on the floor beside her own for the baby fox. He'd had a big day, and although he whimpered a bit, he seemed to adjust well enough.

As Cali lay in bed, she looked down at the little fox. "We'll have to find a good name for you. What do you think? We'll give it a few days and see what name fits you." She scratched his ears and drifted toward sleep.

∞   ∞   ∞

Cali woke as the light came in through her window. The little fox had climbed on her bed and curled up against her during the night. The first smells of breakfast came floating in, and her little fox woke up sniffing too.

"Come on, little fella, let's go see what Mum's cooked up for breakfast."

"Good morning! I see our new family member is still doing good," Cali's dad said as she came into the large kitchen.

"Morning, Da, Mum. He's doing great. I am going to give it a couple days to see what name suits him. He seems to like it here!"

"Of course he does, honey," Cali's mom said. "You've always had a way with animals." She smiled as she put a plate of eggs and sausages down in front of Cali.

"Bodric has already headed out to the other farms to spread the word about the boar," Erwin said. "You stay around the house today and help your mother out to get things ready for the gathering."

"Sure, Da. I was going to start training the little fella, and I wanted to work on that hide," Cali said.

Smiling, Erwin shook his head at his daughter and her new fox. He stood, giving Bethal a quick kiss, and headed out the kitchen door. Cali thought it was sweet how her parents wore matching pendants. She would have to remember to ask her Mum about them sometime, she thought to herself.

"Mum, do you need me to do anything now?" Cali asked.

"Not much, honey. But if you could bring me some fresh carrots and onions from the back garden, that would help," Bethal replied.

Cali and the little fox headed out the kitchen door to the small garden next to the kitchen. Grabbing a basket, she headed to the carrots first. The little fox jumped and tried to play with the carrots as Cali shook the dirt off. He scampered and hopped around the garden, chasing bugs and butterflies as she worked.

Cali let out a low whistle to see if the fox would respond, but he kept right on playing in the garden. She stood, walking to the row with onions, and as soon as the little fox saw her walking, he ran over to follow her. She let out the low whistle again. He looked up at her with his head cocked to the side.

"Good boy! When I whistle, that means you come to me. But don't worry, we'll work on it." Cali smiled.

She took the vegetables back to her mother. "Anything else I can do, Mum?"

"No, mostly it's just cooking to do. Why don't you go check your hide, and train up your little friend there?"

Cali grabbed an apple and headed out toward the small barn. Even in the dark, she had done a good job cleaning and racking the hide. In the clear morning light, the boar looked even larger than when they carried it home last night. She was thankful she hadn't gotten any closer to it when she rescued the baby fox.

Examining the hide closer, it was very thick. It was a good strong hide, and Cali was anxious to work with it. She was already imagining a new quiver, belts, and...

"A collar!" Cali said. Scratching the little fox behind the ears, she said, "I'll make you a collar, oh, and maybe some armor to protect you from any future boars!" she laughed.

Cali and the little fox spent the rest of the morning playing in the field near the fire pit. The fox was a quick learner and seemed to pick up on Cali's instructions well. They shared the apple and headed back to the kitchen to see if her mom needed any help.

"Ah, perfect timing, Cali! Can you bring me that basket of potatoes by the door, please?" Her mom said.

As Cali carried the basket of potatoes, one fell and rolled across the floor. The little fox instantly gave chase, tackling the potato and playing with it with happy little barks.

Bethal laughed. "Well, he seems to be making himself right at home, eh? Any luck starting to train him?"

"He's doing great, Mum. Watch!" Cali let out a low whistle. The little fox looked up from his potato, looking at Cali. She gave another whistle and he hopped up and ran over to her. "Good boy! And good job chasing down that potato!" Cali laughed, scratching him behind his ears.

"That's it!" Cali said. "I'll call you Chase. What do you think, little fella?" The little fox rolled over looking up happily at Cali. "What do you think, Mum?"

"Well, he does seem to like to chase things. And he seems to like it. Chase it is! Welcome to the family, little Chase," her mom replied as she began cleaning potatoes.

Several of the wives gathered to help with the cooking the next morning. They expected the gathering to be bigger than the last. The weather was perfect, the heat of the day had eased, and farmhands and neighbors from nearby farms started arriving mid-afternoon. They marveled at the size of the boar and complimented Cali on a fine hide.

Jenkins from the closest farm asked if she had enough hide left if she would make him a new set of straps for his plow. Cali was excited, this would be her first real paying job in leatherworking.

Everyone helped themselves to the delicious boar and food and sat around the fire pit late into the evening talking and comparing farm stories. The young ones ran around the field playing and having fun with Chase. The sense of relief over the boar was obvious with all the farmers.

Cali and Chase sat a bit away from the fire pit with friends from the neighboring farms. The Jenkins boys, Rowan and Jorah, Sarah from the Calbert farm, and Flora and her two young twin sisters from the Nomarr farm. They all loved hearing the story of how Cali rescued Chase.

"I would've shot that boar right between his big eyes if I'd been there with you, Cali!" Jorah boasted.

Rowan, his older brother, punched him in the shoulder and shook his head.

"Right, Jorah, and when the arrow bounced off its skull and he charged you down?" Rowan asked, laughing.

They all laughed and joked about how they would have taken down the boar and saved the fox at the same time. Then started making plans to go to the lake soon.

As the night wore on, their friends began to leave, heading back to their own homes. With congratulations and pats on the back to Bodric and Erwin, they left, fading into the darkness until only Bodric and her parents remained around the fire.

Chase climbed up on Cali's lap and fell asleep. "Mum, Da, I'm going to turn in."

"Goodnight, honey." They called back as Cali carried Chase into the house.

She didn't bother putting Chase on his blanket, instead curling up in her bed with him next to her. Hearing her parents and Bodric outside talking, she soon drifted away into a deep sleep.

∞   ∞   ∞

"Are you sure this boar was what attacked the animals, Erwin?" Bethal asked.

They were still sitting around the fire with Bodric as the others had all left. Bethal fiddled with her pendant, staring into the flames.

"Fairly certain. It seems the likely culprit. It had blood on its muzzle. And an animal that size would explain how many of the livestock had been killed or gone missing." Erwin replied.

"Aw, don't you worry now, Bethal," Bodric said. "That old boar was trouble. And if there are any others, we'll find them and roast them up too!"

Bethal laughed. "True. And I'm sure we'd get no complaints from everyone if we had another boar roast! Still, just seems odd that a boar that size would have just suddenly turned up."

Erwin eyed his wife. "Beth, it's just a boar. And at worst, maybe two boars. If there is another we'll get it. But don't worry yourself about it. There's nothing to show that it's anything more than just that, they probably just came down from the mountains."

"You're right, Erwin. You both are right. I'm just tired I think." Bethal replied.

Bodric laughed, "I would say you should be given how much food you put together today! I'll be heading home, myself. Day will be here before we know it."

Erwin took Bethal's hand and stood up. "We're calling it a night, too. We'll see you in the morning, Bodric. No hurry though, get some rest."

Bodric raised his hand in a wave as he left, as Bethal and Erwin headed into the house.

CHAPTER
3

"Mum, I'm going to head over to the Jenkins farm this morning, if that's okay? I've finished those plow straps he wanted, and I was going to take them over to him," Cali said.

"Yes, honey, that's fine. Are you going to ride over so you can get back by lunch?" Bethal asked.

"Yes, Mum. And Chase has gotten very good at following with me when I'm riding, so he can come along."

"I didn't expect anything else, Chase is always with you!" her mom laughed. "Just be careful and come back as quick as you can. Oh, and take Jenkins some of this jam that I made."

Cali packed the jars of jam along with the new straps into the saddlebag of her horse. Her mom had surprised her with a sort of a sling so that she could carry Chase while still having her hands free. He was growing fast, but sometimes still wanted Cali to carry him.

She adjusted her bow on her back and put Chase in the sling, so he could ride with her for a bit. They climbed up into the saddle and set off towards Jenkins' farm. It was a bit of a trip, but on horseback, she shouldn't be gone past midday. She was anxious to get back, she wanted to start working on her new quiver, and the collar for Chase.

Passing through the east fields, Cali waved at the farmhands. Ahead, the trees grew thick and closed in around the road that led to other parts of Edelaine, including Jenkins' farm. She urged the horse on to a trot, excited to deliver the straps to Jenkins and get her first pay.

It had taken slightly longer than normal to fully prep the boar's hide for working since it was thicker than the hides she normally worked with. She was surprised that it wasn't much more difficult to work than the thinner hides though.

Cali hoped Jenkins would like the new straps. She had cut the straps and embellished the edges with thin rawhide stitches for reinforcement.

It was cooler here on the road under the thick trees, but the day was going to turn hot. Cali wanted to make quick work of this and head back home before it got too humid. She decided once she got back, she would work on Chase's collar first.

Chase seemed content in his sling and didn't want to run alongside, he alternated between napping and looking around.

Cresting the top of a hill she could see the small road to Jenkins farm ahead on the right. Unlike Cali's family farm, you didn't have to go through fields before getting to his house. She rode up, tying her horse to the post as Jenkins walked around the corner of the house.

"Young Miss Cali!" Jenkins shouted, raising his hand in welcome. "How are you on this beautiful day?"

"Hi, Jenkins! I'm doing great, thanks. Mum sent you over some jam, and I've brought your new plow straps."

"Oh, Cali, you have made my day! I'm not sure which I'm more excited about. Those old straps of mine are about worn through." Jenkins replied. "Come on in the house, let me get your pay."

They walked inside when Chase poked his nose out to look around. Cali sat at the kitchen table as Jenkins went to get her pay. He stopped by the back door telling Rowan to go say hello to Cali.

"Father, really, Cali is a bit young, don't you think? I'll not be married off yet!" Rowan complained but did as his father asked.

Rowan walked into the kitchen nonchalantly, with Jorah running in excitedly right behind him.

"Hi, Cali. Oh, your mom sent jam?" Rowan asked seeing the jars on the table.

"Cali! It's great to see you! Hey, when are we all going to head over to the lake?" Jorah asked, his words coming out all in a rush.

"Hi! Yes, that is from Mum's latest batch, and there's more where that came from." Cali smiled. "Hi, Jorah, it's been so hot, we ought to get everyone to the lake soon before summer is gone."

"Here you go, young lady. My, that little fox is growing! He's almost twice as big as when I saw him at the gathering! You've got him trained up good?" Jenkins said as he came back in the room.

"Yes, sir. He's a great friend, smart too," Cali replied. "Wow, Jenkins, this is more coin than I expected, are you sure?"

"Cali, you did fine work on these straps, you deserve no less. Oh, tell your father that old man Jossin was rambling on the other day about losing some sheep again. It's probably nothing, but I know he'd want to know."

"I sure will, Jenkins. I better be heading back, I told Mum I'd try to make it back by lunchtime!"

"Then you better be off, young miss! And tell your mother no one makes jams like her!" Jenkins laughed.

With several shiny silver coins jingling in her small drawstring purse, Cali and Chase pointed the horse back toward their farm and set off.

Chase ran alongside Cali on the ride back, jumping at bugs and the occasional leaf. With the sun at its peak and no breeze, it felt stifling even in the shade of the thick trees on the road. She was thrilled at the money she made from Jenkins and couldn't wait to tell everyone at home.

Suddenly, Chase stopped in the middle of the road with a low growl, looking into the forest. Cali jumped down from her horse thinking he may have hurt a paw and knelt beside him. He was trembling, fixed on whatever it was he sensed in the woods.

"What is it, boy?" Cali looked around at the trees but didn't see anything.

There were no sounds. Not even the rustling of leaves in the heavy air. Breaking out in a cold sweat she could feel eyes on her, but there were no eyes she could see. She scooped Chase into his sling, brandished her knife and got back on her horse. Something was not right here. Not right at all.

"Who's there?" Cali demanded. "I know you're there, come out!" She hoped she sounded more confident than she felt. A tremble of fear crept across her skin raising the hair on her arms. She needed to get away from there.

Urging the horse to a full run with her heels, she leaned forward to protect Chase and gain speed. Once she entered the east fields she finally slowed and rode on to the house. Bethal saw Cali ride up and met her by the back garden.

"Hi, sweetie, I'm glad you made it back before lunch. Are you okay, you look a bit shaken?" Bethal asked. A farmhand came over and took the horse to the barn.

"Mum, I've got some great news, but I have to tell you something else first."

They walked into the kitchen. Cali sat at the table, Chase hopped down and sat beside her. Bethal poured a cold drink and handed it to her daughter.

"Mum, there was something in the woods about halfway back from Jenkins. I think there's another boar or something out there. And Jenkins said to tell dad that old man Jossin said he had some sheep go missing." Cali said in a rush.

Bethal's eyes widened. "Did you see this animal, Cali?" she asked, then called out the door to the worker to go find Erwin.

"No, Mum. I didn't see it. Chase sensed it first and was mad and scared. And I could feel it looking at me, I know it was there, I could feel it there, Mum, I could!" Cali said, trying to convince her mother.

"Cali, honey, it's okay, I believe you. You and Chase are safe and back home. It's okay. Here comes your dad, let's tell him and then you can tell us your good news." Bethal smiled. Her smile didn't quite reach her eyes though.

Cali told the whole story to her dad and Bodric who had come in too. Erwin and Bodric planned to ride over to see old man Jossin the next day and would look along the road to see if they could see any signs of the animal.

"Now, what's this good news?" Bethal tried to lighten the subject.

"Oh, Mum! You aren't going to believe this!" Cali jumped up and jingled her drawstring pouch around. Chase bounced around at her feet. Cali proudly poured her coins out onto the table for everyone to see.

"Well, looky at that, Cali girl!" Bodric said. "You're a gonna be richer than all of us soon!" he laughed.

"That's good pay for those straps, Cali." Her dad said. "Did you see Rowan while you were there?"

Bethal lightly smacked Erwin's shoulder. She knew that Jenkins not-so-secretly hoped that Rowan and Cali would eventually be married. She also knew that Cali had no interest in Rowan, even if he was a handsome older boy.

"Sure did, Da. And Jorah, too. We are going to get everyone and go to the lake soon," Cali said.

"You know, honey, that Jorah is a good boy, and he's only a year older than you," Bethal said slyly.

"Mum!" Cali rolled her eyes and headed to her room. She put her coins away, then headed out to the small barn to work on Chase's collar.

She had forgotten all about the animal in the woods, and was focused on what she was going to make next, and if she should start making leather items to sell to the other farms.

∞   ∞   ∞

"Erwin, you and Bodric go and check that place out tomorrow. And you let me know what it is." Bethal said once she knew Cali was out of earshot heading to the barn.

"Beth, dear, it's just animals. I'm sure of it. Of course, I'll let you know either —"

"I think we need to sit her down and —" Bethal started.

Erwin held up his hand, interrupting his wife. "No, Beth. No. If we run into any sign this is anything other than just hungry, wild animals, then we'll talk about that. But right now? No."

Bethal wasn't convinced, but she trusted her husband.

"Bethal, I've known you all since we've been little sprouts, listen to Erwin on this one. You've got nothing to worry over. And that's a heavy burden to put on anyone, you know that best of all," Bodric said, trying to ease Bethal's mind.

"I know, and you're right. I just can't shake it. I guess I'm just jumping at shadows or boars in this case." Bethal laughed. "No, we won't tell her, no reason to."

"It's been generations since it was needed. Since well before our time. And there's no need now. Don't worry yourself." Erwin stood, giving his wife a kiss on the forehead.

"Bodric, come on, let's get a couple of the hands to go with us tomorrow, we'll stop by the other farms too and camp overnight at

Jossin's."

Bodric laid his hand on Bethal's shoulder. "Only thing to worry about is all that cooking for another boar roast coming up!" He winked, laughing as they headed out the door.

CHAPTER
4

Cali and Chase headed to the small barn right after breakfast. "Come on, Chase, we are going to finish your collar today!"

Chase happily bounced at her feet. She had oiled the collar yesterday and only needed to finish the sizing holes and fastening the buckle. As she was clamping the buckle onto the leather, Bodric walked up.

"Hey, Cali girl! I brought you a little something before we head off to find our next boar to roast!" Bodric smiled. He handed Cali a small leather pouch with a drawstring.

Excited she opened the pouch and poured the contents into her hand. A shiny tooth, encased in silver on the large end hanging from a thin rawhide string, and a smaller tooth with the same silver, but with no string, just a silver ring.

"One for you, one for your foxy!" Bodric smiled. "Here, let me put that on his collar for ya!"

Cali slipped the necklace around her neck, adjusting the rawhide sting to the right length. Then put Chase's new collar around his neck.

"Oh, Bodric, I love it! And Chase does too, look!" Chase

bounced around in the grass.

"Well, you and wee beastie there helped with the first boar, it was only right that you had a trophy from it!" Bodric replied.

Cali, Chase, Bethal and several farmhands were in the yard near the back garden to see Erwin, Bodric, and the others off on their trip. Bethal had packed plenty of food, dry clothes, ointments, and about anything else she could think of. She was nervous about their trip, but she knew Erwin was right to take the extra time to stop by the other farms.

"Cali, honey, you stay near the house and help out your mother while we're gone," Erwin said.

"Sure, Da, I will! If you find another boar, can you bring me the hide?" Cali asked, excited at the prospect.

They all laughed, Cali caught the leatherworker bug ever since selling the plow straps to Jenkins and wanted to try her hand at making more things.

"I sure will, Cali, don't you worry!" her dad laughed. And with a long look at his wife, they turned and headed up the road toward the east fields.

Before mid-morning, the group reached the spot where Cali had the encounter with the other boar. Dismounting, they looked around next to the road. There was no sign on the road of a large animal.

"She never saw the beast, but I believe we're looking for

another boar, boys. Let's head into the brush a piece and see what we can find. Stay within eyeshot of each other." Erwin said.

They spread out and headed into the undergrowth. The brush and thickets in this part of the woods were dense and heavy and made moving around difficult, but it would also make finding evidence of a large boar easy.

"Aye, fellas, come over this way, and step light," Bodric yelled.

They all met where Bodric was standing. Broken branches and twigs, leaves strewn about, and an obvious path back deeper into the forest. Kneeling, Bodric ran his hand over the ground, finding prints from what could be a boar, and looking up at Erwin.

"If this path and print are any sign, this boar is bigger than the first." Erwin rubbed his face, looking around at the thick, shadowed woods around them. "Let's set up a few traps, and head on up to the Jenkins farm. We'll stop by here on our way back."

As they were riding up to Jenkins' house, Jorah came quickly around the corner of the house and scanned the group. There was a flicker of disappointment on his face that Bodric couldn't help but smile at.

Jenkins came out on his porch. "Hello, Erwin! What brings you out on this beautiful day?"

"Hi, Jenkins, we are heading around to all the farms to see if anyone's having any more animals go missing. Have you had any problems here?" Erwin asked as he looked around at the farm.

"No, can't say as I have. It's been quiet. Do we have another wild animal around?"

"We believe so, Jenkins. Cali ran into something on her way

back from here yesterday on the road and —"

Jorah looked shocked and angry. "Is she okay, sir, it didn't hurt her right?"

Bodric coughed to keep from chuckling. Erwin smiled. "No, lad, she's perfectly fine, just had a little scare is all."

Jenkins gave his son a stern look. "No, Erwin, I appreciate you stopping by, but we haven't had any animals go missing. I know old man Jossin said he was missing some sheep, but that's all I've heard."

"Good, good. Jorah, you and Rowan stick close to the house here and make sure you all keep your weapons handy. If we're right, this boar looks larger than the first," Erwin said.

"Yes sir, we will, I'll make sure to tell Rowan as soon as he's back. We'll watch for it," Jorah replied. "Do you want me to ride over to your farm to check on things since you are heading further out?"

"That would be fine, Jorah. But if you do, make sure to take Rowan or a hand with you. No traveling on the road alone until we take this one down." Erwin smiled.

Rowan may have no interest in his daughter, but it was obvious to anyone with eyes that Jorah certainly did. He was a good boy, strong, tall, he looked young, but he was a capable lad.

As they turned to go, Erwin said, "Thanks, Jenkins, keep a sharp eye out and we'll let you know what we find."

The news was the same at both the Calbert farm and Nomarr's farm. Neither had any missing or dead animals, although Nomarr's farm had more broken fences than usual. Erwin warned them of the large boar that was roaming, and to keep the girls close to the farm and the hands armed when out in the fields.

They camped over at Nomarr's, heading out to the farthest farm, old man Jossin's, the next day. He had the best vineyards and sampled his own wines a bit more often than proper, but he was a good, honest farmer. Making steady time they reached Jossin's farm with plenty of day left.

Tired and dusty from the ride, Erwin and the group dismounted as Jossin stepped out of his barn.

"Oye there! Erwin Flynn, Bodric, it's good to see you, boys! What brings you all the way out here?" Jossin said, walking towards the group. He motioned for a farmhand to come take the horses.

"Jossin, it's good to see you! We think we have another boar roaming around, and got word that you've had some missing sheep again?" Erwin said, shaking Jossin's hand.

"Yeah, yeah, come on inside, all of you, my hands will water your horses. Let's go inside where it's cooler and we'll get you some drink from my latest barrel!" Jossin motioned for them to come in the house.

"I'm glad you came, Erwin. Yes, I've had some animals go missing again. But one that didn't get dragged off I found dead in the fields. But I tell you, I don't think this was any boar. It wasn't gored." Jossin shook his head.

"Oh? What then, a bear?" Bodric asked.

"Oh no, no, I don't think it was a bear either. I think we have some wolves running around. There weren't no claw marks, no goring, but plenty of ripping bites. I haven't found the others yet. I'm a bit too old to go hunting wolves, and I won't send my son out there alone."

Erwin rubbed his chin. "No, that's good, no one needs to be out in the woods alone till we get these animal attacks dealt with. Point us to where you think they are, we'll go check it out before it gets dark."

∞   ∞   ∞

"Jorah, you are seriously going to make me ride over to Cali's with you?" Rowan complained.

"Erwin is going to be gone until tomorrow sometime. They are there by themselves. And there's a large boar roaming around. We are going to the Flynn farm." Jorah wasn't taking any excuses.

"Brother, you know they have a small village of farmhands, right? I doubt they need our protection." He punched Jorah's shoulder. "Come on, let's go check on your sweet girl."

Jorah's face turned red as he punched Rowan back. "We'll be back soon, Father. We're going to ride over to the Flynn farm," Jorah called out.

They rode fast, not wanting to stay long. As they galloped up to the house, Bethal came out to greet them.

"Hi, boys! What can I do for you? Everything okay over at the farm?" Bethal asked.

"Yes, ma'am. We knew Erwin and the others would be gone to the other farms, so we wanted to ride over and check in on you," Rowan replied.

Bethal tried to hide her smile. "That's kind of you, come on in and take a rest. I've got some snacks."

Jorah and Rowan came in and sat at the kitchen table as Bethal set out a basket of fresh biscuits and different flavors of jam she had been making.

"Is Cali around, ma'am?" Jorah asked. "I know Erwin was telling everyone to stay close to their houses until this boar is caught."

"Oh, she's out in the small barn with Chase working. You say that Erwin said it was a boar?" Bethal asked, looking at the boys.

"Yes. They stopped by yesterday." Rowan answered.

"Jorah, why don't you go see about Cali, and tell her to come on back in the house as soon as she's finished up, would you?" Bethal asked.

Jorah jumped up and headed out of the kitchen in a flash. Both Bethal and Rowan smiled.

"Rowan, I know what your father thinks about Cali… and you. But I have to ask, what do you think?" Bethal looked at Rowan pointedly.

"Ma'am. Cali is a great girl, don't take me wrong." Rowan was caught off guard by her direct question.

"But?" Bethal prompted him to go on.

"But, she is like a younger sister to me. Please don't be mad. She is wonderful, and she would make some farmer a perfect wife, better than perfect!" Rowan stammered. "But, well, it's not me who is crazy about her."

Bethal smiled. "That's what I thought too, Rowan. Thank you for confirming it for me. So, now tell me what my husband said about this boar."

$$\infty \qquad \infty \qquad \infty$$

"Cali?" Jorah called out when he reached the barn. There was no answer. "Cali!" He called a little louder.

Cali stepped out from the corner of the barn, surprised to see Jorah.

"Jorah? What are you doing here?"

"Oh, hi, Cali. I was… well, your dad stopped by and told us about the boar, and that he would be gone until tomorrow, so I, Rowan and I, we came over to check in on you. And your mom." Jorah answered. "Oh, and your mom said to come in the house if you are done."

"I'm about finished, come look if you want," Cali said, turning to go into the barn.

She had cut several large pieces of the boar hide and soaked them. Now they were formed around a thick branch to form the shape of the quiver she was making.

"Cali, you are really good at this. Are you going to start selling the things you make?"

"I think so, Jorah. It's a lot of fun, and the coins I made from your father made me want to do more!" Cali laughed.

"Hey, what's that?" Jorah pointed at her necklace.

"Oh, this is one of the boar's teeth! Look, Chase has a matching one. Bodric made them for us, do you like it?"

"I do, it's great! Oh, we better get inside before your mom worries." Cali turned off the lanterns, leaving them in an almost darkened barn as they headed back to the house.

"Cali, there you are. Rowan was telling me about what your dad found with the boar." Bethal smiled at them.

"Cali, you and your mom be careful and keep an eye out. Jorah, we need to get back home before it starts getting dark." Rowan said.

Jorah looked at Cali, "We can ride back over in the morning to check in on you again."

Rowan glanced sideways at Bethal trying to hide his smile. "That's a good idea, Jorah. Would that be okay with you, ma'am?" he asked Bethal.

"Why, yes, Rowan, I'd appreciate that very much since Erwin won't be home until late tomorrow at the soonest. Thank you, boys," Bethal said.

∞   ∞   ∞

Erwin and the men rode into the fields with Jossin to the area where he found the dead sheep. "Here's the place." Jossin pointed to the repaired fence. "From what Tad and I could tell, they came from the area toward the foot of the mountains."

"Okay, Jossin. We'll go in a piece and see what we can find. You and Tad stay here with the horses and wait for us," Erwin said as he and his men dismounted and headed to the tree line.

It was clear from the smaller area of broken branches and the path disturbed in the underbrush that Jossin was correct and it was likely a wolf. Erwin nodded to Bodric and they set off with their farmhands to see what they could discover.

"Spread out, but not far, keep each other within a few paces distance. We don't know what we might run into out here." Erwin told the men softly as they headed into the woods.

A hundred or so paces in, they heard it. A low howl that seemed to come from ahead of them closer to the mountain. The men came back together and decided to go in two pairs to get the wolf from two different angles.

As Bodric and Erwin were the most experienced fighters, they each took one farmhand and headed further in. They quietly closed in on the area, shocked to discover it was not one wolf, but two.

Erwin silently motioned to Bodric for them to take the smaller of the two wolves, while he took out the larger wolf. The wolves caught their scent and started pacing anxiously, and in the second before they could strike, both wolves lunged, running full speed at Bodric.

Bodric and the farmhand took down the smaller wolf as it ran at them, and although Erwin and his man shot the larger wolf twice, it was still going for Bodric. It happened fast. Erwin heard Bodric's scream as he loosed two more arrows at the wolf fast as lightning.

Running fast, he dropped to his knees beside Bodric. The wolf tore a massive gash in his arm.

"He was a fast monster, eh?" Bodric laughed weakly.

"Hang on Bodric, we've got you, that wolf won't get anyone else. Hang on." Erwin said calmly as Bodric's fell into unconsciousness.

Erwin pulled off his shirt, ripping it in half, tightly wrapping one half around Bodric's arm.

"You, go back quick as you can and grab my horse, bring it here. Go!" Erwin shouted. "And you, keep your bow ready in case there are others."

He took the other piece of shirt and wrapped, then tied it tightly around Bodric's upper arm, slowing the flow of blood coming from the gaping wound. "Come on, Bodric, we've got you. Come on." But Bodric was still unconscious.

The man arrived back with Erwin's horse, and to the surprise of the men, Erwin lifted Bodric and put him on the horse with ease. He climbed on the horse behind Bodric and let out a yell, spurring the horse into a full run.

The farmhands followed, jumped on their horses, and along with Jossin and his son, Tad, followed Erwin back to Jossin's house.

They put Bodric on the long kitchen table. Jossin brought pillows and blankets to keep him warm. Tad started a fire in the cookstove and placed a large pot of water on the fire to boil.

"Jossin, do you have anything we can rip up and use?" Erwin asked.

"Of course, I'll get them." Jossin hurried into the other room.

"Tad, go to my saddlebag. There's a large jar of green ointment." Tad ran out the door to Erwin's horse.

Jossin came back in with a sheet he was already ripping into strips and putting half of them into the boiling pot of water. And then got a large bottle of dark liquor from the cabinet.

Erwin nodded at Jossin. Tad returned with the ointment.

"I need all of you to take a spot and hold him down. He's unconscious, but he may not be here in a second." Erwin uncorked the liquor with his teeth, and unwrapped Bodric's arm, fresh blood started oozing from the wound. He loosened the other piece tied around his upper arm, then poured the liquor over the wound. A shriek like a banshee's cry brought Bodric back to consciousness, but only for a moment.

"Here. My knife, heat it in the fire." Erwin handed his knife to Tad as he kept the pressure on the cleaned wound. There was a lot of blood on the floor, on Bodric, on Erwin.

"One more time, hold him down." Erwin took the heated knife and gently laid it flat along the edges of the jagged cut. Thankfully for him, Bodric remained unconscious as the skin sizzled under the heat of the blade. The blood flow stopped. Erwin had managed to cauterize it successfully.

Jossin took strips of the sheet out of the boiling water, letting them cool slightly and handing them to Erwin. The first one he poured some of the liquor on and gently cleaned Bodric's arm and around the wound to see if he had missed any other spots.

He then slowly loosened the shirt piece that was tied around his upper arm. Loosening it a little at a time to allow normal blood flow back into his arm, Erwin wanted to make sure the wound wouldn't start bleeding freely.

He liberally applied the green ointment to one side of another strip and wound it around Bodric's arm tightly enough to hold the wound closed. Erwin finished cleaning the blood from Bodric, then took a strip rinsed in cold water and applied it to Bodric's forehead.

Bodric's eyes fluttered open. Looking around in a bit of a daze he said, "Did you give that hellish beastie a sharp arrow for me?"

Erwin laughed a little. "I sure did, my friend. I sure did." They got him onto the couch in the other room and helped him lay down. Then made him drink some of the strong liquor.

Erwin went back to the kitchen. "Jossin, thank you. All of you, for your help. I think we got it in time." Erwin looked tired. From the other room, they heard groaning and headed back in to check on Bodric.

"You okay, Bodric?" Jossin asked as he knelt next to him.

The liquor had started working on Bodric, but he mumbled. "Get the hides. Erwin. Get hides for Cali." And then he fell asleep.

They all laughed. "The hides. He's worried about getting the wolf hides for Cali." Erwin shook his head at his friend.

"Me and the hands will go back out and bring the wolves in," Tad said. "You and dad stay here and watch over Bodric."

Erwin stood and shook Tad's hand. "Thanks, Tad, truly. Watch yourselves out there, I don't think there were others, but be safe."

As Tad and the hands headed back out, Erwin took the bottle of liquor and poured himself and Jossin a large cup.

Erwin stayed by Bodric's side the entire night, taking short naps in the chair next to him and checking on his arm while his friend slept.

It looked like they had gotten it in time, there was no unusual swelling, redness or heat. But he would wait until Bodric woke in the morning to see if he thought he would be okay to travel back home.

The next morning, the smell of frying sausages and coffee woke Erwin. He immediately checked on Bodric, no fever, pulse felt good and strong. He left him to sleep and walked into the kitchen.

"You did good, Erwin. Bodric looks to be doing fine if a little pale." Jossin said setting a huge pile of sausages on the table beside of an enormous bowl of scrambled eggs. "You should try to wake him and see if we can get him to eat a bit." He handed a plate of food to Erwin. He went back to Bodric and pulled his chair close.

After Bodric was sound asleep out the night before, Tad had lifted Bodric into a sitting position while Erwin tied Bodric's arm in a sling against his chest.

The sling was still holding Bodric's arm securely, but Erwin was careful not to jostle him when he tried to wake him up. Bodric squinted opened his eyes and groaned.

"How do you feel?" Erwin asked.

He groaned again, closing his eyes. "Like I went into a giant wolf's mouth and came out the other end!"

Erwin couldn't help but laugh. "Well, the wolf didn't eat your sense of humor, I see."

Bodric opened one eye and then promptly shut it again. "By the

Mother, did the foul beastie bite my head too? It's splitting!"

Erwin, trying not to laugh more said, "No, my friend, that would be the liquor we gave you last night for the pain and to help you sleep. Besides, your head is too hard for even a giant wolf!"

Bodric sat up with a little help from Erwin, as the other men came in to check on him. He ate some of the eggs and devoured several sausages. "Did you get the hides for Cali?"

"Yes, don't worry, we are taking the biggest one, and the smaller one stays here," Erwin said.

"I want to head home this morning, we still need to check on the boar traps," Bodric said, feeling stronger now that he'd eaten.

"I don't know, you may want to give it another day. That was a nasty attack," Tad said. "What do you think, Erwin, Dad?"

"He's not fevered, there's no swelling, and he's not incoherent, if Erwin thinks he's strong enough, then I'd say it's okay," Jossin replied.

"Jossin, do you think we could use your large wagon? I can put Bodric in the back with the hide, and then I can have one of my hands bring it back over to you." Erwin asked.

"Nonsense. You take the wagon, I'll send a couple of my hands along with you to bring it back themselves. Send a couple jars of Bethal's jams back with them, eh?" Jossin smiled.

"Thanks, Jossin, that sounds great." Erwin shook his hand and headed out to pack the wagon. They placed the large wolf hide flat on the wagon, Tad added more salt to the hide for the trip. Jossin came out and had Tad load up two barrels of wine and two more of whiskey to take back.

They helped Bodric onto the back, and Jossin gave him a silver flask full of the liquor for the trip. "This wagon rides a bit rough, you'll need a few nips of that before you get home." He smiled at Bodric.

"Jossin, thanks again, and you send word if you run into any more animal problems," Erwin said. And they headed off on the trip back home.

CHAPTER 5

"Good morning, Rowan, Jorah," Bethal called out as they rode up to the house. "I didn't expect to see you this early today!"

"Yes, ma'am. We finished up our morning work, so we could come check in on Cali. And you. And make sure you hadn't had any boar sightings," Jorah said, blushing.

"No boar sightings. But we do have a lot of sausage and some fresh biscuits still on the table. Come on in and help yourselves!"

Cali and Chase came into the kitchen, joining the group. "Mum, you really do make the best jams, and gravy of course!" Cali laughed.

"Do you think your dad and Bodric will bring back that boar today?" Jorah asked.

"Maybe, I would love to have another boar hide to work! I'd make straps to sell to everyone!" Cali said, excited at the idea of having an even larger boar hide.

They sat and talked until Bethal ran them out of the kitchen, so she could start prepping for lunch. "Why don't you go work on your quiver. And you can keep an eye out for your dad."

The three of them went to the barn to see if the leather had dried and was ready.

"Jorah told me how good you are at this, Cali. He was right, you really are. Do you take requests?" Rowan asked.

"For you all? Sure, of course, I do! What are you thinking?"

"I'd love to have a decent sheath for my sword. I don't carry it often, Jorah or me either one, but with the increase in animal attacks, I think we should. And it would be nice to have a decent belt sheath for it," Rowan said.

"Are they short swords, or long?"

"I have a longsword. Jorah now, he's fancy," Rowan joked, "he has a longsword and a short sword."

"Really, Jorah? Do you use them both?" Cali asked, surprised.

Jorah turned red at the attention. "Yes, I've been practicing. But we don't use them much, mostly just bows for hunting, you know."

Rowan laughed at his brother. "Ah, he's being modest, Cali, he's really good. He'll be a much better swordsman than me soon."

"I'd love to make you new sheaths. I've not made those before, so no promises!" Cali laughed.

"I know they'll be great, everything you've made so far has been!" Jorah said, still blushing.

Cali started cutting the remaining hide into pieces she would need for sword sheaths, while they sat around talking about the possibility of having the next big boar gathering at the lake. Or at least part of it at the lake, then the feast at the Flynn farm.

It was mid-afternoon when they heard what sounded like horses coming up the road. They walked out of the barn and toward the house as Bethal walked out from the kitchen.

"That's old man Jossin's wagon," Rowan said. "You're dad's driving."

They were watching, wondering if they had a big boar on the back of the wagon.

"Wait. That's Bodric's horse. Where's Bodric?" Cali asked, a knot forming in her stomach.

"Oh no," Bethal said, running out to meet the wagon. Cali, Rowan, and Jorah followed close behind.

They reached the wagon, all breathing a sigh of relief to see Bodric in the back. Injured, and in pain, but alive.

"What happened?" Bethal asked.

As Erwin came down from the wagon Bethal grabbed him looking him over to make sure he wasn't hurt then wrapped her arms around him tightly.

Jorah and Rowan helped Bodric down from the wagon gently. He was shaky, Rowan put Bodric's good arm over his shoulder and helped steady him.

"Come on," Rowan said, "Let's get you into the house."

They all went into the house and got Bodric relaxed and comfortable on the couch as Erwin told them the story. The farmhand broke in, "I've never seen anyone shoot a bow that fast or pick up a grown man so readily. Erwin was incredible, Bethal.

We would've been wolf food if he hadn't been there."

Bethal shared a long look with Erwin, thankful that her husband had been there, but even more that he was safe.

"Cali girl, I made your dad bring you back the pelt. It's a silver wolf, real large. Would make a nice cloak." Bodric smiled at Cali.

"Yes, it's on the back of the wagon if you want to get it to the barn, honey," Erwin said. "Jorah, maybe you can help? I'm sure she'll want to get it on the rack."

"Yes, sir, I'd be happy to help! Come on Cali, let's check out this giant wolf hide!" Jorah said.

Erwin ran his hand over his tired face. "The boar is still out there. We'll not go after it right now, but we will have to hunt it down soon. Until then, everyone stays in pairs, stays armed, and doesn't stray far from the farms. Rowan, you make sure to spread that word over on your farm, okay?"

"Yes, sir. I will let Father and everyone know. I'll go get Jorah and we'll head back now to spread the word," Rowan replied.

"Thanks, Rowan. And thanks to you and Jorah for coming over and checking on things." Erwin smiled.

Bethal brought a blanket in and covered Bodric's legs. "You are going to rest, and you're staying here until we get you fixed up."

"I know better than to argue with ya, Bethal." Bodric smiled. "Now before you go getting your hackles all raised, this was animals, plain and simple. Something has them riled to be sure, but it's likely nothing more than a new alpha in the area somewhere."

Bethal didn't look convinced.

"Honey, he's right. I know you're worried. I'd say it's this larger boar. From what we saw it looks to be a real monster of a beast," Erwin said. "We'll track it down and have another gathering soon, but first we could all use some rest."

After the initial rush of visitors checking in on Bodric, life settled down into its normal routine over the next several weeks.

Bodric healed well under Bethal's care and her "smelly, magic" salve, as Bodric called it. Cali had been working on a pattern to make the silver wolf hide into a cloak. And there had been no more sightings of the massive boar, or any other animal attacks.

Erwin and Bodric gathered several farmhands and set off to begin tracking the boar. They started in the area where they first saw evidence of it along the road. Each time they went to scout for the boar, they took a different path from that starting point. On their third outing, they found it's trail.

"There!" Bodric pointed.

They had gone a fair distance into the forest where the underbrush had grown dense. It was clear the large beast had been through recently. Small branches were bent and broken, the underbrush trampled down, and hoof prints were noticeable in the soft dirt.

"Okay men, here is where we start. We stick together and watch our flanks. A beast this big can't sneak up on us, but we may stumble over him." Erwin spoke confidently to the men. "Bodric, how's the arm?"

"Good as new if not a little more decorated." Bodric smiled showing off the jagged red scar above his bracer. With that, they headed deeper into the woods, following the trail left by the boar.

The path was easy to see if not quite so easy to follow, and the men had stopped to take a breather when they heard the rustling nearby. They slowly inched toward the sound, taking care not to make any sudden moves or noise. It was gloomy under the thick cover of trees, but they could see the massive shape ahead of them.

Each man took a spot behind a tree in case the boar charged, and as they were preparing to aim, the wind shifted, and the beast caught their scent. Turning to face them, the men could now see the boar clearly.

Over half as tall as Erwin, it's tusks could easily skewer a man clean through. It sniffed the air, pawing, then let out an awful bellowing screech before charging toward them.

"Now!" Shouted Erwin.

The men all shot at the creature then drew to shoot again. It still rushed forward, even with arrows sticking from its shoulders.

"Aim for the neck with me now! Shoot!" Erwin commanded.

The men all aimed for the neck as the boar screeched and lumbered closer. Erwin got off two more arrows and finally, the boar stopped and fell onto its side. They slowly approached, and Erwin stabbed his dagger into the boar's heart to finish it off.

"By the Mother, I've never seen a monster that size," Tom, one of the farmhands said.

"Nor I," Erwin replied. "In all my years, I've not seen one that big."

Bodric laughed, "aye, he'll make a fine roast! And Cali will be thrilled with this hide. Why she'll be rich with all the straps she can make from this monster!"

Bodric prodded the beast with his boot. "Why don't you two head back out and prep the wagon, we'll gut this thing and start dragging it back out."

Erwin, Bodric, and the two remaining hands cleaned the boar. It was much too large to carry on a spit between them, so they made a makeshift sled, pulling the boar behind them back out of the forest.

It took a much longer time getting back to the road with their haul, but they had enough daylight left to wrestle it onto the wagon and start making their way back home.

∞   ∞   ∞

As the sound of horses approached, Bethal stepped out of the kitchen. "Hi, boys!" she waved at Rowan and Jorah. "Good to see you!"

"Hi, ma'am. Any word on the boar hunt?" Rowan asked as they dismounted.

"No, nothing yet. But I don't think they'll come back empty handed!" Bethal replied. "Cali is out in the barn, and if you get hungry, there's plenty of food."

"Thanks! Cali told us to come over today, so we'll go say hi." Jorah smiled. Rowan smiled, rolling his eyes and followed his brother toward the barn.

Cali was just walking out from the barn when she saw them walk up. "Jorah! Rowan! Glad you stopped by. Come on in the barn, I have something to show you!"

They walked into the barn, and she handed each of them a box. "Go on then, take a look!" she said.

Opening the boxes, they saw the gleaming leather sheaths. A longsword sheath for Rowan, and one long and one short sword sheath for Jorah. In addition, she had made each of them a belt that matched.

"This is amazing, Cali," Rowan exclaimed. "You really are incredible at this!"

"Cali, thank you! These are, I don't know, they are beautiful!" Jorah smiled as he ran his hand across the oiled leather.

"Aww, come on guys, these are just my first try, I'm sure I could do better once I have more practice," Cali said. She was trying not to blush but was secretly thrilled that they seemed to love them.

"So, when Da and everyone gets back with this big boar, we will need to plan the party. I still think we should get everyone together and go to the lake first. What do you think?"

"Rowan and I were talking about that too, we could get everyone, make a whole day of it, it would be a lot of fun. Have you talked to your mom about it, Cali?" Jorah asked.

"No, but I'm getting hungry, so let's go talk to her about it now," She said as they started walking from the barn.

"Well, sweetie, I think that is a great idea," Bethal said after hearing Cali's plan for having a big get-together at the lake for the next gathering. "But we should probably see if your dad and Bodric bring back a boar first." She laughed.

They sat around the kitchen table eating and making plans for having a huge get together at the lake before the actual gathering and feast.

Cali wondered if she would be able to get more orders for plow straps, or maybe some other items. If the boar really was as big as they said, she would have a lot of hide to work with.

As the sun started sinking lower and the evening light came in through the kitchen windows, they heard the horses and wagon coming up the road. Excited to have her husband back, Bethal tossed down the potatoes she was peeling and headed out the door, the others close behind her.

Bethal gasped. "Well, I've never..." she trailed off.

Even with a bit of distance, they could see the hulking shape of the boar in the back of the wagon. Cali grabbed Jorah's arm in excitement, jumping up and down, then took off running to meet them.

"Da, Bodric, how did you ever get that thing on the wagon?" Cali asked.

"Cali girl!" Bodric smiled. "Oh, this beastie, he put up a good fight, but we wrestled him up on there. You ready to get rich making straps for people?" Bodric winked as he hopped down.

Erwin pulled the wagon closer to the barn, so they could unload the boar. Jorah and Rowan pitched in and helped, but even with all of them, it was still not easy. Cali was so excited she was beside herself, she ran into the barn to grab her skinning knife.

"Okay, guys. Let's start spreading the word tomorrow that we're having another gathering!" Erwin exclaimed, clapping his hand on Bodric's shoulder in celebration.

"Beth, honey, are you ready for another feast?" Erwin winked at his wife.

"Absolutely! I'll have some of the ladies come over and help too, we'll make this one even bigger than last time. And Cali and the boys had a great idea to have a party at the lake before the feast." Bethal smiled at them.

CHAPTER
6

Word spread fast about the killing of the boar, and the day of the feast families from around Edelaine started showing up early at the Flynn farm. Some joined Bethel to help with the cooking, while the younger ones headed off to the lake for some fun.

The farmhands tended the boar on the spit. The savory smell of the roasting meat could be picked up almost all the way to Jenkins' farm.

The gathering was huge. All of Edelaine came, some brought instruments and sat around playing music while others danced. Men stood around talking about the hunt for the beast, and the women mostly sat around resting and enjoying the time after all the cooking had been done.

The relief of finally having the beast dead that had been terrorizing the farms was felt by everyone. The worried lines on the farmers' faces eased as everyone relaxed and enjoyed the feast.

Cali and her friends returned from the lake as the sun started to set. They had come back to the feast earlier to eat before heading back to the lake.

Cali let everyone know her newest boar hide was curing, and she would be ready to take on any leather jobs. Mr. Calbert, her friend Sarah's dad, wanted a pair of the plow straps like Cali had made for Jenkins, and Old Man Jossin wanted three new water skins made. Of course, everyone knew they were actually going to be wineskins.

Cali, Chase, and their friends settled in around the bonfire as the celebrations started winding down for the evening. Everyone knew they had to get back to work tomorrow but were happy to celebrate for a bit longer. Even Bethel looked calm and unworried, Cali noticed, and her mom seldom looked relaxed. The farmers were pleased the beast had been dealt with and looked forward to things getting back to normal.

Cali and Chase spent most of their time over the next weeks in the small barn working on leather jobs. The wineskins turned out better than she expected, so she made a couple extra.

Rowan and Jorah rode with Cali to deliver the skins to Jossin and the new plow straps to Mr. Calbert. They visited with Sarah while at Calbert's farm for a bit too.

What Cali was most looking forward to though, was working with the silver wolf pelt. She decided to take Bodric's advice and make a cloak out of it, it would be beautiful and warm for the coming cold season.

Surprised, she found she had enough of the wolf pelt left to test her skill at making gloves, and a small section that she was going to use for a warm bed for Chase.

Starting to work with more of the boar hide, she surprised her dad and Bodric with new belts, and her mom with a new knife sharpening strap for the kitchen. She didn't want to use up all the leather, but Cali was so excited she wanted to make a few more items. She made new gloves for Rowan and Jorah too, and then on a whim since there was so much of the massive boar hide left, she made new saddlebags for her horse.

Summer was starting to wind down, and the harvests had begun. All the farms were making extra preparations this year.

Cali wondered about the 15-year winter coming, she had been too young to remember much of the last one. A long cold season happened once every fifteen years. Much colder and harsher than the others.

The older farmhands said it was the Mother's way of cleaning the earth, so it could grow fertile again until the next fifteen-year winter. She shivered at the thought, grateful that she would have her new cloak and gloves. She decided to make herself some new boots, and a few extra pairs of gloves in case anyone else needed them.

Every day wheat was coming into the grind-house and bags of flour were being sent back out to all the farms. Racks of meat hung in the smokehouse to cure. The wood that had been drying in the sun all summer was stacked in neat rows in the barns, more wood than Cali could recall ever seeing in the barns. Many of the older women spent time with Cali's mom making wonderfully warm scarves, socks, and sweaters from the sheep's wool. Those were also sent back out to all the farms.

They then turned their attention to preparing and storing all the harvests for winter. Jars upon jars of jams, fruits, and vegetables were made, sorted, and divvied up. It was great to see everyone come together to make sure that all the farms were fully stocked and ready for the upcoming season.

Cali pondered how it came to be that her family had been made the unofficial leaders of the farms of Edelaine. Her mom and dad had always ensured everyone was taken care of. Most of the goods that went across the mountain pass came through their farm first. And whenever there was any problem, it was always her dad and Bodric that handled it. Maybe her mom would tell her the story, but after the harvest season, everyone was too busy right now.

"Cali, honey, after breakfast you and I need to start working on batches of salve," Bethal said.

"Sure, Mum. Are we running low?" Cali asked.

"No, honey, we just need to make emergency supplies for the other farms in case they need them over the winter," her mom replied.

Cali went out to the gardens to fill a large basket with comfrey, aloe, a sweet mint, and some other plants she couldn't name from memory. Her favorite was the fresh beeswax. Cleaned of most of the honey, it still smelled, and tasted very sweet.

Her mom's salve was praised as a miracle cure around the farms. Although Cali thought it looked more like something you might find in a swamp with its odd green color and slimy feel. They worked the entire day, alternating between stirring the salve over the fire, and cutting strips of cloth that could be used as bandages.

She had helped make the salve before. Bethal was insistent that she knew how to make it in case she ever needed to make it by herself. Cali couldn't remember all the names of the plants right off, but she could easily pick them out. The recipe had been passed down through the family for generations, her mom told her once, and it was imperative that it continued to be known and passed down.

There were so many jars of salve once they were done. One for each house on each farmstead, and a couple extra for the main farmhouse for each family. They separated the cloth strips evenly between all the jars and put them all in crates to be delivered. Her dad and some farmhands were going to load them up on the wagon along with some other items to take to the farms the next day.

Each of the farms always sent back extras of their goods. From the farmers who had come to get provisions, many also planned to send back hides for Cali with requests for things to be made before the cold set in.

∞　　∞　　∞

The day was bright and warm. The sunlight had a different tone, summer was definitely over. But breakfast smelled warm and delicious so Cali bounded downstairs with Chase at her heels.

"Good morning, Mom, Da," she said as she settled in at the table.

As she was spearing sausages from the platter, Bodric came in the kitchen.

"G'morning! Hi, Cali girl!" Bodric called as he sat down.

"Erwin, there's a mighty big smoke coming up from the east. Looks about by Old Man Jossin's area."

Cali's dad looked thoughtful. "It's a bit early for him to be burning his vines, but that's probably all it is. I'm heading out in a bit with the supplies, I'll check things out."

"You wanted me here to handle anyone coming for provisions. Do you want me to ride out with you instead?" Bodric asked.

"Nah. No reason for it. You stay, handle things here. He's probably just getting a head start is all."

They finished breakfast and Erwin headed out to make sure the wagon was loaded and ready. Bodric headed to the supply house. Bethal and Cali went out to see Erwin off. Making the rounds to all the farms would take several days. Traveling with the loaded wagon to deliver and pick up supplies to bring back was slow work.

Erwin gave Bethal and Cali a hug, then hopped up on the wagon with one of the farmhands in the front, and another sitting in the back. Passing by the supply house, he gave Bodric a wave and headed toward the road.

"Cali, honey, will you go get a basket of potatoes and carrots from the storehouse? Oh, and some herbs on your way back in too." Bethal said.

"Sure, Mum. Come on, Chase!" Cali headed to the storehouse.

The storehouse beside of the kitchen garden was loaded with vegetables. Potatoes in their bins, onions, and garlic hanging along one wall. Jars upon jars of preserved vegetables and fruits, with almost as many jars of extra salve that she and her mom made. Cali picked several bunches of herbs, filled the basket with potatoes and carrots, and headed back to the kitchen.

"Thanks, Cali," Bethal said as Cali set the basket on the table. "Are you headed to the barn to work on your leather?"

"I sure am! Do you need anything else before I go?" Cali asked.

"No, honey, you go on." Bethal started scrubbing potatoes in a large wash bin on the counter.

Cali was excited for her dad to get back with all the hides from the farms. She had no idea how many she would end up with, but she knew several of the farms planned to send some for straps and other items. She had a few days to work on the leather she already had before her dad would get back and she would have to start filling orders. Today she would finish making her new boots.

CHAPTER
7

The morning started bright and cool with a pale blue sky that whispered of the approaching winter.

Cali's dad had been out visiting all the farmsteads for two days now, and she was excited for him to return with more hides for her to work with. When she came downstairs, Bodric and her mom were already at the kitchen table talking.

"I hope everything's okay out at Old Man Jossin's place. The smoke, I don't know, Bodric." Bethal shook her head.

"Hi, Cali girl! Ah, Bethal, Jossin has probably just fired up those vines, and may even be smoking some new barrels. I'm sure everything is just fine," Bodric said.

"You're probably right, Bodric. I just worry you know. Cali, what are you and Chase doing today?"

"I was thinking I'd head up the hill and do some reading, Mom. Unless you need me to stay close by?" Cali said.

"No, honey. Things are starting to quiet down. That would be fine if you want to go read. Take some snacks with you, okay?"

"Sure, Mum! I wouldn't mind taking a few extra sausages!"

Bethal laughed. She wrapped two fat sausages and a huge biscuit in a towel and set on the table. "No gravy, I'm afraid."

Bodric and Cali both laughed at that.

"Aww, that's okay, it would be a bit messy anyway." Cali stood, took the snacks, and grabbed her book off the shelf near the door as Chase followed close at her heels.

Bethal looked out the window to the east, worried at the smoky haze in the bright morning sunshine.

"Bethal, if the smoke gets worse, I'll ride out tomorrow and meet up with Erwin. Okay?"

"Thanks, Bodric. That would make me feel a lot better."

Erwin had unloaded several jars of salve and jam and some other provisions as Jenkins farm. Both Jorah and Rowan bragged on the sword sheaths Cali made for them, and Jenkins sent back some supplies and several rabbit hides for Cali for gloves.

The smoke was still in the air, heavier than the previous day, so Erwin wanted to head to Jossin's stead after stopping by Calbert's this morning.

If they made good time, they could be at Calbert's before midday, then on to Jossin's by nightfall. Then they could stop at Nomarr's on the way back.

They started on the winding road that led to Calbert's house, the smoke growing denser. As they rounded the bend and came in view of the house, Erwin knew something was terribly wrong. He reined the horses in hard, stopping as he saw the dead cow and heard a scream.

Erwin and the two farmhands leaped from the wagon and ran toward the house. They weren't armed but for daggers and single bow between them.

"Calbert!" They yelled.

"Stefen! Calbert! Sarah!"

One of Calbert's farmhands came stumbling around the corner, blood running down his arm and dripping from his hand. Erwin ran to him.

"By the Mother, tell me what happened here!" Erwin caught him just as he was falling.

"I don't know. They came from nowhere." He gasped, trying to catch his breath, but it was a deep rattling sound.

Death rattle, Erwin thought.

"There were many, goblins maybe, trolls, I don't know. Never saw nothing like them, Erwin. They got Stefen. Burned the barns. I set loose the horses."

"Sarah. What about Sarah?" Erwin looked at the wound in his chest and shoulder. There wasn't much time left for him. Erwin pulled a flask from his pocket, pouring small sips into the farmhand's mouth.

"Sarah. I hid her. She was bloody... not hurt... Stefen's blood... hid her in the hay, in the haystacks. Get her safe, Erwin. Get her," and with a choking cough, he went limp in Erwin's arms.

"You two, go out back and see if anyone else made it. Stay together. Swing around and meet me at the haystacks. Go. Now." Erwin said.

His two farmhands took off around the other side of the house, daggers drawn, as the smoke from the barn grew heavier.

Erwin made his way to the haystacks. Rounding the corner past the burning barn, he saw one of them. Quietly he readied his bow, the arrow lodged in its skull with a dull *thunk*! He crept slowly forward, but there were no others.

"Sarah!" Erwin said. "Sarah, honey, it's Erwin Flynn. Come out. We are going to get out of here!"

He heard her muffled crying in one of the stacks ahead of him and went to help pull her free. She fell into his arms, sobbing. He picked her up and carried her back toward the wagon just as his farmhands came around the corner of the house. They both shook their head at Erwin.

"None others. One, he was almost gone when we found him. Said they came from the east, didn't steal anything, just killed and kept heading west."

"West," Erwin said. His stomach dropped. Fear and anger like he'd never felt took him.

"Here, get Sarah on the wagon and head back toward home. Make sure she gets there safe. Here, take this bow, you can be the lookout while he drives the wagon. Go. Go now!"

"What are you going to do, Erwin?"

"I'm grabbing that horse over there and I'll get there faster. Just go. Keep her safe. I'll see you there."

Erwin ran toward the field and jumped on the first of Calbert's horses he could find. They were loose in the fields but thankfully didn't run from him. They were off, galloping at dangerous speed across the field and toward the woods beyond.

It occurred to Erwin that he had left himself with only his dagger.

No matter, he thought, *I just need to make it back home.* And he urged the horse even faster.

Erwin and the horse came bursting out of the woods onto the backside of Jenkins farm.

Oh no, they've been here already!

"Jenkins! Rowan! Jorah! Hello!" Erwin called.

Jorah came running when he heard Erwin yell.

"Jorah! You okay?" Erwin hopped off the panting horse.

"Yes, sir. But they, they got Dad. Rowan, he's hurt, but he's alive. What were they? Those, those monsters!"

Jorah looked like he was in shock, but Erwin knew he had to keep going. If they had already passed through Jenkins farm, they couldn't be far from his own.

"Jorah, I'm taking a fresh horse, I have to get home," Erwin said.

It was as if Jorah suddenly woke up from a daydream. His eyes grew wide, then hard.

"Ride swift, sir. Go! I'll get Rowan and we'll make our way to your place and bring any we can with us." Jorah said.

Erwin took a fresh horse and spurred him on hard. He was at a full run toward home. Shortly before the gate, he heard the *clang* of metal on metal and dull *thunk* sounds that he didn't want to think about. He had caught up with them. He rounded the curve and headed through the gate as fast as the horse would carry him.

His thoughts were on making it to Bethal and Cali, he was going to cut through the field just past the first tool shed at the east field. Coming up on the shed, he didn't see the imp until the arrow came burning through his shoulder and he hit the ground.

Stunned, he shook his head to clear it, breaking off the shaft of the arrow and pulling the dagger from his belt as the imp charged at him. His feint worked, and the imp went sprawling into the dirt as Erwin thrust the dagger into its chest.

Erwin stood, trying to clear his head and stumbling in the direction of the house. There were dead and dying farmhands, only a few dead imps. Closer to the house there were more imps dead, and as he yelled for Bethal, an arrow flew past, followed by another which grazed his leg.

He went down but quickly stood back up, turning to meet the imps head on.

Bodric just finished loading provision onto a wagon when he saw the smoke.

"Oye! Everyone to the barn, bring water, get the horses out!" Bodric shouted.

He started running toward the barn with several farmhands

when he heard the subtle slap of a bow. He turned to the east woods in time to see the flaming arrow headed for the large barn, and a host of creatures running out from the shadows of the trees.

They closed the distance quicker than he would have thought possible, Bodric saw they were imps. The group split, some heading for the barn, some headed towards the fields where the farmhands were running in, and some straight towards him and the house.

Bodric unsheathed his daggers and shouted, "Men! To Arms! To Arms!" He raced across the field toward the imps.

Bethal heard the shout, then other screams and metal on metal. A cold chill raced up her spine as she ran out the kitchen door. Farmhands were on the ground bleeding. Others fighting imps near the barn as the horses and animals came running out of the burning building. She ran into the kitchen, grabbing her knives, then ran back out into the yard.

She saw Bodric in the near field fighting imps. "Bodric!"

An imp rounded the corner and charged at her. In a flash of speed, she sent the knife flying, embedding in into the imp's eye. She ran to the imp, barely slowing to yank the dagger out then headed toward the field, knives in hand and more in her apron.

Bodric started backing across the field as Bethal fought her way toward him. *There are so many*, she thought.

An imp leaped onto Bodric's back, ready to plant a dagger into his shoulder when Bethal's knife landed squarely between the imp's shoulder. It fell to the ground with a thump.

"Bodric, Cali. Cali! She went to the hill, you have to go get her. Go!" Bethal said.

"We'll both go," Bodric said.

"No, we've thinned these out, but some made it past, go, go get her now, I'll handle these!"

Bodric gave her a look, nodded, and turned, heading toward the hills. He knew Bethal was more than able to hold her own. Better than himself.

The hill was off to the west, where the heavy forest began past the farm. Beyond that, it was just more forest, unused and untouched for ages. And beyond that the sea, if anyone ever wanted to attempt to make the trek that far.

As Bodric reached the far side of the house, he looked back hearing a wild sound. Another host of imps emerged from the trees yelling, followed by an imp astride a huge boar mount.

Bethal turned to give him a look, shouted "Go!", then turned to meet the imps. He could see blades flying as imps fell before her as he turned, sprinting toward the forested hill.

Cali and Chase were enjoying their biscuit and sausages sitting against a massive tree near the top of the hill. She looked up, thinking it must be at least midday already. She absently scratched Chase behind the ear.

"We'll stay a while longer I think, then head back before dinner time," Cali said.

Chase curled up on her lap and fell asleep as she opened her book again. She loved coming to this spot to read, and the weather was perfect for it.

It was definitely getting cooler, but still comfortable to be outside. Knowing the 15-year winter was right around the corner, she planned to spend as much time out as she could before it came.

The tide of battle had indeed turned in favor of the hero of her story. The sounds of distant blades-on-blades and battle shouts started to subside as the enemies were driven back from the castle.

Suddenly, Chase jumped up, sniffing the air and making a low, throaty growling sound. Startled, Cali laid a hand on his tensed back.

"Chase, what is it, boy?"

She looked around but didn't see anything out of the ordinary. The smoke had gotten heavier in the air, and she hoped her dad had found everything was okay at Old Man Jossin's farm.

Clank!

That sound was not in her imagination. Chase was still tensed and on alert.

"Come on, boy. Let's go ahead and get back to the house."

Cali stood when she heard the distinct sound of metal on metal again. And shouts.

"Chase, let's go, something's wrong!"

Cali and Chase took off running down the hill. The forest was heavy here, but there was little underbrush, so little chance of tripping or getting caught up in brambles. The further down the hill they went, the smoke became thicker.

The forest started thinning toward the bottom of the hill, and through a bare spot in the trees, she saw one of their horses run by toward the fields. A chill ran over Cali, and the hair on the back of her neck stood on end. They ran faster.

As Cali came sprinting from the woods, she stopped, feeling like the wind had been knocked out of her. The barn was on fire. She could see people laying in the field. She was too far away to make out anyone specifically. Their animals were out of the barns and either standing around or running. Far off to her left, there was a small group of... something, they looked to be about the size of large children, but they didn't seem to be human, running into the woods to the west.

Mom! She thought wildly. *I have to find Mom!*

She took off running as fast as she could, with Chase keeping pace right beside of her. She was halfway to the house when she saw several bodies. A few of them where creatures like she saw running into the woods, the other was a man. He was lying face down, dirty and blood covered. Chase growled again, but Cali didn't slow down to look.

Suddenly a hand flashed out and grabbed her ankle and she went sprawling into the grass. Chase let out a bark and went to pounce on the hand when she heard the voice.

"Cali girl," Bodric said.

He sounded weak, his voice strained. She rolled over to get a better look at him.

"No, get Chase make him sit. Then lay down and don't move. Stay still. Don't speak. We need to make sure they're gone."

Cali did as he said. Chase laid down beside her head, and she stayed as still as she could manage. Terrified and confused. It seemed like hours passed although it must have only been a few minutes.

Bodric slowly raised his head and peered around. Satisfied they were gone he let go of Cali's ankle and tried to raise himself up on his elbow.

"You're hurt! Oh, Bodric, what happened? Where's Mum?"

Chase went over and licked Bodric on the cheek, then turned, looking around as if he were guarding.

"Cali girl, I don't know. They came from the east. There was no warning. They were just there."

"But, Mum! What about Mum?"

"I don't know, sweet girl. Your mom, she can take care of herself better than you know. If anyone could make it, I'm sure she could."

"What about you, Bodric? Let's get you back to the house. I saw a few of those things heading into the woods when I came down the hill. What are they?"

"They are imps. Never seen them in Edelaine. They must have come over the mountains."

"Can you walk? Let's get back to the house and check on Mum."

"I think I can walk. I need to tie up this leg first, but I can walk a bit after."

Cali looked down at his leg. There was a gash in his thigh that was oozing blood. She took the kitchen towel from her pocket and used it to tie around his leg.

"It's not great, but it will do until we get to the house. Come on, Bodric, I'll help you. Chase, guard us."

Cali helped him up. He needed to lean on her and he limped badly, but he was able to walk. Chase walked right beside of Cali, warily looking around and sniffing the air.

It seemed to take them ages to reach the house. The closer they got, Cali started to cry. The farmhands! Many were dead, others injured. Of the few that were able to stand, several were working on putting out the barn fire, then they saw her and Bodric, and two of them ran over to help.

The hands took Bodric's weight from Cali, one on each side of him.

"Mum, where's my mum?" Cali asked.

One of the hands gave Bodric a hard look, and then just shook his head.

Cali took off running toward the house. She rounded the corner heading toward the kitchen door when she looked toward the field.

"Oh Gods, no!"

Cali ran so hard she thought her lungs might burst and fell to her knees in front of her mom.

"Mum!"

Bethal's eyes fluttered open. She had been stabbed several times and had part of an arrow sticking out of her stomach. When her eyes finally fixed on Cali's face, she gave her a weak smile.

"Cali, honey. Are you hurt?" Bethal asked.

"No, Mum. No. Hold on, I'll get the salve and some bandages."

"No, Cali, honey. You know it's no good."

At that, Cali laid her head on Bethal's leg and started sobbing.

"Honey, it's okay. You have to listen to me now, I don't have much left. Listen, child, come close."

Cali sat up, putting her arms around her mom, and leaning in close to her.

"Listen. You need to know who our family is, where we come from, and what we do." Bethal winced as a shudder ran through her body.

"No time. My dear sweet girl, I've no time left. Listen. I hoped never to tell you, and now that I have to, I've no time to tell you the whole story."

She took a ragged breath, "just know this, your father and I love you more than all the kingdoms. We never wanted this for you, but it's come for us regardless. We are shields of the realms. For countless generations…"

Bethal let out a hacking cough, blood running from the corner of her mouth. Cali stayed close, looking her mom in the eyes while she tried to continue talking.

"All the generations of our family, shields, guardians. It's our legacy. Our curse. Listen. Bodric. He's alive?"

Cali nodded, unable to find her voice.

"Good. Good. Bodric can tell you what I can't. It is on you

now, Cali. I'm sorry I didn't prepare you for this. I never wanted you to… I never thought you'd need to know. We've had peace for generations upon generations. But now it's your time. You must be strong, and you must learn. Eaparius."

Bethal's eyes closed as she lost consciousness.

Cali cried. "Mum. Mum! What is eaparius? How do I learn eaparius? I don't understand. Mum!"

Bethal came to, opening her eyes, and smiling at Cali.

"Cali, I'm sorry I didn't tell you before now. Remember. Learn. Eaparius. Find Bodric, he'll help you find the legacy."

She was slipping away and didn't seem to be making much sense. Feebly she tugged at the unusual necklace she wore, pulling it off and giving it to Cali.

"Here. Get Erwin's. Bodric. Learn. Love you, Cali."

The last of her breath slipped from her as she went limp.

CHAPTER 8

Cali hadn't heard Jorah ride up, nor the hands walk up behind her. They stayed far enough back to give her and Bethal privacy in her last moments.

It was Jorah who walked up and placed a hand on her shoulder. She felt like she had been sitting there with her mom for days. She looked up at him, and broke down, sobbing. He knelt beside her holding her while she cried.

"Bodric, where is he?" Cali said.

"He's alive, they took him in the house."

Cali sat, wiping the blood from Bethal's hands. The familiar pale scar across her palm.

"I never knew what gave her this scar."

Placing her mom's hands back on her lap, she began wiping the blood from her cheek.

"Jorah, I have to clean her up. I won't have her looking like this."

Jorah nodded and helped Cali stand up.

They walked toward the door, passing shell-shocked farmhands, smoke still heavy in the air, though the fire had been quenched.

Looking around, everything felt dreamlike but out of focus, covered by wisps of hazy smoke. Cali didn't remember walking, although she knew she must be with Jorah guiding her toward the house.

Walking into the kitchen, Sarah Calbert sat crying at the kitchen table. Two farmhands were at the sink, filling a large kettle with water. Another was stoking the fire in the grate.

Moving into the sitting room there were more people, turning to look at her as she came into the room. The shock of seeing Bodric's motionless body on the floor shook Cali out of her stupor.

"Bodric! No!"

Cali ran, dropping to his side, pushing his blood-soaked hair back from his forehead.

"Bodric, Bodric, you are okay. Bodric!"

A low grunt came from Bodric as he regained consciousness.

With a feeling of relief that overwhelmed her, Cali sobbed into Bodric's chest. He weakly placed his hand on her head.

"Cali girl," he whispered, pained.

"Bodric, you are going to be okay. You are going to be fine." Cali smiled at Bodric, still crying.

"No, Cali girl. Listen to me now. Send them out, there's things you need to know."

At this, Jorah stepped back from Cali and motioned for everyone to leave the room.

"No, Bodric, I am going to take care of you. You are going to be fine. I swear it. I swear it! You two, go get sheets, rip them into strips. Jorah, bring boiling water and whiskey. Bring knives from the kitchen. Move, go!" Cali shouted orders at the farmhands and Jorah as they all jumped into action.

"Cali, you have to listen to me now. Your mom and dad, they weren't just your parents. They were guardians. Protectors of our world." Bodric coughed.

"What? No, Bodric, rest, you can talk later."

"Cali, just listen. I'm the only one left to tell you. Bethal. Her entire family, through every generation for countless ages. All guardians. Your dad, brought into the prophecy when they married. Their necklaces, you have to get them — "

"Bodric, Mum wasn't a fighter, just rest now, rest. I'm going to fix you." Cali cried, trying to get Bodric to save his energy.

"She was, hun, she was. You saw her, you saw all the imps dead near her. She was brilliant. I've never seen anyone like her. And your Da, too. Listen." Bodric coughed, wincing in pain.

"The prophecy falls on you now. You are the guardian. Go get their necklaces. Together they are a key. A box in the small barn, under the floor. The key and your blood will open the box. Go get it. You have to get it. Go, now! Go get the keys, get the box, and come back quick as you can."

"No! I'm not leaving you. I'm going to make you better, and you can tell me all this nonsense then." Cali tried to smile at him.

"Cali, you love stories, but this is real. Please listen. Go get the box, it's your fate. I'll wait for you. I'm not leaving yet." Bodric tried to smile at her.

Cali searched his face, he seemed lucid. Cali nodded.

"Don't you leave me, Bodric."

Cali stood up, turning back toward the kitchen, seeing Jorah in the doorway. He had been keeping everyone out of the room to give them privacy to talk.

"Jorah, please give him some whiskey, and begin cleaning him up so I can tend to his wounds. Where's... where's Da?" Cali swallowed hard at the lump in her throat.

"He's in the back of the wagon past the garden. I'll tend to Bodric, go on." Jorah said, with his hand on Cali's shoulder.

Sarah was still crying at the table. The hands tore sheets into strips and boiling water, which they took to Jorah in the other room. Cali could hear them in the room behind her comforting Bodric and jumping into action. Other farmhands were beginning to stumble in the door in twos and threes helping the other wounded people into the house.

Cali felt beside herself as if watching the entire scene from outside her own body. But it wasn't hazy and dreamlike this time, it was sharp, bright, as if from some unseen harsh light. She pushed out into the smoky air, walking toward the wagon.

There were two forms lying in the wagon, covered by a blanket. Climbing onto the wagon, someone had moved Bethal onto the wagon beside of Erwin, covering them carefully. She knelt between them in the back of the wagon.

Was Bodric right? Were these two people more than her parents? Looking at them each, in turn, they looked like her parents. They were just her parents.

She shook herself mentally. *No time for tears right now, I have to get back to Bodric, he's still with me*, she thought.

Being careful, she removed the other necklace from around her dad's neck. Looking at the pendants closer, she could see that the one flat edge of each seemed to fit together. Pushing them together, there was a minuscule click as they connected.

It is a key!

At this, Cali jumped down from the wagon and sprinted to the small barn. She ran past where she worked on her leather to the back of the barn. Looking around, she had no idea where the box could be. Under the floor, he had said, but where?

Closing her eyes, Cali took a deep breath. *The back, right corner*, she thought. She immediately headed to the corner, and pulling her knife she pushed loose hay out of the way and began prying up floorboards.

It didn't take long. After lifting a few boards, she saw the corner of a box in a hollow space beneath. Prying up the remaining boards, she reached down and pulled the box out. It was much longer than she expected. And although it had the dust that had filtered down from the barn, the wood looked unmarred. To her surprise, as she wiped the dust from the stop, it was unscratched.

The light filtered in through the barn windows, but she could tell that it would be getting dark soon. There was still enough light to see that the box was a dark reddish-brown wood. On the lid were engravings in the corners, and another in the center. The center engraving had a deep blue stone set into the wood.

The hair on the back of her neck raised, and the feeling of fear stirred in her, like a snake coiling in her stomach. She suddenly didn't want to open the box.

This prophecy that Bodric talked about killed her parents, and who knows how many others. But she knew she had to open it.

The keyhole wasn't on the front of the box, but on the top, right below the inset blue stone. Her hands were shaking so badly that she couldn't fit the key into the hole the first time. After what seemed like an eternity, she steadied her hand and placed the key into the hole.

Nothing happened, the lid was still sealed shut.

My blood! Cali remembered Bodric telling her the key and her blood would open the box. But how was that supposed to work? Taking up her knife again, she made a small cut on the palm of her hand, then placed her hand over the blue stone.

The box vibrated, startling Cali. She jumped back, landing hard against the barn wall. She had not imagined it, the box continued to vibrate, clattering softly against the wood floor, then came to a stop.

Breathing hard, Cali crept toward the box. It gleamed oddly in the dusty, fading light as if polished since she touched it. Her blood was no longer on the stone, but the stone looked as if its depths had a darkly swirling light of its own.

Her hands, shaking worse than before lifted the lid of the box, the snake-coil of fear inside her felt as if it would consume her.

The inside of the box was pristine as if it had just been made new. It was lined with a rich, dark blue cloth, the same color as the stone. The cloth felt soft like a buttery soft leather, but at the same time, felt as if it had a fine covering of fine fur.

A bow, made of the same dark reddish-brown wood as the box, covered with the same intricate engravings, and polished to a high shine lay in the box. There was the same blue stone set into the middle of the bow above where her hand would rest. It was strung with some sort of silvery looking bowstring, which looked like no string she had ever seen before. The bow seemed to call for her, beckoning Cali to reach in and pick it up.

On either side of the bow was a leather bracer. The leather was the same reddish-brown color, both with engravings in the leather, and a single, deep blue stone inlaid at the wrist. They looked freshly oiled and new.

This box has been here for who knows how long, how can these be new?

Cali reached into the box, her hand hesitating, hovering above the bow. There was a comforting feeling of warmth emanating from the bow. Taking a deep breath, she grasped the bow and stood, holding it in her hand in the dusty light.

A jolting shock of heat seared into her hand, then immediately eased to a soothing warm feeling. It reminded Cali of once when she had stuck her frigid hands into a sink of warm water, that initial shock of the heat, then the warmth as it spread through her hands.

But it didn't stop at her hands. The bow seemed to have its own inner light somehow glowing from inside the polished wood. The warmth and an accompanying vibration circled itself around and up her arm, just like the snake-coil of fear had done in her belly.

By the time the warmth enveloped her, a knowing came over her that this was her bow. It was hers alone.

Cali slung the bow over her shoulder, pulling the bracers from the box. They were stunning in their beauty. She slipped them around her arms, the blue stone resting on her wrists, fitting perfectly as if she had made them for herself.

Bodric! Cali started, looking up at the light coming in through the window. She could have been in the barn for days, although the light was the same. She placed the lid back onto the box and removing the key, the box vibrated and sealed itself. Placing the box back into its hiding spot, she replaced the boards, scattered the hay, and headed back to the house, separating the pendants and placing both around her neck.

CHAPTER
9

Cali walked back through the kitchen door. Sarah stopped crying and looked up at her.

"Sarah. I'm glad you are safe. Do you think maybe... would you mind making some food for everyone? I have to look after Bodric." Cali said.

"S...sure, Cali. Are... are you okay?" Sarah looked shaken but was staring at Cali in an odd way.

"Yes, given what..." Cali gestured. "I'm okay, Sarah. Thanks."

Cali gave Sarah a small smile as Sarah got up and moved toward the sink, and Cali headed through toward the living room.

"Cali," Jorah said, relieved she was back. He stood up, giving her a curious look.

"Bodric's unconscious again. He's alive, but he's... his injuries are bad, Cali."

Cali knelt beside Bodric, removing her bow and laying it beside them. Jorah knelt on his other side, and pulled back the blanket from Bodric's right leg, showing a massive gash below the kitchen towel she had tied earlier.

She hadn't seen how bad it actually was. It went from the outside of his upper thigh to above his knee on the inside of his leg. The skin on his calf below flayed open on the side from an arrow.

There was another long slice across his chest, though not as deep as the one on his leg. And the remnants of an arrow still poked through his left upper arm.

Cali looked up at Bodric's unconscious face. Picking up a clean cloth she dipped it in the cool, clean water then wiped his face.

Looking over at Jorah, he shook his head at Cali, then lowered his eyes back to Bodric.

"No, Jorah. Don't you do that. I will bring him back. I'm not losing him too. I won't," Cali said, determined.

Chase licked Bodric on the cheek and laid by his head.

Cali tied her hair back away from her face.

"Jorah, bring me fresh boiling water and more whiskey from the storehouse, and several more jars of salve, and get the next room set up for others that need help."

Jorah looked at her for a moment, nodded, then set off to get what she needed.

Rowan limped in from the kitchen, carrying another bottle of whiskey. "Thought you may want a spare in here with you." He gave Cali a little smile.

Cali jumped up and went to Rowan. "You're hurt! Is it bad, are you okay?" She began looking over him to see if he needed help.

"No, no, Cali, I'm fine. A little hurt, nothing that won't heal." He handed her the whiskey.

"What about your Da, Rowan?"

Rowan looked sadly at Cali, suddenly looking much older than his years and shook his head.

"Oh, Rowan! I'm so sorry! Come rest on the couch, come sit." Cali said.

"I'm okay, Cali, really. I'm going to go help with the others that need tending." Rowan started toward the next room, then turned back, "Cali, I'm sorry about your parents, they were good people." Rowan went into the next room to help other injured.

Cali stood, frozen for a moment, fighting back the painful lump in her throat. That was the first time someone had said it out loud. But she knew she needed to focus on Bodric and the rest who were still alive and needed help.

Just then, Jorah came back in with fresh supplies, and Sarah brought in a large bowl and a bucket of steaming water. Cali knelt next to Bodric who was still unconscious, his breathing shallow.

"We have to tend this leg first. We have to get ahead of any infection. He's lost so much blood," Cali said.

Determined she was not going to lose him, she took a fresh cloth, ladled some of the steaming water into the bowl, and set to cleaning the gaping wound on Bodric's thigh. The hands had closed up the wound by tying strips of cloth around his leg. Leaving the tourniquet on, Cali and Jorah removed the strips one by one, cleaning the wound as they went.

Cali looked up at Jorah, her eyes wide.

"Jorah, run out to the barn, bring my leatherworking tools and as many spare strips and pieces as you can carry. Go quick!"

Realizing what she planned, he ran out of the house, returning with an armload of spare leather strips, small rawhide strings, tools, knives, even a jar of salts.

"Perfect, thanks. We are going to mend him, Jorah. We are going to save him. Get some fresh water in the bowl, and pour some of those salts in it. Get a couple of the guys, we may need to hold him down if he comes to."

Jorah looked surprised but did as she said. Watching as Cali went back and cleaned the wound again with the hot, salty water. Several men surrounded Bodric, holding him down if he should wake, while Cali sterilized her leather tools in the fire, then cleaned them with whiskey.

She took a deep breath and began stitching up Bodric's leg. She moved on to the flayed calf, cleaning and closing it, working as fast as she dared.

Turning to Tom, one of the farmhands, Cali said, "Tom, run out to the garden and bring me back a big basket of comfrey leaves and a small bowl, fast as you can."

She ladled fresh, hot water into the bowl, adding more salt, and cleaned the newly closed wounds on his leg.

"Jorah, put a big dollop of the salve in that bowl. Tear up and crush those leaves in there, and then add a swig of whiskey for good measure. I want it thick, like a paste, not runny."

Taking another deep breath, Cali loosened the kitchen towel tourniquet. She loosened it a small bit, then checked Bodric's thigh to make sure it didn't start bleeding, then removing the tourniquet completely. She waited to make sure no bleeding started while the circulation came back. Then she checked his entire leg and foot to make sure the color was returning to normal.

Satisfied that her sewing job seemed to be holding, she took the paste from Jorah and gently spread a thick amount over both leg wounds. Covering the wounds and paste with fresh bandages, she turned her focus on his other wounds.

Cali was thankful that Bodric remained unconscious while she tended his wounds. Her mom was good at this, but this was the first time she had tended wounds this severe.

Together, they removed the stub of the arrow from his arm, cleaning and wrapping the wound as she had the others. Then his chest, which somehow was the least serious of the wounds.

By the time she and Jorah had finished with Bodric's wounds, his left arm, chest, and almost his entire right leg were wrapped in fresh bandages. She bound his leg with wooden garden stakes so when he awoke he wouldn't be able to move his leg.

"We won't move him, not yet. I'll tend him here until he is strong enough for us to move him without hurting him worse," Cali said.

Jorah took the bowls, buckets, and dirty cloth strips to the kitchen. Rowan and several others had been tending to the less injured in the next room.

Others went to the barns and brought back hay, spare blankets, and anything else they could find to be able to give people places to sleep and bunk down.

Sarah gave everyone bowls of soup and bread while they worked on Bodric. After they finished, she brought a bowl to Cali and

Jorah.

"Thanks, Sarah, I don't think I can eat though, give it to one of the guys," Cali said.

"No, you are going to eat this. Jorah, you make sure she eats it, I'm serious," Sarah said, sounding stronger than she looked.

Sarah could see that Cali was getting ready to complain. "Cali, listen. I get it. I do. My Pa, he..." Sarah sniffed and could only shake her head.

She took a deep breath, trying to steel herself.

"I understand, Cali. But if you truly want to save Bodric, you have to be strong enough to do it. Eat." And she turned and went back to the kitchen.

Cali knew she was right. She and Jorah ate, sitting on either side of Bodric. He remained unconscious, his breathing still shallow and fast.

After she ate, Cali realized she was utterly exhausted. She looked up toward the window, seeing the light which looked like sunrise.

Jorah nodded, "Yeah, it's morning. Most everyone has found a place to try to sleep. Some of the men camped outside to keep watch. You take the couch and get a couple hours sleep." Jorah held up his hand to stop Cali resisting.

"Don't argue. I'll watch Bodric, and then we'll switch. Later, you can tell me about that." He said, nodding toward her bow still laying on the floor.

Cali was too tired to argue, and she knew he was right, just like Sarah was right. She had to keep herself strong to make sure she could take care of Bodric. She lay on the couch falling into the blackness of sleep.

CHAPTER
10

Cali woke with a start, disoriented. Looking around she realized it hadn't been just a bad dream. She looked down at Bodric's still form, unmoved from before as Jorah wiped a cool cloth over his face.

"Take some sleep, Jorah. I'll watch over him a while. Are you okay? How's Rowan?"

"We are okay, Cali. They got everyone else patched up and bunked down around the place. There's been no movement, it seems we are all clear out there," Jorah said.

Jorah took her place on the couch. She sat beside of Bodric checking for fever. She looked over at Jorah, but he had already fallen into an exhausted sleep. Rowan was sleeping in the chair in the far corner of the room, and Sarah had fallen asleep in front of the fireplace.

Several people came in to quietly check on Bodric and the others. Cali began to avoid their eyes. She could see her own sadness reflected in them, and she wasn't ready to look at that part of herself yet.

Some bit later, Sarah woke, coming over to sit beside of Cali.

"Would you like me to go start cooking so we can get everyone fed this morning?" Sarah asked.

"Thank you, Sarah. Truly. That would be great. Would you like some help?"

"No. You stay here and watch over Bodric. Some of the wives can help. You stay."

She could hear Sarah in the kitchen beginning to work on breakfast. It seemed most people in the house were still asleep.

Cali wondered about the ones who camped outside, and who else they had lost. Chase stayed by Bodric's head all night, keeping his own watch.

As the smells of breakfast began wafting through the house and out the windows, everyone began to stir and wake. The morning was clear and cool. Cali was having a hard time reconciling what looked like a normal fall morning with the reality of what had happened. As others passed through to the kitchen, she saw the same thought on their faces.

Jorah joined her on the floor next to Bodric as they ate breakfast. They took turns wiping Bodric's increasingly warm brow with a cool cloth.

"Jorah, can you stay with Bodric? I need to… I need to go tend to Da and Mum." Cali said, her voice cracking.

Rowan came back and was sitting on the couch. "Cali, why don't you take Jorah with you to help? I'll stay with Bodric."

Jorah nodded to Rowan. "Thanks, Ro. Cali, can I come with you? I'd like to help if I can."

Cali nodded, and they got up to leave as she slung her bow over her shoulder.

"Chase, stay with Bodric, boy."

As they passed through the kitchen, Tom told them they had moved them into the big barn.

Jorah and Cali left the kitchen, seeing a large pile of burning imp corpses in the field, bringing back the horror of what happened the previous day. They turned, heading past the kitchen garden toward the big barn.

"So, do you want to tell me about that bow and your new armor now?" Jorah asked.

"I don't know all of it, Jorah. How much did you hear?"

Jorah looked sideways at Cali.

"It's okay if you heard. I would have told you anyway."

"I heard all of what Bodric told you. It sounded... well, it sounded a bit far-fetched to tell it true. But, seeing your Da after it all started, I... I had never seen him look like that. I thought what Bodric said might just be —"

"You saw Da? When? What happened, what did he say?"

"Cali, are you sure you want to hear this right now?"

Cali just nodded, fighting that lump in her throat again.

"He was, I don't know Cali, he seemed... more. I know, I know that doesn't make much sense, but that's how he was. It wasn't just Erwin on that horse that came bursting out of the woods. He was bigger somehow, he was fierce, almost scary. A man that no one in his right mind would go against."

Jorah shook his head at the memory before continuing.

"The horse he was on was winded and frothing. He took a fresh horse. He was frantic and determined to make it to you and Bethal."

"He jumped on a horse, no saddle, nothing. Just jumped on the horse and took off like, well, like nothing I've ever seen before. The horse just obeyed him. That horse would have bucked anyone who tried to rein him by the mane. Then they blasted into the forest toward your farm."

He looked at Cali, who stared at him looking torn somewhere between tears and pride. Jorah put his arm around her shoulders.

"Come on, let's go tend to them."

After they had cleaned the battle from her parents, Cali and Jorah were met by a running Chase halfway back to the house.

Jorah knelt to rub Chase as he bounded up to them.

"Jorah... Bodric!"

Cali, Jorah, and Chase took off running back to the house, fearing the worst. They burst into the kitchen to find several people standing near the doorway to the sitting room.

Cali pushed through and dropped beside of a conscious Bodric.

"Bodric! You're awake. Jorah, get me some cold water," Cali called.

Bodric's head was feverish, and his eyes were bright. But not bright from alertness, the far-off bright from a fevered consciousness. He grabbed Cali's arm, with little strength in his grip, as Cali lifted the water to his lips.

"Drink a bit, Bodric. It'll help, drink a bit. Sarah, make me a strong tea, with honey, whiskey, and drop a spoonful of the salve in it to melt," Cali said, turning back to Bodric.

"Cali. The box. Box!" Bodric said.

"It's okay, Bodric. I found the box, it's okay. Don't worry." Cali smoothed his hair back from his forehead.

"Cali, I have to tell you. There's more. You know it's true now, right?"

Jorah shot a look to Cali from his spot on the other side of Bodric.

"Bodric, it's okay, calm down. Really, I know it's all true and right. You need to rest. Don't worry. I'm going to mend you, remember?" Cali said, tears starting to form in her eyes.

"Cali girl. You'll heal fast. Don't know how. Its aim is true. Save the keys." Bodric sounded panicked and confused.

"Bodric, it's okay. Cali's here, I'm here too. We are taking care of you. You've got a fever, don't try to talk right now. We are going to look after you till you're back on your feet," Jorah said, laying his hand on Bodric's shoulder.

Bodric turned his head, looking at Jorah, for the first time realizing all the other people around him.

"Jorah?" Bodric looked at him.

"Yeah, man, I'm here. We all are. You are going to be fine, but you have to rest. You have to save your energy. Okay? Do that for Cali, okay?" Jorah tried to calm him down.

Bodric turned his head back to Cali. With a small smile, "Cali girl. You won't leave yet, right?"

Bodric let go of her arm and held her hand.

"More to tell, Cali girl. More to tell." Bodric's eyes closed.

Cali laid her head on Bodric's hand that she was still holding, and Jorah rubbed her shoulder.

"He's fallen unconscious again. We have to work on this fever or he won't make it, Cali."

Everyone started filing out through the kitchen, many of them stepping out into the garden. Cali wiped Bodric's forehead with the cool cloth again.

"Rowan, can you watch over him for just another few minutes please?"

"Sure, Cali, of course," Rowan said.

Cali stood up, motioning Jorah who followed her into the kitchen and outside.

Several of the farmhands and their families stood around talking. There was muttering, they were worried about Bodric, feeling that he may not pull through his injuries, but they fell silent when they saw Cali step out.

They turned to Cali expectantly. For a moment she stood there, Jorah on one side, Chase on the other.

"We've been through a nightmare. We've lost a…" Cali choked back tears as she looked toward the large barn, then at her friends.

Their exhausted and scared eyes stared back at her.

"We've lost a lot. But I have to ask something of some of you. In a few days, we need to send out a party to the other farms."

Several of the women gasped. In the chaos of what happened here, none had thought about the other farms and if there were injured still there.

"If things were different…" Cali gestured at the house behind her, they all knew she meant Bodric. "I would go myself. I wouldn't ask this of any of you."

Tom stepped forward. "Cali, we'd never let you go by yourself. You don't need to ask, after we… after the ceremony, we'll go to the farms."

Several men in the group nodded or put a hand on Tom's shoulder. Cali knew they would make sure there were none left alone out there.

"I hope it's a wasted trip, Tom. I hope none of the others even saw those monsters. But we have to make sure," Cali said.

"Make sure you are armed. Take the big wagon. We'll load you up with the salve and bandages we can spare. Bring everyone you find back here." Jorah added.

"Yes, what Jorah said. And back here, we'll get the small barn set up to house everyone. But I'll feel a lot better if we can get everyone to winter over here. We don't know what those were, where they came from, or why. Or worse, if there are more, and if they are coming back. I want us all together until we're sure," Cali said.

They all agreed that was the best idea, and began to wander off, talking to each other or to be alone with their grief. Cali and Jorah went back inside to Bodric.

Jorah told Rowan the plan, who also thought wintering over with everyone together was the safest plan. He stood, with some trouble, and said he was going to check on some of the other injured.

"Is he okay, Jorah? Was his arm injured badly?"

"He is okay, thanks, Cali. He took a nasty cut on his upper back and that shoulder and banged up his knee a bit. He told me he felt lucky." Jorah shook his head. He was thankful his older brother wasn't injured worse.

They propped Bodric up on pillows, so they could give him small sips of the medicated tea and water. Focusing on Bodric and trying to stave off the infection took Cali's full attention the rest of that day. Bodric woke from his sleep briefly and didn't try to talk much.

With Jorah's help, Cali managed to change the dressings on Bodric's wounds. They were pleased to see the gash in his thigh was clean, there was no sign of redness or infection. The source seemed to be from the spot where the arrow pierced through his upper arm. It was swollen, red, and hot to the touch.

Jorah and Cali exchanged a dark glance seeing his arm.

"Jorah, I think there was a splinter of that arrow left in his arm. The wound was cleaned. There was no poison. It has to be that," Cali said.

"I'll go get a couple of the guys and have Sarah put on some water to boil. We have to get it out." Jorah stood and left.

Cali was terrified. Cleaning wounds, making poultices, binding wounds, she had no real fear of that. But this. Cutting into Bodric's arm to find a piece of arrow — a splinter that she believed was there but had no real proof, this was something her mom could have done.

She looked at Bodric's pale and feverish face, listened to his shallow breathing, and knew she had no choice. It had to be done.

With boiling water, fresh bandages, and a new mixture of the paste they used on his other wounds, Cali took a deep breath and lowered her knife to Bodric's arm.

CHAPTER
II

Cali walked out of the kitchen and around the corner of the house. Closing her eyes, she leaned against the house, her head in her hands crying.

Feeling a hand on her shoulder she looked up to see Jorah.

"I may have killed him, Jorah. By the Mother, what if I killed him? I didn't know. I guessed that there was a piece of the arrow in there!" Cali sobbed.

"Cali. Calm down, breathe. You probably saved his life. You were right. There was a splinter. It caused the infection. Breathe," Jorah said, pulling Cali into a hug.

"I've never done anything like that before. It was always Mum or Da who did that sort of thing. I could have killed him. What if I made it worse? What if I had been wrong?" Cali turned away from Jorah, crying harder.

Jorah took hold of her shoulders turning her around.

"Listen to me right now. You likely saved Bodric's life. Hear that again. Saved. His. Life. No one will ever fault you for doing what none of the rest of us could have done."

Cali nodded, trying to catch her breath.

"Cali, listen, you've been through more in the past few days than any normal person could bear in a lifetime. You're allowed to break down. And you can't save everybody. But if it's possible, if the Mother wills it, you will save Bodric. I know it. Now, let's get some food, and go check on our patient."

∞　　∞　　∞

The next morning, after another night of switching shifts with Jorah, Cali sat, mopping Bodric's brow with a cool cloth. Sarah came in with another steaming mug of medicated tea, sitting with Cali. She held the cool cloth on his forehead while Cali fed small spoonsful of the hot tea to the still-unconscious Bodric.

"Sarah, thank you. I don't know how I would have done these past days without you here. I'm sorry about your dad."

"Thanks, Cali. I want to help. I can't do this... what you've done with Bodric here, but I can cook and clean, and help out other ways. I have to help. I have to do something." She looked at Cali with sadness in her eyes.

Cali nodded. "I understand. Well, I'm glad you are here." Cali sighed. "He's still so pale, Sarah."

"He's going to be good, Cali. He's a strong man, and you will mend him. You will bring him back from this fever."

Sarah sat, thinking for a moment. "What do you think about feeding him fresh broth? Between the tea feedings? Maybe we can get some more meat in him, even if it's not actual meat yet."

"Sarah, that's a great idea! We can't get any real food into him right now, but that might help him get stronger and fight this. Yes! Let's give that a try."

Sarah headed to the kitchen to start making fresh beef bone broth. Jorah woke and joined Cali, listening to their plan of feeding Bodric some broth too.

Shortly before midday, everyone gathered outside the house. Tom's wife volunteered to stay to watch over Bodric. The rest headed out to the field where they'd had the feast gathering what seemed like a lifetime ago.

The large wagons made their slow procession to where they gathered. Bethal, Erwin, Stefen Calbert, Jenkins, and several farmhands made their final journey across the farm. The wagons led the group toward the lake where they stopped. The fresh-hewn wooden boxes came to rest under the massive tree near the lake edge.

It was hard for everyone, taking turns talking about the loved ones lost in the attack. Many who tried to speak couldn't find the words, so instead sang, or recounted memories. Sarah, Rowan, Jorah, and Cali sat together in the front.

It was a mild fall day, sunny, with a cool, gentle breeze from the lake which swirled around them as they sat, trying to come to grips with what had happened.

In their own time, people started making their way back toward the farmhouse, while others stood around talking. More than one came up to Cali to thank her, and tell her that had it not been for Bethal, more would have died. They were at once proud and grateful for Bethal's bravery, yet shocked that she fought and killed the monsters. Cali politely smiled and thanked them as best she could.

Tables had been set up in the yard outside of the kitchen. Several roasts, potatoes, pies and other dishes had been cooking for everyone to gather together after the long day of saying goodbye.

Making their way back to the house, Rowan sat at one of the tables, Sarah headed into the kitchen to check on the bone broth, and Jorah and Cali headed back to Bodric. Cali felt older and more tired than she had ever felt in her life.

As they came into the house, Tabitha, Tom's wife, jumped up and ran over to them.

"Cali, Cali, come on. Bodric's fever - his fever has broke!"

Sure enough, as Cali sat next to Bodric, his face still covered in a sheen of sweat, but his breathing was deep and even. She laid her hand on his head, the heat that had been emanating was much lower than it had been earlier in the day.

Tears that had been stuck behind Cali's eyes fell freely as she smiled in earnest for the first time in days. Looking up from Bodric she saw Jorah smiling at her, nodding.

"Callera Flynn. Dear, you may turn out a better healer than even your sweet mama." Tabitha took Cali's hand, squeezing it hard and giving her a kiss on the cheek before leaving her and Jorah with Bodric.

Sarah brought a huge plate of food in for Cali and Jorah, and a small bowl of broth in for Bodric, while everyone else began their feast outside at the tables. Rowan and Sarah brought their food in and sat on the couch to eat. But word spread fast that Bodric had turned for the better, and many others came in and sat around the room eating too.

Bodric was still unconscious, but Cali was hopeful now that he may pull through. Jorah was convinced that his body was working so hard fighting the infection and mending that there simply wasn't energy enough left for him to wake right now.

The sadness still clung to each of them, but there was a small spark of hope too. No one wanted to say it for fear of jinxing it, but it was there, in the back of everyone's mind. Hope was still alive.

The next morning, Cali woke up to a pale, exhausted, but awake Bodric. Jorah had been watching over him as everyone slept, and he had woken shortly after sunrise. Excited, Cali jumped down onto the floor next to him and held his hand, tears spilling down her face again.

Bodric gave her a weak smile and croaked out "Cali girl."

"Don't try to talk right now, Bodric. Save your energy to get better. Here, drink." She helped him take sips of water. The first time he had been awake to do it since the attack. Bodric fell back asleep, his breathing deep and even.

Sarah and some of the ladies were preparing a huge breakfast for everyone. Today was going to be a busy day. Tom and the others were preparing to head to the other farms, and there was much work that needed doing.

Cali was thankful that those injured were recovering, as their stores of salve were running short. She would work with Sarah and the other women to teach them how to make more, and they could replenish their supplies for the upcoming winter.

Tom came in after breakfast and sat next to Rowan on the couch, smiling.

"I knew you would do it, Cali. I knew you would help Bodric get better."

"Thanks, Tom. He's not out of the woods yet. Still, a long way to go, but I know he'll pull through," Cali said.

"Cali, I was talking to some of the men, and we had an idea. I wanted to run it past you though and see what you thought." Tom looked at her seriously.

In shock, Cali didn't know how to respond. She hadn't considered that now, after everything, that she, Cali, was the Flynn farmstead. And that the hands and all the others would be looking to her as they had to her parents before her. The realization slammed into her as hard as if she had been hit by a board.

"Ri... Right, of course, Tom. What is it?"

"Well, I know that the folks staying here were going to work on turning the small barn into a bunkhouse of sorts. But I was thinking. We have more than enough people to build onto your farmhouse here. We could build a proper addition, where each family could have their own rooms and such. It would be much more comfortable and secure than using the barns, too," Tom said.

Cali was suddenly very aware that everyone in the room was looking at her. More than that, they were looking for her to consider all the options, make a decision, then execute it.

Only hours before, Cali had felt older and more tired than she had ever felt, now, she felt like a child again, with the sudden shock of realizing that she wasn't.

She took a quick glance at Jorah, and Rowan, and saw that Rowan gave her a tiny nod, almost unnoticeable. Cali cleared her throat.

"Tom, I think that's a wonderful idea. You're right, we have more than enough materials to build it, and we have a good number of people healthy enough to jump in and make this happen."

Cali thought fast. "Here's what we're going to do. You are more knowledgeable at building than me, so please tell me if any part of this won't work, okay, Tom? The addition needs to be at least large enough to house all the people, whether single or families we have here now, of course. But we are going to triple that."

Surprised, everyone looked at her. Cali continued.

"We have no idea what we are going to... what we are going to find at the other farms. We need to plan for as many people as possible, in the hopes that the other farms were spared."

"Also, Tom. When you and the men head out to the farms, I have another task for you. I want you to take both large wagons, and one of the smaller ones."

Tom and the others looked even more surprised but continued looking at Cali listening to her orders.

"At each farm, I want you to bring back as many supplies as you can load on the wagon. If we are going to have everyone winter over together here, we are going to need as many provisions as we can gather."

Tom looked at her thoughtfully for a moment, running his hand through his hair.

"Cali, that's spot on. I'll have the men prepare the other wagons, and start organizing the building. We'll plan on leaving first thing in the morning to give me time to get everything running." Tom stood and walked back out through the kitchen.

Sarah brought a kettle of tea and several cups and sat beside Rowan on the couch.

"Cali, I think you are going to be just fine handling all this," Rowan said with a smile.

CHAPTER 12

Early the next morning, as Cali and Jorah sat with Bodric helping him drink some tea, Tom came in.

"Bodric! Old man! About time you decided to rejoin us, we have a lot of work that needs doing around here!" Tom winked at Bodric.

Still weak and exhausted, Bodric managed a smile and a dirty look at Tom. But Cali could tell he was getting some of his strength back.

"Cali, I wanted to report in. The men are going to start working on the addition this morning, so there will be a lot of noise and comings and goings. I put Dorin in charge of the building team because he knows his stuff. And Rowan in charge of materials so they'll be in to see you."

"Tabbi and some of the ladies are going to start sewing up blankets, pillows, curtains, all those things we'll be needing. And I set another small crew to gather more materials from the forest."

Seeing the look of alarm on Cali's face, Tom continued, "Now don't worry. They're all armed, they're going to stick together, and they aren't going in any further than the tree line. But we are going to need to materials. What doesn't get used for the building will be used for the fires over the winter. It'll still be green wood, but it will do."

"Tom, thank you for all you're doing. Do you think three wagons will be enough?"

"I'm sure it will, Cali. Besides, we'll be bringing back the other farms' wagons too, so we'll have plenty of room to bring back people and provisions. We've loaded up the medicine and bandages, and we're all armed and ready. Don't worry, Cali, I'll bring them all back safe."

Tom stood, giving Bodric another wink and left. Bodric looked at Cali questioningly, his eyebrows raised.

Jorah, Cali, and Rowan spent the next hour telling Bodric all that had happened since the attack. Catching him up on what all they had done, the decisions made, and the plans put into action. Bodric looked at Cali, pride showing out of his eyes.

"You've done good, Cali girl," he said.

His voice was still rough, and Cali could tell he was still pained, but to her, it was the best sound in the world.

The next couple days passed in a blur. Bodric was improving, even if he was becoming a bit grumpy. And everyone was busy making preparations.

Piles of blankets, pillows, and curtains were stacked around the house. Cali taught Sarah and some of the wives how to make salve, and they were beginning to replenish their stock. Logs were being brought to the house, milled into timbers, and constant pounding was happening on the new addition.

"I can at least go outside to help oversee things, answer questions, something!" Bodric fumed.

"Bodric, you can't walk yet. It's too soon on that leg. I know you hate being cooped up in here, but the most important thing is for you to heal," Cali said.

Bodric's bad mood continued, he wasn't used to doing nothing. And seeing everyone else busy working and preparing for the new housing and people made it worse.

In the afternoon, Jorah pulled Cali aside. "Me, Rowan, and Dorin are going to carry Bodric outside for a while this afternoon."

"What? No! He can't be moved around yet, Jorah."

"Cali. Yes, he can. He can't walk on his own yet, sure, but you know we'll be careful, and he needs to feel useful. He needs to feel like he's helping you shoulder all this."

"Jorah, I don't know. I don't think it's — "

"Cali, listen to me. The one thing that Bodric would do, before anything else, before his own health even, is to swear to himself to take care of you after losing Bethal and Erwin. You have to let him help."

"I..." Cali sighed. "You are right, Jorah. I know you are. Okay, but we have to bring a chair and stool out there, his leg has to stay propped up."

"Great, thanks, Cali. And I'll tell Dorin and the men if they have any questions to go straight to Bodric." Jorah grinned and turned to leave before Cali could complain.

Sarah and Cali sat at the kitchen table after lunch as the next batch of salve simmered over the fire. The flurry of work outside had resumed after everyone ate, and the next batch of logs was being hauled in.

The hammering in the addition continued, but would soon quiet down, the men were talking about raising the first walls later in the afternoon.

Bodric was happily talking to the men outside in his chair. Cali had made Jorah and Rowan promise to keep him there and not let him try to get up and move around on his own yet. But she knew he was ready to try. Never being one to sit around, he was antsy and restless, but at least his bad mood had subsided being out around the men and feeling useful.

"I was thinking, Cali," Sarah said, pausing a moment to drink her tea.

"We need to start making arrangements for who is going to go where in the house." She finished.

"There are several bedrooms here in the main house, I was thinking that Bodric could have my room since it's downstairs here, and I know he'll be trying to walk around on his own soon." Cali sighed, shaking her head.

"I think you need to move into your parent's room," Sarah said, trying to see how Cali would react. "Jorah and Rowan can each take a room and Bodric of course. Then we can figure out how to arrange everyone in the addition once we know who all we're dealing with."

"I don't know, Sarah. I mean, I'm not sure about Mum and Da's room. The rest is fine though."

"Cali, look. You are the Flynn farmstead now. You know that. And don't take me wrong, you're doing amazing! But you need to accept your new role. And getting settled in is the next step."

"Yeah, maybe. I wonder how Tom's doing. I'm starting to get anxious, I hope they don't run into any trouble," Cali said as she looked out the kitchen door.

Together they walked out and joined Bodric in the yard. The weather was still holding out, bright and sunny as the men worked on the addition.

Cali was surprised at how large it actually was, and how much the men had accomplished in such a short time. The framing was in place. The rooms roughed out, stairs built, and the floors put in on the upper level. It stretched out to one side but was in an "L" shape that wrapped around the back of the main house.

Seeing Cali's surprise, Bodric told her they made some slight design changes. Wrapping it around the backside of the house would allow them to continue building if they needed more space after Tom and the men returned.

The rooms roughed out on the ground floor were larger and would be for the families with children. These rooms were going to have a small partition wall, so the parents and children could have their own areas. The rooms on the upper level were for couples and individuals and were smaller, but still spacious. There were fireplaces spaced throughout the addition to evenly heat the building.

Bodric and Rowan were discussing plans for a large kitchen and dining area separate from the main house. It would make feeding everyone easier if it wasn't centered around the farmhouse kitchen alone.

Cali knew in that instant that Jorah had been right in bringing Bodric out to help. He looked stronger and was sounding more like his normal self. And she had to admit that it was a relief having him to help be in charge.

After the next load of logs came in, the men from the wood crew stayed to help raise the first exterior wall. Everyone had stopped to come watch as the addition was beginning to take form. Cheers erupted from everyone as the first wall went up.

The addition was taking shape, and would soon be home to many of their friends and family from Edelaine.

That evening after dinner, it was decided that Bodric would take Cali's old bedroom. Cali and Sarah had cleaned it out and readied it for Bodric.

"Thanks, Cali girl, and you too Sarah." Bodric smiled.

"It will be nice to be in a real bed again, rest these old bones. And what about you lot? What rooms are you moving into? Cali, you need to take your folk's room. Sarah, you could have that next largest bedroom up there. The other two could go to Rowan and Jorah, if that sounds okay to you, Cali?"

Again, Cali felt their eyes on her, waiting for the decision.

I don't think I'll ever get used to this, she thought.

"Right. Yes, that sounds good. Makes more sense than us sleeping in the living room," Cali said.

She smiled, even though she still wasn't comfortable with the idea of taking her parent's room. *I guess it's inevitable.*

Rowan cleared his throat. "So, uh, Dorin made something extraordinary today."

Everybody murmured in agreement. Jorah and Bodric smiled.

"He really did, it's incredible what you all and the men have done in the past few days," Cali said.

"Thanks, and yes, Dorin and the men have pulled the addition together quickly," Rowan added.

"But no, he made something else. He made a new wooden brace for Bodric's leg."

Cali eyed them suspiciously. "Really?"

"Yeah, it's ingenious actually, Cali. It will support most of Bodric's weight so that he can stand, but the weight won't fall directly onto his injured leg."

Cali jumped up. "Oh no, no way. That leg is not ready for standing and walking around. No!"

"Cali girl, I don't want to sound ungrateful and all," Bodric said, "but don't you think this is my decision?"

"I… but your leg…" Cali was livid. "Fine. It's your leg. But I expect each of you to make sure he has help and someone with him just in case!" she jabbed her finger at each of them in turn.

Bodric just grinned at Rowan and Jorah, obviously happy about this victory. Chase leaped up on the couch beside of Bodric.

Cali glared at Bodric and Chase. "You too, Chase? You've all been scheming behind my back!" Everyone laughed.

CHAPTER
13

Bodric took his time learning to use the brace and a sturdy cane that Rowan had made for him to stand, and walk short distances. Cali could tell it pained him, but even she had to admit that it didn't appear to be hurting the wounds, and it would help strengthen him.

The work continued on the addition, the other exterior walls were raised, and the interior walls were also coming together. Some of the builders broke off into another crew to bring in stone for the fireplaces, as the builders continued on the interior.

The final decision on the new kitchen and dining area came to Cali, who agreed that if we had the materials, it made sense to go ahead and build it. And with that, they added two more rooms. A large kitchen stretched the width of the addition, while the dining hall stretched the length along the side.

Cali and Sarah had gone out to walk around the addition. It had turned into something far beyond the size that Cali imagined, and the work going into it was tremendous, but she knew it was the right thing to do. She never knew why or how her parents came to be the ones the others looked to as being in charge. But she now felt that weight plainly and heavily on her own shoulders.

They sat at one of the tables, watching the work continue.

"I'm beginning to worry about Tom and the others," Cali said.

She and Sarah had become close since the attack, and she was grateful to have someone to talk to about her worries.

"I am too," Sarah replied.

"It's been seven days. I remind myself that with provisions and families in tow, they will be moving much slower than normal, but I can't help but worry. I have to keep everyone safe, Sarah."

"You don't have to do it alone, Cali. You have us to help you, and we want to help. You are right, they will be moving slower than if it were only a wagon or two and a few people. I'm sure it's nothing to worry over. But if you are still concerned, bring it up with Bodric."

Just then, Bodric, Jorah, and Rowan turned the corner of the addition heading toward the tables. Bodric was moving better with his brace, but still slow, and still with difficulty. They joined Cali and Sarah at the tables.

"Well, Cali girl, what do you think?" Bodric asked.

"It's incredible. It's huge. I hadn't thought about how large it would be, it makes sense. But still."

"Everyone's worked tirelessly. You brought everyone together, Cali," Bodric said.

"This wasn't just me, Bodric. This was all of us. It's just incredible. I'm worried though. It's been seven days, and we've not seen anyone."

"Aw well, they'll be moving slow-like, Cali. Even if the other farms were spared, they'll have to explain what happened, gather provisions, get everyone together, packed, and ready to move."

Bodric rubbed his beard, thinking to himself.

"We know they hit Calbert, Jenkins, and our steads. That's all we know for fact. The others may not have no idea what happened. Or they may. We don't know."

"There was smoke coming from the direction of Jossin's place. But that's not a knowing. We can only go on what we know. And that is what you are doing here." Bodric waved his hand at the house.

"No need for worrying for at least another few days. Then we can talk worry."

Bodric paused for a moment as if he were wanting to say more, rubbing at his beard again.

"And about that, Cali, we have to do some talking, you know," Bodric said with a serious look.

Sarah, Rowan, and Jorah got up to leave, turning to head back to the kitchen.

"Jorah, son, you stay if you will," Bodric said.

They sat for a long time, not speaking. They listened to the workers in the addition, the logs being brought in, the stones being dumped in a pile nearby.

Sarah walked back from the kitchen carrying a tea kettle and some cups. She set them on the table, gave Bodric a little smile and also set down a small bottle of whiskey.

"Just in case," She said, turning back to the house.

Chase jumped up on the bench beside of Cali and fell asleep. Bodric looked across the table at Cali. He looked sad, and more than a little tired.

"Cali girl, I know you know at least some of what I told you is true now." He motioned toward her bow.

Bodric continued, looking at Jorah. "And I know you know at least some of what I told her."

Jorah nodded, keeping silent.

Bodric tried reached across to the kettle wincing, but Jorah did it for him. Pouring three cups of tea, and with a tired smile, added a large swig of whiskey to each one.

"Now listen, now that you are sure I'm all here in my right mind," Bodric grinned, "as much as I've ever been… I'll tell you everything I know."

His smile looked tired, and his eyes looked sad.

"I don't know all of it, Cali girl. Only the pieces Bethal and Erwin — mostly Bethal — could explain. And of course, the bits I saw with my own eyes."

"Bethal was a guardian, a protector of sorts. Of the whole world, so the legend goes. One from each generation of her family, how far back only the Mother knows. I've never seen anyone fight like she did, Cali. Never. I never thought those bastard imps would take her."

Bodric's voice cracked. He took a swig of his tea, shaking his head.

"She never told you, never wanted to tell you. And why should she really? Edelaine and the world's known peace since before any of us, for ages past. The stories were just that. A legend passed down through her family. Stories of the history. But the evil had gone. There was none left. Her and Erwin never wanted you burdened with it, and never believed in their heart that you would need to be."

Bodric paused again, collecting his thoughts.

"Oh, they would have told you the legend eventually, passing on the keys and such. But there was no danger. No evil left. So, we all thought. Can you... can you pick up your bow and hold it out for me, Cali?"

Cali looked a little surprised. Jorah looked from Bodric to Cali, confused.

Nodding, Cali stood up. She took a deep breath and removed the bow from her back. The warmth filled her hand, encircled her arm, enveloped her completely.

Jorah jumped up with a gasp.

"Jorah, son, it's all right, Cali's fine, aren't you, Cali girl?" Bodric smiled.

She slung the bow back over her shoulder, sitting back down at the table.

"What in the name of... the light... a bow can't... what was that?" Jorah looked shaken and pale.

"That, Jorah, was the prophecy. See, from what I know, as soon as Bethal was… as soon as she passed on, the prophecy fell onto Cali. She is the next in line. Only the one bearing the blood of the prophecy can call on the power of that bow. Or that armor." Bodric tilted his head toward Cali's bracers.

"So… so, if I were to take her bow, would it like, kill me, or do something bad?" Jorah asked, still shaken.

"No, no, nothing like that. I held it before, you know what happened?" Bodric grinned at them.

"Nothing. It was a bit of a letdown after seeing Bethal with it!" he grinned at the memory.

"No, Jorah, in your hand, mine, or any other's it is just an ancient wooden bow, nothing more. Same with the key. Just a key that won't open nothing, not without the blood of the prophecy."

Cali took the bow and laid it on the table between them. "But it's not ancient, Bodric. Look at it. There's not a nick. Not a scratch, a mar, there wasn't even dust!"

"Cali girl, like I said, I don't know it all. But I do know that bow is ancient. The stories tell that it is as old as time itself and that it was time that strung it."

"What?" both Cali and Jorah said.

"What do you mean, it was time that strung it?" Cali asked.

"I can't say for sure, but you tell me what kind of bowstring that is." Bodric nodded toward it again.

He was right, none of them had ever seen a bowstring like the silvery one that was on Cali's bow. It almost looked as if the air itself had been made solid.

"Alls I know is when Bethal showed me the bow the first time, and I watched her shoot with it... it was as if time had stopped. Well, time had stopped for everyone but her. In the blink of an eye, she loosed half a dozen arrows. In barely the span of a breath." Bodric shook his head again, seeing the memory in his mind.

"Okay, but that still doesn't explain how an ancient bow can look new," Cali said.

"It heals, Cali girl." Bodric looked at her.

"It what!" Jorah looked as if Bodric had gone crazy.

"Jorah, son, hear me, I thought it was far-fetched when they told me too. But it heals itself. And those heal its owner too." He motioned at the bracers again.

"That's just, that can't be, Bodric," Cali said.

But she remembered cutting her hand to open the box. Glancing down at her hand there was nothing more than a tiny white line on her palm as if a cut had been there years before. A scar, just like Bethal's.

"Can it not be? You opened the box after all."

"Cali, what's he mean, you opened the box after all," Jorah asked.

"I had to use the key and my blood to open the box. I cut my hand to do it," Cali said, still staring at her hand.

Jorah grabbed her hand, turning it over and again looking for the cut.

Bodric pulled out his knife. "Do you trust me, Cali girl?"

"Of course, Bodric."

"Well, this is gonna hurt both of us a little bit, but just watch."

Bodric took his knife and cut into the wood of the bow, dropping his knife and shaking his hand.

"Stings a bit, that." He grinned.

Sure enough, there was a cut in the surface of the bow.

Bodric reached for Cali's hand, he nodded at her, and when she nodded back, he put a shallow cut in her palm.

"What the… Bodric, what are you doing?" Jorah yelled.

"Just wait son, you know I mean no harm here. Now, Cali girl, feed the stone on your bow."

Cali placed her bleeding palm on the deep blue stone inlaid in her bow. At first, nothing happened. Then, the blood slowly disappeared, the stone took on a darkly swirling look, and the knife cut in the bow slowly vanished. The bow looked new.

"Now your bracer." Bodric nodded toward her bracers.

She put her bloodied palm on the stone of the left bracer. Just as with the bow, the stone absorbed the blood, seemed to darken for a moment, and her hand tingled sharply.

Gasping, Jorah grabbed her hand, there was still some blood on her palm, but no cut could be seen. Only a tiny, almost unnoticeable scar.

They all sat, staring at the tiny scar for what seemed like a long time.

Jorah reached over and added another swig of whiskey to each of their cups.

Bodric laughed, nodding. "That's exactly the same thing I did the first time, Jorah."

Cali's tears fell into her upturned hand.

"Cali girl, what is it?"

"These, these could have saved Mom, couldn't they?" It was barely a whisper when she said it.

Bodric reached over and took her hand with a wince.

"No, Cali girl, no. They can help heal a wound, but they can't… they can't stop death. They don't make you indestructible. You saw your hand, you can still be injured. They can heal, but the worse the wound, the harder it is to heal, and the longer it takes. And some wounds… well, some wounds just can't be helped." Bodric looked at her sadly.

Cali stood, putting the bow back on her shoulder and walked off without a word. Chase following at her heels.

Jorah stood to follow, but Bodric grabbed his arm.

"Let her go, son. She's safe enough, and she needs to deal with this."

CHAPTER
14

Sarah was already awake and in the kitchen starting breakfast when Cali came downstairs. She poured two cups of tea and headed for Bodric's room, knocking softly on the door before she went in.

Sarah continued making breakfast as a couple of others came in to help before the men were to start working for the day. It was a chilly morning, gray, but since the addition was walled and under roof, rain wouldn't slow down the work.

The slamming door was felt through the house and Bodric's angry voice reverberated.

"Absolutely not, Callera. No. That is not an option."

The women looked on from the kitchen doorway, as Rowan and Jorah hurried down the steps, stopping at the bottom.

Bodric had come limping out of his room, his face red, angry, and pacing as best he could in the living room.

Cali, looking equally angry shouted back.

"I don't remember asking your permission, Bodric. In case you forget, I am the one who helps people heal and recover!"

"I am fine. I don't need no more of your healing if that's the price of it. No."

Wincing, Bodric sat as well as he could on the couch, propping his leg up on the nearby chair.

"Right. It appears you are in perfect condition!" Cali snapped back and stomped from the room, out through the kitchen door.

No one knew quite what to say or do. They all stood wide-eyed and staring at Bodric. No one had ever heard them argue. Sarah and the others hurried back to the kitchen to work on breakfast, talking amongst themselves.

Rowan walked through the living room into the kitchen, and Jorah came over and sat on the couch by Bodric.

"I know she has been tense since we talked about... everything the other day, but what was that about, Bodric?"

Bodric was still angry.

"Silly girl! That's what it's about!"

Bodric took a deep breath and lowered his voice, looking at Jorah.

"She wants to use her bracers on me," Bodric said, shaking his head.

"She what?"

"Exactly. Did she not hear me when I told her she had to feed the stone! That only the blood of the prophecy could use those powers! No, Jorah, no. I know she means well, but no! I will not agree to this."

Jorah took a deep breath of his own, running his hands over his face.

"No, Bodric, I agree with you. Would that even work? Can it do that... heal like that for someone else?"

"I don't know exactly. The stories say it can, but think, man! It would take her blood to make it work, and this..." Bodric motioned at his leg, "is not a light cut!"

Bodric looked as tired as Jorah had ever seen him. He closed his eyes and put his head back on the couch, again lowering his voice to talk to Jorah.

"Go talk to her. She won't hear me right now, but she listens to you. Talk some sense into her."

Jorah found her sitting at the farthest table, near the corner of the new addition. He wasn't sure if she looked more mad or upset. Chase was on the table, and they were almost nose-to-nose since Cali was resting her head on her arms.

"Let's walk, what do you say?"

Cali looked up at Jorah and nodded. They walked in silence for a bit, Chase running ahead and pouncing on bugs in the damp grass.

"Cali, Bodric told me what you wanted to do. Now wait, don't start arguing. Just listen."

He gave her a minute to calm back down and took a deep breath.

"Bodric's right, you know. You can't risk it. You did a

miraculous thing bringing him back and tending to him like you did. Now you have to let him heal and get strong on his own. What you want to do - I get why you want to do it. I do. But you have to keep yourself strong."

They continued walking, not speaking. Jorah couldn't tell if he was getting through to her or not. He pressed on.

"You know the condition of his leg, it's mending, but if you do have to actually... feed... that stone, how much of you do you think it would take. Really?"

He watched Cali from the corner of his eye, he knew she was listening, but she wasn't responding. At least she's not yelling at me, he thought.

They came to the graves near the big tree by the lake edge.

"Cali, what were you thinking? I'm being serious. He's fine, sure it will take him a while to completely mend, but he's fine. Why would you risk yourself without even knowing what it would take to do it, or what the outcome would even be?"

She sat at the base of the tree, looking at the fresh graves, not speaking as the morning light continued to brighten.

"Jorah, I don't feel somehow all great, or strong, or powerful, or, or... certainly not like some protector or guardian! I don't know what any of this is. I don't want it! Sure, the bow has a power, and I feel it. But I don't understand it. I don't, I can't... I just... I don't know what I'm supposed to do now, Jorah."

Covering her face with her hands, she cried.

Jorah let her cry until she was able to cry it out, then took her hand.

"Cali, I don't know either. But maybe... maybe you're not supposed to *do* anything right now. Maybe, you are already doing exactly what you need to be doing, which is taking care of everyone that you can. You can't save everyone. And... you can't bring them back."

Cali nodded, tears still running down her cheeks as she stared at the graves of her parents.

"There are people who are still here who need you. Besides, if you are some incredible protector now," he grinned and poked her in the side, "don't you think you should keep yourself healthy and strong and not take unnecessary risks?"

Cali almost laughed. "You're right, Jorah. I know you are. But he's... Bodric's the only almost family I have left. I just wanted to..."

"I know, Cali. And so does Bodric. He understands why you wanted to do it, but he would never let you do something that could hurt you to help him. You know that. Now, come on, let's go back to the house and have some breakfast before it's time for lunch."

Jorah pulled Cali up and they walked slowly back to the house.

∞　∞　∞

They were now eleven days out from when Tom and the others had left to go to the other farms, and the worry was starting to show on everyone's face. Even Bodric was beginning to worry.

Cali, Sarah, and some others busied themselves making more salve and bandages, and working in the garden on the cold-weather vegetables. The wood-cutting crew continued bringing more wood in from the forest edge, most of it now being split to dry for later in the winter. The builders had split, part of them working on the new kitchen and dining hall, and the rest putting the finishing work inside the addition.

They spent a good part of the evening taking the blankets, pillows, curtains, and some other items to each of the quarters in the new addition. Starting to get them ready for everyone to move into. The families were still haphazardly camped in the main farmhouse and small barn while the addition was being worked on. Plus, everyone was still hopeful that at any moment a caravan led by Tom would be coming up the road around the bend.

The last stores of wool were processing in the barn, to be used to make more winter items needed for the others coming.

But the nagging worry hovered in their minds, why weren't Tom and the others back yet?

Tabitha, Tom's wife, had come into the kitchen and overheard some of the ladies talking worriedly about it. They hushed as soon as they saw her, of course, but it didn't matter.

Tabitha told them that Tom was perfectly fine, she felt in her heart that she would know if something had happened to her husband. And Cali believed she was right. But that nagging worry still plagued them all.

That evening as they sat around the fire in the living room, Cali said, "I am going to ride out if they aren't back in the next two days."

She said it so calmly that they didn't realize what she had said at first. Of course, they all told her under no terms would they have her ride out to anywhere for any reason.

"No, Cali girl, you can't ride out to see what's going on. I know you're worried. We all are. But if there is a reason to be worried, then none of us should go. And if there's not a reason to worry, we won't need to go."

"Fair point, Bodric," Rowan said.

"None of us could stand against those… things anyway, you are right, Bodric, we are best here," Sarah said.

Jorah stole a quick glance at Cali, but they both knew she wasn't ready to be any kind of protector, they didn't even understand what it all meant.

"Right. So, no talk about riding out, Cali girl. They are fine, I am betting on it. The best we can do is make sure we are ready for them when they get here."

"I almost forgot. Dorin told me earlier that the dining area and the kitchen would be ready tomorrow!" Sarah said.

"That's amazing. It's incredible the work they've put in on all this," Cali said.

"Sarah, what would you think about this? Let's get together in the morning and prepare a feast for everyone to break in the new dining area?"

"Cali, that's a great idea! We'll have to use our kitchen until the new one is ready tomorrow, but that would be great!" Sarah replied.

CHAPTER
15

"Sarah, what are you thinking for the feast today?" Cali asked.

The workers filtered in and out getting breakfast and drinks and the news of the feast had spread fast. Everyone still carried the nagging worry about Tom and the other farms. They were doing what they could to help ease everyone's stress with the breaking in of the new dining hall.

"I'm thinking we'll make a few roasts and fresh breads. Tabbi is making some fruit pies too," Sarah said.

Everyone loved Tabitha's pies, she was a brilliant baker, with the pies being her favorite to make.

"It sounds so strange to me to hear people say we are eating in the dining hall tonight. I never thought Flynn farm would ever have a dining hall!" Cali laughed. "Sound rather formal, doesn't it?"

Cali left the kitchen to go look through the new kitchen and dining area, and check out the quarters now that they were being finished up.

Opening the door to the hall, Cali was again surprised at how large it was. On one end of the space was a massive stone fireplace. On the opposite end, another fireplace, and turning to the left, a large doorway which led to the new kitchens. All along the walls were counters, with hewn stools and chairs spaced around the area.

The men began carrying the tables from the yard into the hall, spacing them in two rows down the length of the room. It was hard for Cali to imagine that they would ever fill the hall, but she knew she'd made the right decision to try to accommodate everyone.

Dorin carried in firewood for both ends, with a large stack of extra. Bodric limped in, beginning to get around better with his brace and cane. He seemed as impressed as she had been.

"Pretty amazing isn't it?" Cali said.

"Have you inspected the quarters yet?" Bodric asked.

"Not yet, should I?"

"Yes, Cali girl, it's your farm, you want to inspect it," Bodric said in a lower voice walking up to her. "And make sure to tell the men what you like, or what you want changed."

"Really? Okay, thanks, Bodric, I will. Let's go look at the kitchen then inspect the quarters."

If the dining hall was impressive, the new kitchen was magnificent. A massive stone fireplace and oven sat in the middle of the front wall. Surrounded on both sides by smaller wood-burning iron ovens. There were solid wood-block counters, with shelves both below and on the walls above the counters.

"The ovens, where on earth did we get ovens this fast?" Cali said.

"From the old farmhand bunkhouses. With everyone wintering here, we used what we needed from those buildings." Bodric said.

The housing quarters were sparse to start but would begin looking more like home once they brought in more furniture. The curtains had been hung, the new blankets and pillows stacked on chairs ready for use. Simple hay-stuffed mattresses were in each room. Everyone had pulled together and accomplished an incredible amount of work in less than two weeks.

Several of the quarters were being moved into as Cali and Bodric walked through. It was a busy day for everyone. Cali and Chase helped move people's belongings from the temporary barn shelter into the new quarters. It felt good to stay busy and help and it gave her a chance to see what they still needed before winter set in.

The day passed in a blur. The kitchen work was being finished, the dining hall prepared for the dinner, and people moving into their new homes for the winter.

That evening, people filtered into the dining hall, resting from the day's work and waiting for the feast to start. A large table had been set in front of the fireplace on the kitchen end of the hall.

Sarah, with help from the wives, Jorah, Cali, and others brought bowls and platters of food and set them on the table. Everyone found a place to sit, chattering among themselves.

Jorah elbowed Cali, "You should say a few words to everyone or something, Cali."

Surprised, Cali looked from Jorah over to Bodric, who nodded.

Taking a deep breath, Cali walked toward the front of the hall at the food table and looked around. Feeling the weight of their eyes on her, the quiet filled the room as surely as the chatter had just moments before.

Looking at her friends, Sarah gave her a smile, and Bodric nodded encouragement.

"I don't know… there's not a single thing I can say to you about what's happened." Cali suddenly felt that same feeling of being a child suddenly forced into adulthood. So many pairs of grief-stricken eyes looked back at her. The fire crackled and hissed behind her.

"I can say this though. Thank you. Just thank you. To see how everyone came together…" Cali motioned her hand around the room.

"It is incredible what you've built here. How you all helped. We will weather this like we will weather the coming winter, and it's because of you all that we can do that. So, thank you." Cali bowed her head to them all. "Now, let's enjoy this food!" She smiled.

Bodric stood and gave her a smile and put his arm around her shoulder as she walked back to their table. People passing by gave her a pat on the shoulder on their way to the food table. With tears in her eyes, Sarah hugged Cali, then turned to go with the others to the food table.

"See, I knew you could handle all this." Rowan smiled.

As everyone filled their plates and mugs, the chatter was only broken by the sound of forks and knives, and the occasional toast at some of the tables. For the first time since the attack, they felt almost normal. Almost hopeful.

Tabitha and Sarah left the hall, returning with huge pies to the cheers of everyone. As they were making room on the table to set the pies, Tabbi looked up and out the window. The light had grown dim, she walked to the window to get a better look at the movement that caught her eye.

Tabbi let out a high, wavering scream, and ran toward the door leading outside.

Frightened, everyone jumped up running out the door behind her.

Cali ran outside to see Tabbi running as fast as she could to the line of wagons that had just turned the bend heading toward the house.

Tom was on the front wagon.

A sigh of relief and a raucous whooping cheer traveled through them all as they began walking to meet the wagons.

Thank the Mother, Cali thought, leaning up against the corner of the dining hall, her relief making her weak-kneed. Bodric clapped her on the back, the relief evident on his face too.

Tom swung down from the wagon in time to catch Tabbi as she propelled herself at him crying and laughing.

There were many more than the three wagons that had left almost a fortnight past. The two large and one small wagon were piled a man's height with provisions, blankets, sundries, clothes, foods, barrels and more. Six more large wagons behind were also stacked dangerously high with items. On the three wagons behind those, Cali could see Flora Nomarr, her younger twin sisters and parents, Tad Jossin, and a large crew of hands and their families.

"Good thing you had us triple the size of the addition." Jorah leaned over and whispered to Cali.

Cali's eyes were huge at all the people Tom had brought back. Stuck between tears and elation, she couldn't move for a moment, standing there her eyes trailing over the caravan of wagons.

The last wagon in the line was a smaller, odd-looking wagon that Cali didn't recognize. The lanterns mounted on the top front swinging as it came to a stop on the road.

"Tom, who is that?" Bodric had made his way over.

"Bodric, man! You are up and around after we left on our quest, I see!" Tom slapped Bodric on the back laughing.

"Oh, him? Odd fellow, not seen him before. We met him on the road, he was making for the Flynn farm here almost running the wheels off his wagon." Tom eyed the man climbing down from his wagon behind all the others.

"Said he heard what happened, was an old friend of Bethal and Erwin's and came to help." Tom shook his head, his shoulders drooped. "Had to tell him what happened, and he stayed with us to help. Odd, but he seems okay, Bodric."

Bodric watched the old man talking to his horse and giving him an apple.

Bodric grunted. "Did he tell you his name?"

"Yeah, funny kind of name. Eepan, Eapas, something like that."

"What did you say?" Cali turned to Tom, her heart racing. "Was… was it Eaparius?"

"Yeah, yeah, that's it!" Tom smiled.

Everything felt distant and far-off like she were seeing everything through a long tunnel. The sounds of everyone talking faded into the background as she watched the old man and his horse.

"Flora!" Sarah shouted, running toward their friend who was being carried by her father.

Sarah's shout shook Cali from her stupor. Bodric looked at her with a sidelong glance. She followed Sarah to meet Flora and her parents, greeting people along the way.

Flora suffered a broken leg during the attack, and her dad had a broken arm, but the twins and her mom were unhurt. Tad Jossin walked up, looking older than Cali remembered, nodding at Cali and walking on toward the front of the caravan.

As they all walked back toward the front of the line of wagons, the newcomers had shocked looks on their faces at the now much larger Flynn farmhouse.

"Tom, we christened the new dining hall, and there's plenty of food still. Let's get everyone in there to take a rest and get some food in them, I'm sure you're all exhausted," Cali said.

Cali turned, looking for Jorah. "Rowan, Jorah, can you round up a few of the men and let's get these wagons parked over near the big barn, and get the horses stabled and watered?"

"Sure, Cali, we'll take care of it and meet you back in the hall." Rowan smiled.

It was almost full dark by the time everyone made it to the dining hall. The new people were filling themselves on roast and potatoes. Sarah had carried in several more pies that Tabbi had made.

As they ate, Cali and Bodric took turns telling them about the new addition on the house and having everyone winter over at the Flynn farm. Slowly the talk turned back to the attack.

The Nomarr's had lost many of their farmhands, all but four of their horses, and their house. Their spared sheep and goats were tethered and led along with the wagons. Besides Flora's broken leg she had several cuts, her dad beaten and bruised with a broken arm getting Flora out of harm's way.

Tad told how his father, affectionately known to everyone as Old Man Jossin, fell when the attack first happened. He was in the vineyards readying the fields for winter when the horde burst out of the mountain forest setting fire to everything in their path. Tad Jossin's house was lost, as were both of his barns, and a good number of the farmhands. Their large storehouse had been spared.

They all sat for a long time in silence, taking in the enormity of all that had been lost. An overwhelming, crushing loss.

And for what? Cali thought.

"Cali, the men and I will go start unloading the wagons." Dorin finally broke the silence.

"No, Dorin, it'll keep till morning. You've all put in enough work the last bit." Cali smiled at him.

"But we can do this, let's get people settled into rooms, I know everyone must be utterly exhausted."

At that, they got up, leading the newcomers to the quarters and beginning to get them settled in, talking about the attack, and how this was built so quickly.

Cali stood, catching the old man's eye, and walked toward the hearth fire at the far end of the hall.

She had never met anyone who looked like this man. He was older, his skin had that sort of aged, leathery look about it. He wore robes, and a long, slouching hat that Cali may have thought was a sleeping cap.

No one Cali knew from the farms ever wore robes, the closest was a sleep shirt. Only the old wizards in the fae-tales she used to read ever wore robes. But what caught Cali's eye was the large walking-stick he carried, and a small brooch at his shoulder.

Both contained a dark blue stone.

CHAPTER
16

"**Y**ou are Eaparius, then."

Cali sat, staring into the fire as the old man sat at the table across from her. She wasn't sure why, but she felt angry at this man she had never met. But her mom had told her to learn from him, so she must.

"I am, young Callera."

His voice was deep, yet soft-spoken, surprising Cali. She had thought it would be rougher somehow, rather than the kind voice she heard.

"I am sorry I did not arrive at your farmstead sooner, young one. It seems peace and plenty have dulled our awareness." He continued.

Neither of them spoke. Eaparius pulled a flask from a satchel Cali had not noticed before, taking a large drink. She noticed the brooch at his shoulder fastened a long cloak. And while his walking stick hand was free, the cloak draped over his other shoulder, effectively hiding the satchel.

"Would you have saved them, then? Had your awareness not been dulled? Had you arrived sooner, as you say?" Cali looked directly at him.

Noticing from the corner of her eye, both Bodric and Jorah had situated themselves at the next table, keeping a close eye on the old man. Cali motioned for them to come join them.

"Bodric, Jorah, this is Eaparius. He... he knew my Mum and Da. I think," Cali said as they sat down.

Eaparius nodded to them both, returning his gaze to Cali.

"Can we talk, about all that has transpired? Here and now?" Eaparius asked.

"Yes. These two know, I trust either of them with my life."

"As you say, young Callera. As to your question, no, I am sorry to say. I could not have saved Bethal or Erwin unless I had arrived well prior to the attack. And even then, perhaps it would have mattered not. The Fates said their piece, and their will is always done."

"I trust your mother taught you all she knew, then?" he continued.

"My Mum taught me many things. How to cook, how to tend wounds, though cooking was never my best skill. But all this? What I know... what little I know... I heard from Bodric, and a few fleeting words before Mum died in front of me." Anger tinged Cali's voice.

The old man's eyes widened as he looked from Cali to Bodric and back again. "Truly? You knew not of your family and the prophecy prior to the attack?"

Sensing Cali's growing frustration, Bodric told Eaparius all that he knew of the prophecy that he passed on to Cali after her parent's death.

Eaparius sat, smoking a pipe he had lit while Bodric spoke, looking thoughtfully into the fire.

"Young Callera, we will need to waste no time in beginning your learning. It is unfortunate that your training should occur now that the evil has returned to this world, but there is no call for regret on the matter. We begin on the morrow."

Cali jumped up from the table, back stiff, pointing at the old man.

"Now, just you wait a moment. My Mum told me I had to learn from you, and I will do that for her. But you cannot come in here presuming what I know and what I need to learn. I don't know you. I know nothing more than your name. And as I see it, this... this prophecy is what killed my parents, and I'm none too sure I want to hear more about it!"

"Cali girl." Bodric laid his hand on her arm. "We need to know the bits of this prophecy thing we don't know yet."

"Eaparius, you said you need to teach Cali. But she already has the bow, she knows about the stone, saw how it heals. And she is a great shot. What could you teach her other than the legends?" Jorah asked.

"Young sir, Jorah, is it? Yes, there are the legends as you say, more accurately said, the history of her family and the prophecy. The stone can heal, that is true. But where there is light, there must also be dark. I dare say you or Bodric here could shoot her bow well enough, but that does not give you the ability to harness its power," Eaparius said.

Looking over at the bow on Cali's back, Jorah nodded.

"Young Callera... Cali." Eaparius placed his leathery hand over hers, "I am truly and deeply sorry about your mother and father. For my part, I am sorry I did not sense the danger sooner. Saved them it would not mayhaps, but you would at least have not felt the crushing weight of the prophecy in addition to their loss."

Cali truly saw Eaparius for the first time then, her anger vanishing as quickly as it came. The kindness and sadness in his eyes could not be faked. Swallowing back the lump in her throat, she nodded at him.

At that moment, Sarah came walking down to them bringing a fresh hot kettle of tea and mugs, along with the bottle of whiskey. She set them down, gave Cali a small shrugging smile, and left again.

"Are you a wizard of sorts?" Cali asked.

Eaparius's eyes crinkled and he laughed a deep, happy sound.

"No, child, not in the way as you may know from books and tales, at least. I am a scholar, a teacher, a watcher, and what you may hear the old folk refer to as an Elementalist or a mystic, but I am not a wizard in the fae-tale sense."

"So, how did you know my Mum?"

"I first made acquaintance with Bethal much like I am with you. The difference was Bethal's mother had told her the prophecy legends from a young age and had trained her in the martial skills. She was gifted, you would probably like to know."

"Gifted how?" Cali's curiosity was winning out.

"Young Bethal, while brilliant in archery, your bow, her innate skill lay in steel. Daggers, specifically. Even in my long years as Watcher, I had never seen dagger skills such as hers. It was born with her, you see. We are all, each of us, born with a particular set of innate skills, and with our own individual purpose. Even those outside of the prophecy." He looked at each of them in turn.

"Cali girl, he speaks true there. Bethal with daggers was like nothing I'd ever seen. All the dead imps, she took them all with her kitchen knives!" Bodric looked both sad and proud.

"Kitchen knives, you say? But what of her daggers?"

"She didn't have any daggers, none that I ever saw," Cali said.

"Hmm." Eaparius looked thoughtful. "No, young Cali, she most certainly did have daggers. A fine set of throwing daggers that she made herself, with a leather belt that held them. I know this because I helped oversee the process, and imbued them for her once complete."

Cali looked at Bodric and Jorah. Bodric just shook his head and shrugged.

"She made daggers and a belt? And you imbued them? How? What does that mean? Did you train her too?" Cali felt a thousand questions flood through her, not sure which to ask first.

Eaparius smiled. "Young Cali, I expect you will have many questions for me. I give you my word as Watcher, I will answer them all, but we will not get through them this night. I would suggest we all take rest and begin again on the morrow?"

"Okay, Eaparius. I'm sure you're tired from the journey, we have had a long day, too. We can talk after breakfast," Cali said.

"Come on, we'll show you to one of the rooms where you can

make your home while you're here."

They went through the large door leading from the dining hall into the new quarters. Cali gave him one of the larger suites on the first floor.

"One question, sir, if I may?" Jorah looked at the old man as they walked.

"Of course, young Jorah."

"News of the attack must have reached the other regions, the capital? Will they send armies?" Jorah asked.

"Ahh, young Jorah, how I would hope that were the case. But no, I'm afraid. News of the attack is known no further than the steads here in Edelaine alone." Eaparius sighed, dejected, his shoulders slumped.

"But, then how did you know?" Bodric looked pointedly at Eaparius.

"Ahh, young master Bodric, I am the Watcher, not so different from yourself, after a fashion." He smiled as Cali showed him into his new rooms.

As they walked back to the main house, Jorah leaned over to Cali grinning, "Have you noticed he calls us 'young'? How old do you think he is if he calls Bodric young too?"

Cali snorted a laugh, and Bodric smacked Jorah in the back of the head.

CHAPTER
17

Cali lay awake most of the night, getting up before the dawn began to break over the mountains. She slipped downstairs, hoping to find Sarah starting her morning routine in the kitchen. But all was quiet. A fire was crackling in the kitchen hearth, with a tea kettle steaming.

Cali made herself a cup of tea, wondering at Sarah's whereabouts. It was evident that she, or someone, had been in the kitchen to start the fire and put a kettle on to boil.

The new kitchen, Cali thought.

Cali walked out into the kitchen garden with her tea steaming in the cool morning air. To her right, light blazing from the windows of the new kitchen. Smiling, Cali headed to the nearby door.

Opening the door the smells of sausages, bread, and something else Cali didn't recognize washed over her from the bustling kitchen. Sarah turned giving Cali a huge smile.

"Oh, Cali, this is wonderful!" Sarah spun around looking at the kitchen.

"I can't believe the men built something this... this... perfect! I see you found the kettle I put on?" Sarah was beaming. Cali hadn't seen her this happy since the boar feast back in the summer.

"It is unbelievable, Sarah. I don't know how I can ever thank the men enough."

Sarah grabbed Cali's arm, giving her the tour of the kitchen, showing her where she planned to put all their supplies. With a satisfied smile she pointed out the fresh bread cooking in the massive stone hearth oven.

Stopping short, she turned to Cali. "Oh, I'm sorry, Cali. I'm just so excited. But this is your kitchen, tell me how you want it, and that's where we'll put it all."

"What? Sarah, no, this is... this is for all of us, it's not only mine! Your ideas sound perfect."

Sarah beamed, feeling like Cali had given her the keys to a castle, and turned back to the heavy iron ovens.

"I was going to ask, Sarah, what is that smell? It's not one of the normal breakfast smells."

"Oh, you are going to love this, Cali! Look!"

Sarah grabbed a nearby hook and being careful, opened the heavy iron door to one of the woodburning ovens. Inside were four large pies, the smell of onions, ham, and spices floated from the oven.

"Pies! Tabbi and I were talking last night as we looked over the kitchen here, and we came up with this idea! She made the crusts of course, and I put them all together this morning." She looked at her creation with pride before closing the oven door again.

"Sarah, they look amazing! I can't wait to try it." Cali looked around at everyone busy in the kitchen preparing for the day.

"Um, Sarah, I am going to head down to the lake for a bit, but can you let Bodric, Rowan, and Jorah that I want to talk to you all after breakfast?"

"Sure, Cali. Me too?" Sarah looked at her with raised eyebrows.

"Yes, definitely you too." Cali smiled, giving a little wave to Sarah she headed toward the door at the far end of the kitchen leading to the dining hall.

As Cali left the dining hall and headed toward the lake, the light had begun to creep over the mountains. Chase walked next to her, nudging Cali with his nose.

Cali laughed, "oh, come on you!" as Chase jumped up into her arms, laying his head on her shoulder.

Walking up to the graves she noticed someone had brought a large, flat rock and settled it in the grass under the tree. A perfect place to sit rather than on the cold ground.

Chase jumped down, curling up between the graves of Bethal and Erwin and drifting to sleep.

The silence was only broken by the occasional bird and the distant small splash of a fish from the lake. Holding her still-warm mug of tea between her hands, Cali closed her eyes, leaning back against the tree. Visions of a younger Bethal making daggers floated into her mind.

"Mum. Da. I don't understand all this yet. Eaparius is here, Mum. And I brought everyone from the farms here for the winter. I don't know, it seemed like the right thing." Cali shook her head, sipping her tea.

"There is so much that I don't know. So much I wish I could ask you now. Bodric is doing loads better. All that salve you taught me to make really works, Mum. And Da, I'm glad you and Bodric taught me to shoot, I guess I'll be needing that now."

"I don't think things will ever be, they won't ever go back to the way they were. But, Mum, I'll do as you told me. I'll learn from this Eaparius. He seems genuine. Though I don't think Bodric trusts him much."

"I'm going to make a few changes. Well, a few more changes." Cali took a long breath, clutching the pendants around her neck.

"With everyone here, there's a lot to account for and manage. In a dream last night, Mum, you told me to 'set them to manage it'. I thought about that a lot, and it came to me what you meant."

Chase snuggled against Cali's leg, and she scratched his ears, continuing on.

"I don't know if the others will understand, but I know you are still here. I know you are. Please help me make the right choices for everyone, they seem to be looking to me now. But I'm not you, I don't know how to do all this. But I can start with this, at least."

She sat there a while longer, the morning officially started. Mist rising from the lake behind her.

"I need to go meet with the others and let them know my, your, ideas. But I'll come back as often as I can."

Cali felt warm and content, the presence of her parents felt closer than they had since the attack. Taking a deep breath, Cali and Chase started back toward the house.

∞   ∞   ∞

"There you are!" Sarah stood motioning for Cali to join them at the long table.

"I saved you some of the pie." Sarah smiled as Cali made her way over and sat down.

Bodric and Jorah were already seated, watching Cali. Not realizing how hungry she was, Cali dug into the breakfast pie before telling them her ideas.

"Sarah, this is wonderful! We should make this a breakfast standard. You and Tabbi should talk in the kitchen more often," Cali said around bites.

Cali poured herself a cup of tea after devouring the pie, looked at her friends, and took a deep breath.

"I have an idea, and as it involves you all, I wanted to talk to you about it in private first."

None of them spoke, waiting for her to continue.

"As I see it, this is very different than what any of us are used to." She motioned around the room.

"We have a lot of people here, and you all have made this work so far, it's been nothing short of amazing what everyone has pulled together to do. But, we have even more people here now, and it could get out of hand. I can't do it all, and no one would want my breakfast cooking anyway." Cali grinned at Sarah.

"Here's what I want to do." She steeled herself, took a deep breath and continued.

"Sarah, I want you to be in charge of the kitchens and all kitchen duties. You can pick who you want to 'work' for you, but I want you to manage it all. You are brilliant in the kitchen, and I can't think of anyone else who could do what you've done here."

Sarah's mouth fell open. She shook her head to clear it.

"Are… are you sure, Cali? I mean, I've never managed anything before."

"Sarah, I am absolutely sure. It's not any different than what you are doing now, only a bit more organized is all. And you can assign different people for different tasks to take the workload off of you. Tabbi is a master at deserts, let her do those, and she can even take on apprentices if she wants to teach others. And the same with other areas. I leave that to you."

Giddy, Sarah looked at Cali, not sure what to say.

"Of course, if you don't want this, I won't be hurt, Sarah. But I know you'll have no problem with it, and you really are brilliant in the kitchen."

"No, no, Cali! This is… thank you. I would love to! I'm just, I just don't know what to say is all." Sarah smiled.

Cali smiled back, nodding.

"Jorah, you and Rowan are both brilliant with horses. You are both expert riders, with more than a bit of skill at training them too. I would love to have you, and Rowan if he agrees to join in, to manage the stables, the horses, horse breeding, care, and all that entails. Same as with the kitchen, pick those you know are best in the different areas, so we can make sure everything is being taken care of."

"Of course, Cali, I'd be honored, and I'm sure Rowan will jump in too." Jorah smiled.

Cali looked around, "I should have invited Dorin too, it didn't cross my mind though." With a shrug, she continued.

"If you all agree, I can't think of anyone better suited to heading up a builders crew than Dorin. He managed the work of this incredibly well and kept everyone going and motivated. I'm still amazed at how fast they made it happen."

Looking around at them all, they nodded in agreement.

"Bodric, can you sit down with Dorin and let him know, ask him if he would be willing to take on that job? If he agrees, I would like to sit down with the both of you, I have some more ideas of things we are going to need, and he will be the person to take charge of it."

"Sure, Cali girl, and I know Dorin will jump right on that. He's one of the best woodworkers I know."

"Now, Bodric, what I've got for you is two parts. One that starts now, and one that will come over time. I want you to be the main person in charge, for any of the different work crews that have questions or need anything. I want you to be the person that they come to for whatever they need."

"But, Cali girl, you are the person in charge here, not me."

"Right, of course, but I want you to do all the day-to-day type of managing it. Then you come to me with any big questions, or needs or whatever, and we can work those out together."

"That frees up your time to work with Eaparius. Good call, Cali girl. You know I'm in for whatever you need doing." Bodric smiled at her with pride.

"Of course there will be smaller work crews that will be, I guess, a sort of sub-crew of the main ones. Cleaning, and home-type chores that would fall under the kitchen. Gardeners that would fall under the kitchen. Wood and materials gathering that would fall under builders. And so on. Everyone will still need to be working together, this is all entwined and needs to come together to make all this work smooth."

With a stony expression, Cali stroked the pendants around her neck.

"Those little bastards didn't get us... not all of us. Not completely. But the winter will if we don't all work together and take care of each other."

They all nodded at Cali, a mix of pride and awe in their faces.

"Oh, and have Dorin get the loggers busy again, we are going to need a lot more wood and stone."

CHAPTER
18

They all stood to start their new jobs as Cali took her tea and headed toward the quarter's door. She wanted to find Eaparius, they had a lot to talk about.

"She put me in mind of Erwin right there," Bodric said with a gleam in his eye. "Let's get to work, sounds like we all have a lot to start doing."

Cali wandered outside after there was no answer at Eaparius's door. The wagons were being unloaded, provisions taken to the kitchen, storehouse, and barns. Personal belongings heading into the quarters. She was greeted by many 'good mornings' as they passed by.

Spotting Eaparius by his wagon, she headed that direction.

"Fine day, young Cali. A fine day indeed," Eaparius said looking at the bright sky. He turned back, rummaging through a wooden chest near the back of his wagon.

Cali hadn't noticed much about his odd wagon the evening before with the excitement. Larger than she first thought, it looked like a strange little house on wheels, more than a wagon. There were small windows with wooden shutters, a curved roof that slanted downward on the sides. On the back was an actual door, though much smaller than a normal door, the height of the wagon wasn't such that a tall person could stand upright fully.

The roof extended over the door as if an eave on a house. Walking around the wagon she saw the front bench was also protected by the curved roof extending over it. From the roof over each side of the driver's bench hung a large metal and glass lantern.

Circling back around, Eaparius stood, one arm clutching a stack of books, the other holding his walking stick. He had shut the wagon's door, and as he had stepped aside, she could see there was a small set of steps to make entering the wagon from the back easier.

What a curious man this is, she thought.

"I thought we would begin today with these. Answers will come, young Cali, but mayhaps you'll learn your history at the same time." Eaparius turned, walking back toward the house.

They sat in the dining hall, Eaparius setting the stack of books on the bench next to him, and with a swish of his cloak, they were hidden from view.

Pulling an ancient looking tome from the stack, he pushed it toward Cali. It was bound in a type of leather she had only seen once, dark blue, soft, but feeling as if it had a fine fur covering it unseen by the naked eye.

Opening the book, she looked up at Eaparius, "What language is this?"

"That, young Cali, is Dranoxian. The only full sample we have of it, that I have found in my travels." He had lit his pipe again, watching Cali as she examined the drawing that covered most of the page above the odd writing.

Running her fingers over the drawing, a sense of dread filled her stomach. "And this?"

"Hmm, yes. Have you not seen one like him before?" Eaparius asked.

"No," Cali said, staring at the drawing. "The monsters that attacked, they, their coloring was like this, but they were nothing like this!"

The tall figure in the drawing was almost completely colorless. Like something seen on a moonlight night that appeared to have its color drained, leaving nothing more than dark shades of slate and black. But this figure seemed to be enveloped in a blackish-purple mist cloak. His sharp eyes mirroring the color, seeming to be lit from behind. Long, clawed fingers reaching out, almost beckoning.

Cali shivered, looking up at Eaparius.

"That, as best we know from the recounting passed down, was Prince Esotan. None living has ever seen his ilk, not even myself, young Cali. He is a Dranoxi demon. Son of Lord Dranox himself. Esotan was reputed to be cruel beyond even his father, and was commanded to rule Dranoxi by Lord Dranox until that time when Dranox would name him Lord."

"But... but what does this have to do with me? With the prophecy?"

"The Dranoxi are, as we Watchers believe, the reason the prophecy was given flesh by the Fates. The first guardian, your ancestor eons past, was charged with defeating the Dranoxi."

"What? These, these things… they were here?" Cali felt as if she had been doused with cold water.

"Oh yes, young Cali. But as said, eons have passed since then, and the prophesied guardians have dealt with other, mundane evils of the world," Eaparius said with a wave of his hand.

"The crux of the problem lies here, young Cali. None of the Guardians through that time were able to defeat Esotan or his people."

"Wait, what? They are still here?"

"No. Your lineage found a way to banish them. Dranox, Esotan, and their hordes were sent to the Undying Night realm, and the doorway sealed upon the banishment."

"Undying Night realm?" Cali asked, her eyes wide.

"Yes. This is the name us mortals gave the place the Dranoxi were banished to. As truth would have it, that plane is unknown to us. The leaders of the world during those times simply named it thus, in their haste and relief to spread the news the Guardians had succeeded. In times since, to those of us who know of it, it is simply referred to as Dranoxis."

"Guardians. There were more than one?"

"Yes, but not as you may think. It was successive, not simultaneous, young one. The Dranoxi were to rule this world, by the will of Lord Dranox. It took many of your ancestors to finally push them from Idoramin. And just as you experienced with dear Bethal, the prophecy does not fall onto the next guardian until the previous guardian passes on the burden."

Cali flipped through the pages of drawings as Eaparius talked.

More drawings of Esotan, one of Esotan with another, even larger demon than himself.

Cali pointed to this drawing, "Lord Dranox?"

"Yes. As you can see from the drawings, the Dranoxi people, if you can call them such, are similar in appearance, but smaller and less dominating in stature than their rulers."

Cali turned the ancient pages in horror. There were drawings of Esotan appearing to burn people alive, a black-purple flame engulfing them. Entire cities destroyed. Dranox and Esotan leering over humans in chains. And the worst, Esotan consuming living people.

Cali looked at Eaparius, terrified. "But how, Eaparius? How did my ancestors banish them finally? And where did they even come from?"

"My dear, young Cali, that I cannot answer with not but speculation. See much is lost in history, especially so when that history becomes mere legend over the eons. What is the urgency or importance of preserving a fae-tale used to scare children into their chores, I dare ask?" Eaparius smiled sadly, shaking his head.

"No, child, there is much we do not know as to fact. Some we have only piece mailed bits of information and lore."

"Eaparius? Are they... have they come back?" Cali felt as if her entire body had been turned to stone. Fear coiling once again in her stomach, threatening to overtake her.

"What attacked your steads were not Dranoxi, as you say, and this I can confirm, seeing but a few of their corpses on our journey to your farm. What these were, are known as imps. Smaller, of course. Malicious. They thrive on pain, misery, enjoying destruction."

"So, the Dranoxi, they aren't back then." Cali felt a small bit of relief.

"That is yet another question I cannot answer, not in totality. See, young Cali, imps by and large are foul but ignorant creatures. They haven't been seen for an age, and imps like these, I don't believe have been seen in a far, far longer time. The one fact about imps I can speak to beyond their brutality and lack of cunning, is they are not oft known to act in cooperation except on the orders of a superior."

A stone seemed to settle into Cali's gut. Her head spinning with all the known and unknown, images of blackish-purple smoke swirling around her thoughts.

With a swiftness that belied his age, Eaparius closed and deposited the book under his cloak as the first people started coming into the hall for lunch.

Cali stood, affixing a smile to her face that felt entirely not her own as people filtered in, waving and saying hello. Chattering among themselves. Sarah, Tabbi, and several others began bringing in food from the kitchen and placing on the long table. Jorah, Rowan, Bodric, and Dorin came in and sat at the table with Cali and Eaparius.

Everything felt entirely normal outside of her skin, but inside, she felt turned to stone.

Word had spread quickly about Cali's plans to institute work crews. Murmurs of agreement passed through the hall, as people stopped by to ask if they could be on certain duties. It seemed the advice of her parents from her dream was overwhelmingly liked.

Rather than continuing to answer individual questions, Cali stood once they had all settled in to eat, going to the front of the hall. She got their attention, explaining how the work crews were divided up and who was in charge of each. She told them that if anyone had any special skills or wanted to help on a particular team, to go see the person in charge of that team or to come to Bodric, or her.

Cali returned to the table, trying to force herself to feel normal. She ate, without enthusiasm, answering a few questions that came from the table. Dorin telling her he could stay after lunch to talk about what projects she wanted him to work on.

Again, she had that disconnected from reality sensation. It was the shock of learning the beginnings of the prophecy she knew, she tried to push it out of her thoughts as best she could.

Best to focus on what I can do right now, she thought.

∞   ∞   ∞

"Dorin, first, thanks for heading up the builders, I couldn't think of a single other person better suited for it." Cali smiled.

"Now, I have some ideas, several things we are going to want to start on. I'll just give them all to you at once and we can begin planning from there."

"Sure thing, Cali. I've got the men out timbering now, and another batch out getting more stone. We'll be ready for whatever you need," Dorin replied.

"Great. We are going to need it. First, the practical stuff. We need to build onto the storehouse. Many of the provisions brought in from the other farms are still sitting in the barn because the storehouse is full to burst. And Tom tells me there is that much more which they plan to go back and get on another trip."

"We should put that one first, what do you think Cali girl?" Bodric asked.

"Exactly, Bodric. We need that one now, so it should get priority. Next, we are going to need to add on to the stables and the big barn. With all the new horses, goats, sheep and livestock, they are crammed in there tight. I want to keep them all housed together this winter for warmth, so we'll just expand what we've already got."

Cali could see Dorin formulating plans as she went through her list. Bodric was nodding agreement, and Jorah and Rowan looked ecstatic that the barn and stables were going to get an addition too.

"If you can spare a few men to do a smaller project at the same time, we are going to need a large indoor washroom for laundering. With winter coming, the barns spoke for, and our lodgings, we are going to need a separate space for that."

"Yes, that is a great idea, Cali!" Jorah said.

"Oh, thank Sarah for that one! She brought it up to me earlier, I hadn't thought of it myself." Cali smiled.

"Jorah, Rowan, I know you've been trying to mend those fences in the paddock, let the loggers know if you need extra wood. We are going to need a much larger area, I think?"

"A larger fenced pasture would be a help. I'll figure it up and let the loggers know." Rowan said.

"Great, Cali, we can get right on all of this. These are needed, and we can get them done quickly," Dorin said. "I can work with Bodric on the final layout and we'll get them to you before we start the build."

"That's good, Dorin. There's one more, and this one is larger than the rest, but it can happen after those are complete."

They all looked at her, expectation written on their faces, unsure what else they could need before winter settled in.

"A new addition on the other side of the farmhouse. Two stories, the full length of the house. Fireplaces of course for heat, but on the outside wall, not on the ends. Three rooms upstairs, one larger, with a lockable door."

They looked at her incredulous and wide-eyed. This was the first she had spoken of this idea to anyone.

Dorin thought for a moment. "Sure, Cali, that should be no problem at all. Is this for more quarters, or kitchens? What furnishings do you want?"

"We'll need some chairs, stools, and a few tables, but not many. What we need most are racks. For weapons."

Eaparius hid his smile behind relighting his pipe, as the others sat open-mouthed staring at Cali.

CHAPTER 19

"S... sure, Cali. We'll get on this. I'll draw up those plans, and Bodric and I will get them back to you." Dorin stood, still a little surprised, and headed toward the door.

The others sat, silent, not sure where this sudden idea had sprung from.

"Cali girl? That's a pretty big hall for you to train in, don't you think?" Bodric said, forgetting for a moment that Rowan was still sitting with them.

But Cali didn't mind, she had a suspicion that before all was done, more than Rowan would know of the uniqueness of the Flynn family.

"Maybe." She glanced quickly at Eaparius. "Or mayhaps not." Cali smiled.

"I know this seems sudden, and I hadn't spoken to anyone beforehand about it. We need to build a training hall, and yes, an armory of sorts. Eaparius, can we pick back up tomorrow?" Cali looked at the old man.

"Of course, young Cali. I must retrieve more things from my wagon as it stands." He nodded to them all, turning to leave.

"Cali, what are you planning for this new area? Don't take me wrong, I'm on board, but what is the purpose beside..." Jorah lowered his voice, "beside your training?"

Cali looked around at their eyes. "It's something we must do. The idea is not fully formed yet, but I know..." she wasn't sure how to tell them that it had been Bethal that told her to build the training area. Not without them thinking her completely unhinged.

"Just trust me on this." Cali smiled as she absently touched the pendants around her neck.

∞　∞　∞

Cali noticed over the next days that the mood around the stead seemed uplifted. The new work crews were busy, and the expansion of the storehouse was making great progress.

They all want to feel useful and to have a purpose, Cali thought.

As Cali walked outside, she saw Eaparius pulling a wooden chest from the back of his wagon.

"Let me help," Cali said.

"My thanks, young Cali." Eaparius smiled picking up one side of the chest by a heavy braided leather handle. Cali picked up the other side, and they walked back to the farmhouse.

"I thought we may use my kitchen today, fewer people coming in and out."

"Very good. We have a lot to speak of and explore today, young Cali."

As they settled at the kitchen table, Cali put a kettle over the fire in the hearth, and put some cheese and bread on the table. Eaparius opened the chest. Cali saw it contained not only more books, but parchment scrolls, pens, and small bottles of differing shapes filled with many different colored liquids.

"Our learning today starts with a question for you, young Cali. Mayhaps you would share the inspiration for the new building tasks for your farm?" Eaparius watched Cali with narrowed eyes as he asked the question.

Unsure how to answer, Cali watched as he lit his pipe. She had the feeling he already knew the answer.

"I… well, we needed the extra storage, and as Tom is taking a party to go back to each farm for the rest of the provisions and animals and other sundries, it seemed practical," Cali said.

"Smart, and practical, yes. And what of the new addition to your farmhouse?"

Cali hesitated, she wasn't sure how to explain getting messages from her Mum in her dreams.

"Child, I am the Watcher of the Prophecy. The one who watches over the Guardian. I am meant to be your teacher, mentor, scribe, and a protector, of sorts. Moreover, young Cali, I would give my life for the prophecy, and for you. I understand you know me not, but your trust is safely placed with me." Eaparius looked at her wisely.

Shocked at his words, Cali looked down at her empty mug, standing to retrieve the tea kettle from the hearth.

"Yes, you are right, of course. I'm sorry, Eaparius."

"No call for apology, young one. We must forge ahead together, and learn the other's ways as we go. Trust will come."

"Eaparius, it will… it will sound crazy, but it was Mum. She told me to build the addition. She told me to protect and teach our people. I couldn't tell the others. I don't think they would understand."

Eaparius smiled. "Young Cali, you are beginning to see some of the power of the prophecy. Young Bethal, and I daresay all your ancestors, will attempt to help you as they can. You see Bethal most clearly and with ease because she is the closest to you, in both blood and time. Do not be alarmed if you see others besides."

"What do you mean, they will attempt to help? Can I ask them questions? Can I meet my other ancestors?"

"No, child, it is not as normal conversation, as you may have seen. They will come when there is need, and try to show you the path forward. But that is all."

"Can I see my Da, too?"

"Sadly, no." Eaparius patted Cali's hand. "While he became part of the prophecy through your mother, it was not his burden to bear. Only the blood of the prophecy can reach through time to this age's guardian."

"It's good to know I'm not losing my mind, at least." Cali managed a weak smile.

"Eaparius, you said that the Fates gave flesh to the prophecy, did you mean they chose my bloodline to be the Guardians?"

"Precisely so, young Cali. The Fates cannot intercede in this world directly, they can only affect the path, and therefore the destiny, of those of us which are of this world. That was why they created the prophecy and chose your ancestors from eons past. See, they could not step in to defeat the Dranoxi, they could only give our world the ability to see them defeated."

"Eaparius, if the Fates created the prophecy, why didn't they tell my ancestors how to defeat them?" Cali asked.

"Mayhaps they did, young Cali, this is one of the answers we do not have. When the history and accounting of the Guardians of old slipped into mere legend, much was lost through the ages."

"Did the Fates create these too?" Cali motioned to her bow and bracers.

"After a fashion. You see, they gave the inspiration and ability to create these to a man who became the first Watcher. Lore tells us it took him many attempts over years to finally perfect them, and it wasn't until he discovered the stones that they were completed."

"So, was he your ancestor?"

"No, the line of watchers is a different path than that of the prophecy, young Cali. Each Watcher must discover the next Watcher from the students sent to him. Within each age, select individuals are chosen, endowed with innate skills and abilities that lend themselves to the path of a Watcher. These become students of the current Watcher, one of which, through studies and practicality, will show themselves as the next in the line."

"What of the others? Your other students? What happens to them if they are not the next chosen?"

"Worry not, young Cali. These are all gifted scholars, and

through their studies, their strengths are divined. They go on to the different schools of magicks or lore."

"Magicks? I thought you said you were not a wizard?"

Eaparius laughed. "Ahh, child, I am not a wizard in the sense of what most know from fae-tales. Many look at our kind and see something beyond reason, and many others fear it. But, young Cali, magicks are not to be feared, or even so highly revered. Magick is simply one having a higher understanding of nature, you see."

"So, do I have magick? Will you train me in it?" Cali looked excited.

"You, young Cali, have your own magick, the magick of the prophecy. Yes, I will be your teacher, in what I know of the prophecy, and the more mundane magicks of this world to an extent."

"Why did it take the first Watcher so long to create the bow and armor?"

"Ahh, that is an interesting tale, young Cali. See, it is made from a wood that came from a rare tree, a tree that cannot be found except by those who are given the eyes to see it."

"The Watchers," Cali said.

"Exactly so, young Cali. The first Watcher tried many woods, none of which were of use for this bow. It took him some time, and a long journey to find the Spiritwood, but find it he did. Once the Spiritwood bestowed a branch to him, he was able to create the bow. It is said the Spiritwood, so impressed by the Watcher's determination also gifted him a single Spiritwood seed. But his adventure was far from through."

Cali poured them both more tea, engrossed in Eaparius's story.

"As lore tells us, while on his journey back from the Spiritwood, he was attacked by a fearsome beast. A wolf-like creature half the size of a horse, with midnight blue eyes that seem to be lit from within. After a long battle, the beast was defeated, and his hide was taken by the Watcher."

Cali looked down at her bracers then to Eaparius, who nodded.

"The bow could not be strung by any normal string, however. The Watcher tried every material he could conceive. The stories tell us he dreamed of a ghostly creature, who beckoned him to a cave. Setting off on another journey, the Watcher traveled to an empty cave in the Gelid Mountains."

"He spent days in the cave, waiting. Until finally a terrifying creature entered and sat opposite his campfire. There was no threat from the creature, and his recounting described it as a spirit spider. A spider as large as the Spiritwood beast, but translucent, ghostly, and intelligent."

"Intelligent?"

"Yes, quite so. It spoke to the Watcher about his quest and the bow. Once satisfied with the Watcher's sincerity and connection to the Fates, he granted the Watcher the silken strands which would be used to string the bow."

"But, Bodric said it was Time that strung the bow?"

"Yes, but what form would you have Time take in this mortal realm, young Cali? Time is a precious and precarious thing, it creeps along, there one moment and gone the next. See, of all the patrons of The Mother, Time is the one that can, and does, in its own way, directly affect everything in this world. So, it was written that it must be Time that string the bow, he was the only one who could."

"But what about the stones? These are not normal gems."

"You are correct, young Cali. To most, they would appear as a highly polished lapis, but as you say, these are not normal gems. As truth would have it, we do not believe them from this realm at all."

"So, how did the Watcher find them?"

"Ahh, yes, that would be the Watcher's final journey, young Cali. He set off to the far south from his home. It is said that he met a young scholar on the trip that he knew he must mentor. He passed on all the knowledge he had gained thus, knowing that his student was meant to carry on the knowledge, as his student was the only other person he had found that could see the Spiritwood seed."

"So, he gained a student, one who would be destined to be the next Watcher."

"Just so, young Cali. They were drawn to a lake on their journey. Located in deep woods, and with water so dark blue as to appear bottomless. It shimmered with a power they did not fully understand. After much time, the spirit of the lake showed itself to them. It set upon them tasks that they must complete to gain the spirit's trust."

"A spirit of a lake?" Cali asked, her eyes wide.

"Yes, child. Everything in this world has its own form of life, you see. Woods, waters, winds, they live here with us. After the tasks had been completed, the spirit agreed to talk to the Watcher and his apprentice of their quest. The apprentice asked the spirit why he had given them such tasks to complete, to which the spirit replied he had to be certain of their willingness."

"What tasks did they have to do?"

"I am unsure, young Cali, the records do not say with any specificity. Once satisfied they were committed to the prophecy, he told them that a trade must be made to collect the final needed pieces. The stones. A sacrifice, of sorts."

"A sacrifice?" Cali looked alarmed.

"Hmm, yes." Eaparius looked solemn. "The sacrifice was that the first Watcher had to join the spirit in protecting the lake's secret. The stone of the Mother. So, it was that the Watcher, ensuring his apprentice learned of all his knowledge, passed the Watcher mantle to him, and agreed to join the spirit of the lake."

"No! But he, wouldn't he die?"

"It may seem so, child, but death to one of this mortal realm became immortality to the first Watcher. His spirit joined the spirit of the lake, and so he lived on. Before joining the spirit, the Watcher and the spirit passed their knowledge to the apprentice, and bid him travel south to find the first Guardian."

"My ancestor," Cali said.

Eaparius nodded. "And so it came to be, the intertwined destinies of the Watchers and the line of Guardians."

CHAPTER 20

The day was bright and clear, but the air had a dry feeling that only comes with fall. Chase bounded around, playing in the leaves under the tall trees of the forest.

"Eaparius, shouldn't I feel, it may sound silly, but shouldn't I feel, stronger, or more powerful or something, as a Guardian?" Cali asked.

Cali and Eaparius wound their way through the trees in the forest near the big barn. He wanted to see her skill with the bow and to begin her training on how to harness its power.

"No, young Cali. Unlike stories, a body does not suddenly know how to be a protector of others, nor know, without training, how to defend or attack. You are still you, child. The difference is you have access to something powerful beyond knowing."

They had spent days talking about the lore and history, learning more of her family and the prophecy itself. But the practical learning of how to harness the powers of her weapon and armor could not be done through books alone.

Bodric and Jorah had protested their trip into the forest, compromising only when they swore to not wander in past eyesight of the house.

Eaparius was impressed with Cali's hunting and tracking skills, even if they were still green. Shortly inside the tree line, Chase had sniffed tracks left by a stag, and Cali had begun tracking it through the trees.

In a low voice, Eaparius said, "see, young Cali, if the imps were still nearby, your forest's natural inhabitants would be in hiding. This gives me some confidence that they have moved on."

"Only some?" Cali asked.

"Yes, lest my maps are wrong, beyond this huge forest lies the edge of Edelaine as it falls into the Great Deep. That begs the question then, where did the foul creatures go?"

Cali stopped, turning to Eaparius. "I hadn't thought of that. So, they are either still out here, or they managed to double back without us seeing."

"Those are both quite possible, young Cali. Or, they could have left by other means."

"Other means? By boat, maybe?"

"Quite so. But while imps are largely ignorant creatures, there are a few among them who can use some limited magic, with help. But speculation is all we have on the matter, which tells us little in truth."

Cali resumed tracking the stag, heading along the forest edge toward the lake. They came on it as the sun blazed high in the sky above them, filtering down through the trees. Cali drew her bow, took aim and the world seemed to freeze.

Cali surprised at first, glanced around.

She looked to Eaparius who seemed to be blinking in slow motion, as did Chase while sniffing the ground. The bow and string seemed to have its own inner light.

The wind still moved the remaining leaves, but they seemed to be floating, dreamlike.

Even the stag, who had caught their scent looked up, moving more slowly than Cali would have imagined.

She saw the stag's muscles tense and bunch, it had sensed them and was preparing to bound away. Cali loosed two arrows so fast her own hands seemed to blur, and the stag fell.

Gasping and wide-eyed, she turned to Eaparius, who now seemed to be moving at regular speed again.

"What just happened, Eaparius? What was that?" Cali felt breathless and excited. The warmth of the bow was still in her.

"What would you say happened, young Cali?"

"I, I'm not sure, did time slow down, or did I speed up? I could see everything clearly, but I was able to sense and shoot much faster than everything else was moving."

"That would be the best explanation of it, I think, young Cali. That is how it feels to use a bow which has been strung by Time."

∞ ∞ ∞

As Eaparius and Cali rounded the corner of the big barn, Bodric and Jorah were leaning against the fence to the pasture. They had been waiting for them to return from the forest.

When they saw the stag that Eaparius was carrying, Jorah ran forward to take hit from his shoulders, and Bodric walked forward to meet them.

"Great find, Cali girl!" Bodric said. "No problems in the forest then?"

"None at all, Bodric. The deer and rabbits were out, and Chase didn't sense anything out of the ordinary. We think the imps have moved on." Cali replied.

"That's good news, but where would they have gone?" Jorah asked.

Eaparius looked at him thoughtfully. "That is indeed the question, young Jorah. We will widen our hunting area and begin to scout further in to look for any signs as we train."

"I'll clean this and take it over to Sarah in the kitchens. Do you want me to rack the hide, Cali?" Jorah asked.

Cali smiled, "yes, of course, I would love to have some leather to work."

"I had heard talk from some others about your skill in working leather, young Cali," Eaparius said.

"Cali girl is the best around! If you see something leather-made here, she probably made it," Bodric said with a satisfied smile.

Eaparius nodded, smiling. "Young Cali, why don't you go on and help with the stag. I am tired. I'll walk with young master Bodric."

As Cali and Jorah headed toward the small barn on the other side of the house, Bodric and Eaparius started their slower walk.

"What can I do to help Cali girl?" Bodric asked.

"I am glad you asked, young master Bodric. The running of the stead is an undertaking which is of great help already. Once your leg mends more, I would ask you help her with working some sword and axe skills."

"Are you not to train her in all the fighting skills?" Bodric asked.

"Oh yes, but I also need to be able to see her train with others to assess her innate battle skills. Each Guardian, while trained and having some level of skill is most fighting stances, will have one which stands above the rest."

"Like Bethal and throwing knives," Bodric said in a quiet voice.

"Exactly so, young master. The bow is the weapon of each guardian, but it is not by default their given skill. When I can see clearly her given skill, if it is other than the bow, I will oversee her in creating her own weapon to be imbued."

Bodric nodded, running his hand over his scruffy beard.

"She's only ever used the bow I made for her and daggers. Of course, Cali girl has never had to fight, only hunt."

Eaparius laid a hand on Bodric's shoulder to stop him. With a quick glance around he spoke in a lower tone.

"Young master Bodric, I feel that you have been much farther than the steads of Edelaine. What do you know of Wanderers?"

Surprised by the question, Bodric replied, "I have met only a handful. Great trackers. A few of them with darker talents."

"Yes, yes, the assassins, those are darker talents, indeed. Necessary at times, but darker. I speak most specifically of the rangers," Eaparius said.

"They were different, as I said, excellent trackers, but tended to keep themselves to themselves. Of the ones I met, most had a likeness for pets and…"

Bodric's eyes widened.

"Wait, Eaparius. Do you think Cali girl is — "

"Her skills certainly lend themselves to those from the guildhalls of the rangers. I cannot say with surety, having not seen her other skills. But it would seem a distinct possibility."

Eaparius turned, resuming their slow pace toward the house.

"Of all of the Guardians I have known or studied, each and every one has fallen into the skills that would be prized by any of the Wanderers. Bethal, in another life mayhaps, would have been a leader amongst those assassins. Her great-grandmother before her a master at healing, and daggers."

"Bethal was… yes, I can see where she could have been that, in a different life. And her healing salve saved more than a few of us," Bodric said his voice breaking.

"You have been a watcher of sorts for young Cali, I hope you will continue to be, she will need us all, young master Bodric."

CHAPTER 21

The storehouse was finished, it was twice the size on the ground floor and now had an upper floor also. The provisions had been moved in from the barn, with ample space left for the other supplies they would be bringing back.

The laundry building was almost finished. Rowan had worked with Eaparius to design a waterway to pump water directly from the lake and river behind the stead to the laundry area. Everyone marveled at what they had built, knowing it would save many hours of people carrying water to and fro.

The builders had already begun work on the barn. Besides building onto the barn and stables, they built several rooms above the stables for stable hands to live, or for supplies if needed.

The farm had fallen into a sort of a routine, with each work crew busy keeping everything running. Eaparius had been teaching Cali herb lore.

"Eaparius, what does learning all about plants have to do with the prophecy and protecting people? Shouldn't we be out there practicing?" She motioned toward the forest.

"Child, where do you think you're mother's healing salve came from?"

"I know, but I already know how to make that, and what goes into it. This just seems like a bit of a waste of time!" Cali said, tapping her fingers on the table.

"Hmm. I understand, young Cali."

Eaparius rummaged in the wooden chest for a moment, pulling out a small glass vial and handed it to Cali. She turned it over in her hands, noticing the thick orange liquid inside.

"Caution, young Cali, you do not want to get that on your skin," Eaparius warned. "Come, let me show you something."

Cali followed Eaparius outside. The days were getting cooler, the occasional breeze carrying red, orange, yellow leaves with it.

Walking toward the woodpile, Eaparius picked up a large piece of the firewood. He set the wood on its end in the open field area, away from anything close by, then walked back away from it.

Carefully, Eaparius opened the cork on the small bottle and pulled a single arrow from Cali's quiver.

"Watch, and learn." He said as he put a single small drop onto the point of the arrow, handing it back to her, and motioning toward the firewood sitting some distance from them.

Cali pulled her bow, the warmth and dramatic time slowing now becoming familiar, and let loose the arrow at the wood. It landed with a thunk!

Cali watched, then looked at Eaparius and shrugged.

Eaparius began walking toward the wood, as Cali turned to follow, she saw what looked like smoke rising from where her arrow had pierced the wood. Running the remaining distance, she saw the small piece of wood smoldering, looking as if it had caught on fire from inside.

Shocked, Cali turned, staring at Eaparius, wide-eyed.

"That, young Cali, is one reason why herb lore is important. You can imagine the uses, and there are many variations you can make. Now, let us go have some lunch."

Cali had a newfound appreciation for plants.

∞　∞　∞

The next morning, Cali and Eaparius headed to the forest. Eaparius showed Cali the first potion she would learn to make, and she was going to gather the plants needed while they were out.

"Young Cali, today you shall make a warming concoction." He held up a small clear vial to her. This one also had an orange liquid, but unlike the other, it wasn't thick but watery, and a lighter shade of orange.

"Does this one go on my arrows too?" Cali asked, bouncing from one foot to the other.

"No, young Cali, but patience, this one is more useful than that and much easier to brew. Alchemy is complicated, you see. And to make the more difficult potions, you need a keen eye, patience, and much practice."

Together they headed into the chilly morning toward the forest. Once they reached the forest edge, Eaparius motioned to the small vial of warming concoction.

"Take but a sip of that, young Cali. See for yourself what it does."

Cali removed the cork from the bottle, giving it a small sniff. It smelled both spicy and sweet. She took a very small sip, replacing the cork. Within a moment, she felt a warmth spreading through her body as if she had been standing in shadow and felt the sudden warmth of the sun on her skin.

"Useful, no? When you are out in the wild, warming concoction can fend off freezing for yourself or others, and without the other effects of whiskey or mulled wine." Eaparius smiled.

"This would be good for the workers that are outside once it gets colder this winter," Cali said.

"Quite so, young Cali."

They ventured further into the forest, looking for any signs that the imps may still be in the area, hunting along the way. Chase was happy to be out in the forest again and gleefully pounced on falling leaves as they went.

"Eaparius, you said that none beyond Edelaine would know about the attack," Cali said.

"That would be true. There were no other attacks in other regions that I sensed or was made aware of."

Cali nodded, hesitating for a moment.

"I think we need to go to the capital and warn them. Have them send out a guard, or at least make the guard ready and get the word out to the other regions," Cali said.

Eaparius stopped to look at Cali. "You are correct, young Cali. I have been considering this and who could make the trek."

"I want to go, Eaparius. I... I think I'm supposed to."

"You saw your mother again, didn't you?"

"Yes. She said they needed to be warned. And she also showed me where she buried something, but I don't know what it was she buried. I'm supposed to go find it."

"Young Bethal would not steer you poorly, young Cali. You should find this place and discover what it is she left for you," Eaparius said.

"Mayhaps take Jorah with you. I sense that he's had many questions for you. He worries about you as much as Bodric, it seems." Eaparius smiled.

∞　∞　∞

Everyone gathered the next morning in the dining hall for breakfast. As the chattering started to subside as people made their way from the hall to begin work, Dorin stopped by the table.

"Cali, the all the additions are complete, and we will be starting on the addition to the house in the next few days. Thanks to the ingenious water contraption from Rowan and Eaparius here, we also built a waterway for the stables too. It should cut down on a lot of work."

"Thanks, Dorin, that's great! And if you need anything for the new addition, just ask." Cali replied.

"Jorah, are you free this morning? I may need some help," Cali said.

"Sure, Cali! What can I help with?" Jorah smiled.

She looked around at them all. Rowan had been unofficially invited into their group. And although the entirety of the story had not been told to him, Cali was comfortable with him there.

"I need to find something that Mum buried and left for me."

"What?" they all asked, looking at her and shifting in their chairs.

"Cali girl, Bethal never said anything to me about this. How did you learn about —"

"Mum told me. In a dream."

At that, they all looked at her with open mouths and identical looks of shock on their faces.

"No cause for alarm, young Cali speaks true. It is a power of the prophecy. The ancestors of the current guardian can reach out to assist when it is needed." Eaparius said.

Cali nodded thanks to Eaparius. "It's true. It was Mum who suggested the new addition to the house too. I've felt her here ever since the attack, but didn't understand it until the dreams happened and Eaparius helped explain it."

"This couldn't be some sort of a trick… this buried item, could it, Eaparius?" Jorah asked.

"No, young Jorah, Bethal would not lead Cali astray or put her in harms path. There are many powers that come with the prophecy, this is just one of those many."

"Cali, let me go get a shovel and some things, and I'll be happy to help," Jorah said, standing to leave the dining hall.

∞ ∞ ∞

Jorah and Cali set off toward the lake. He had gotten a shovel and a pickaxe, and Cali noticed, he had also strapped on his swords into the sheath belt she had made for him.

"Okay, guardian, share your secrets!" Jorah smiled.

"What have you and Eaparius been working on? I smelled something awful coming from your kitchen yesterday, I hope that wasn't your cooking!" Jorah teased.

Cali poked Jorah in the ribs. "No, that was my first attempt at a warming concoction. Needless to say, we threw it out. But my second try was much better. Here."

Cali reached into her pocket and pulled out a small vial of orange liquid, handing it to Jorah.

"Um, what's this?" Jorah shook the bottle, holding it up to the sunlight.

"Take a little sip. You'll see." Cali smiled.

He looked a little hesitant but shrugged and pulled out the stopper, taking a very small sip. His eyes widened in surprise as the warmth spread through him.

"Wow, Cali, that's, what is that?"

"It's a warming concoction. Just a very simple potion made from herbs, spices and such to fend off freezing."

Cali went on to tell Jorah about the fire potion that Eaparius had put on her arrow, and how it had smoldered the piece of firewood. Also about how he showed her how to identify ingredients in the wild.

The spent much of the afternoon talking, Cali catching him up on what she had been learning from Eaparius.

"Jorah, I am going to leave soon to go to the capital with Eaparius. They need to be warned about what happened, so they can ready the guard and warn the other regions."

Jorah looked at her, surprised.

"But, Cali, the farm, and winter will be here soon," Jorah said, running his hand through his hair.

"It's not for long, but we have to warn them. They have to know, Jorah."

Jorah nodded. "You are right." He took a deep breath. "I'm coming too, then."

"What? No, Jorah, it will be a long journey, and it…" but Cali couldn't actually think of any other good reasons.

"No, Cali, I am coming with you and Eaparius. There are, things, in the mountains, I've heard. It will be safer with three than with two."

Cali could see that Jorah's mind was made up. She nodded, planning to talk to Eaparius about it later.

Suddenly she stopped, looking around. They had walked some distance into the woods after turning east halfway to the lake.

"This is the place, Jorah. I recognize this rock near that split tree from my dream." Cali said, swallowing hard.

"Are you sure, Cali? Show me where to start digging." Jorah said, setting down the tools.

They began digging in the cold and hardened dirt between the split tree and large rock. When the hole had deepened to about Cali's knees, the shovel hit something that sounded like wood.

Cali knelt down, digging the rest of the way with her gloved hands, slowly uncovering a dark brownish-red box much like the one that held her bow in the barn.

She and Jorah sat on the hard ground, the large square box between them. It was like the other, but more square where the other had been long and flat for her bow. It also had a blue stone and the same keyhole on the top of the box.

Cali's hands were shaking as she dusted them off. Combining the key pendants, she placed them in the lock. Then, taking the knife from her hip, she made a shallow cut on the palm of her hand, placing her hand over the blue stone.

The box began to vibrate on the ground, as Cali placed her palm on her bracer.

The forest was silent, except for Jorah's anxious breathing, when she realized she had been holding hers. Cali took a deep breath and opened the box.

Bodric and Eaparius both looked at the throwing knives. Eaparius ran his finger lightly over the inscription at the handle end of one of them. There were nine in all, three on either hip and three more on the leather sash that crossed over the chest.

The daggers were made of fine steel but had no ornamentation. They were flat, no handle beyond the wider piece of steel on the end with the inscription, coming to a deadly sharp point on the other, and finely sharpened on both sides of the blade. The braided leather belt had a sheath built into each side for daggers, and a leather pouch that was filled with coins.

"Young Bethal's throwing knives," Eaparius said, his shoulders slumped.

"She made these, you said?" Cali ran her fingers softly over the braided belt and sash.

"Yes, young Cali, it took her some time working with a blacksmith who was a friend of mine. The leather she hunted and worked herself, mayhaps where you inherited your skill in leatherworking from," Eaparius said.

Bodric lifted one of the knives from its holster on the belt, balancing it on his finger.

"They are lighter than they look, and balanced just right," Bodric said.

They all sat in silence, staring over Bethal's weapons.

"Eaparius, my Mum's knives, are they, are they like the bow? Part of the prophecy?" Cali asked.

"Yes, and no, young Cali. The guardian-made weapons of the prophecy are different than the bow in many respects, but in others, very similar. In the hands of anyone other than Bethal, or mayhaps yourself, they would be ordinary throwing knives. Finely crafted, yes, but nothing more."

Eaparius lit his pipe, looking at Cali with his wizened eyes.

"For Bethal, these were an extension of the bow's power, after a fashion. The speed with which she could use these daggers was beyond the normal, much like the bow. They would respond to her touch, would never get stuck in a target, with a range much beyond those of any standard knives, and a true aim."

"And for Cali?" Jorah asked.

"Ahh, young Jorah, only practice will tell us that. But we shall soon know." Eaparius replied. "We have yet to confirm young Cali's weapon gift, but yes, we shall soon know."

Cali cleared her throat and closed the box. "Jorah, could you run out and ask Dorin, Sarah, and Rowan to join us for a minute?"

Jorah, knowing what was coming, nodded and left.

∞ ∞ ∞

"Cali, I just want to tell you again, I love the work crews, I love being in the kitchens, and it's going great! Tabbi is even starting to show me her pie crust secrets!" Sarah smiled as she sat.

"We'll all get fat as the hogs if you both know how to make pies like that!" Rowan laughed, joining them.

"Thanks, you all, for taking a minute for me. I wanted to say thanks for what an incredible job you've been doing, and it seems to be lifting everyone's spirits jumping in and being involved." Cali said.

"Since you all are the ones that really keep the place running right now, I wanted to talk to you directly."

Cali looked around at them all.

"Eaparius, Jorah, and I are going to travel to the capital soon. Word has to be taken to them, they have to be warned so they can ready the guard and other regions."

"What? Cali, I don't know, that seems, can't we send someone else?" Sarah asked, biting at her lip.

"No, Sarah, it has to be us, but don't worry, we don't expect any trouble. Those creatures are long gone, and we'll be on the road," Cali said, trying to reassure Sarah.

"But why? Can't we send some of the men? They could go quicker and be back sooner," Sarah said, unconvinced.

"Ahh, young Sarah, your logic is sound, but worry not. It must be us who takes the trip. A hand from the farm would be far less likely to get an audience with Lord Riston, or even with the general of the guard," Eaparius said.

"Yes, I suppose that makes sense," Sarah said, clearing her throat.

"Cali girl, I don't like this, you know. But I talked to Eaparius when he first mentioned it to me and, even if I don't like it, you two are right. We have to let them know," Bodric said.

"Thank you, Bodric. I am really leaning on you the most to keep everything going smoothly here." Cali smiled at him.

"Dorin, are we still on pace for the new addition?"

"Sure are, Cali, we have plenty of supplies and have already started the foundation," Dorin replied.

Cali nodded. "Good, good, and if you need anything, you know you can always go to Bodric."

"Rowan, how are the stables? Do you need anything?"

"No, Cali, it is in top shape. Several of the hands wanted to be on the crew along with Tad Jossin, who moved into one of the new quarters above the stables. We are ready when Tom and those men return if they have more livestock," Rowan answered.

"Sarah, how about the kitchens, house, and laundry. Is there anything we need to do there?"

"It's going great, Cali. We are thankful for the waterway, especially in the laundry. Everything is working well," Sarah replied.

"I don't expect to be gone longer than absolutely necessary. I want to be back before the hard winter settles in." Cali looked at Eaparius, who nodded.

"Young Cali is correct. We will not tarry long in the capital, none of us wish to cross the mountain pass with the winter bearing down on us."

"You'll be taking your wagon, Eaparius?" Rowan asked.

"Yes, young Rowan."

"I will make sure we check the wagon axles and wheels and prepare your horses. I'd like to send two extra horses along on tether, you can switch them out when they tire."

"Fine idea, indeed, young Rowan! That can certainly help us speed better across the mountains," Eaparius replied.

"Then it's settled. As soon as everything is ready, I would like to leave so we can return. And if any of you need anything until we return, Bodric is the person to go to," Cali said.

∞　∞　∞

The morning of their leaving dawned clear and chilly, the sun not yet visible over the mountains. The wagon had been loaded and prepared the day before, the horses well-rested and fed. Eaparius's horses were hitched on the wagon, with two of the strongest horses on the stead tethered behind.

Jorah had his swords sheathed on his belt, along with a cloak and the gloves Cali had made for him. Eaparius looked as they had seen him each day. A set of his normal robes, long cloak, and walking stick. Cali had put the leather armor she made for Chase on him for the trip.

It wasn't cold enough for it yet, but Bodric insisted that Cali take her silver wolf fur cloak and boots. And at breakfast, he handed her a hastily wrapped gift.

Unwrapping the gift, Cali gasped.

"Bodric, it's beautiful!" Cali pulled out the new dagger Bodric made for her. Like the boar's tusk dagger he made for her before, this one was made from one of the stag's antlers. She was wearing Bethal's braided leather belt and knives and already had her one dagger sheathed. She sheathed the new dagger on the other side.

Rowan walked up, grasping his brother by the wrist in a handshake.

"Don't you get lost in the big city, little brother." Rowan smiled at Jorah.

Bodric clapped Jorah on the shoulder. "You watch out for her, and bring all of you back safe and quick." He shook Eaparius's hand and gave Chase a quick scratch behind the ears.

With hugs, handshakes, and well-wishes all around, the four climbed onto the bench of the wagon and set off up the road. From the farm, they watched until the wagon pulled out of sight around the bend.

CHAPTER
23

They made good time through Edelaine and stopped past Jossin's farm where the road started climbing into the mountains. They had taken turns driving the wagon and hadn't stopped except for the brief rest. Jorah suggested switching to the larger, stronger horses for the mountain ascent they would begin the next morning.

It was still only evening, but Eaparius didn't want to start the mountain path with darkness settling around them. It was decided that Cali would sleep in the wagon, with Eaparius on the wagon bench, and Jorah next to the fire as the first watch.

As they made camp, they helped Eaparius get a small black iron pot, along with some of the food Sarah had packed for them. For the first time, they were able to see inside the curious wagon.

Just as Cali had thought the first time she looked at it, the wagon was indeed like a small house. There was what appeared to be a small bed, which on one end also doubled as a seat for a small table. Down both sides of the wagon were shelves, made with a front panel to ensure the contents didn't spill out. Books, bottles, parchments, along with bags and small containers of various sizes filled the shelves on both walls. A smaller version of the lanterns from the front of the wagon hung from the curved roof.

Seeing their curiosity, Eaparius told them he had cause to travel much over his long years and had the wagon built by his own design.

"It is indeed a small replica of my home and study, you see." He told them, lighting his pipe and stirring the stew he had started preparing.

"As a scholar, and moreover, as a Watcher, I have need to venture far at times, and cannot be without supplies or my basic necessities. It is far easier to make my home like this than in various inns and wayside stops."

"Why have you had to travel so much?" Jorah asked.

"Ahh, young Jorah, the life of a scholar may seem dull and sparse to many, but in truth, there is much adventure in learning the lore of the world. But in learning the lore of the world, one must make their way out into the world. There is only so much learning to be had from books."

Eaparius grinned, leaning closer, "but do not tell the other scholars I said so, they may think unkindly of me!" he laughed.

∞　∞　∞

The morning came, steel gray and colder. Jorah had taken the watch and tended the fire overnight, and had a tea kettle on the fire as they woke.

Cali, as always, shared her breakfast with Chase, who had slept in the wagon with her the night before. They discussed the day's trip while they ate.

"The mountain pass is long, and can be dangerous for those not familiar with its turns," Eaparius said over his tea.

"I've heard there are things that live in the mountains." Jorah said.

"Yes, young Jorah, that is truly spoken. One may find all sorts of creatures in the mountains, from small rodents to large mountain rams, or even bears. Clans of, less friendly creatures, also make their home in mountain ranges, much like these."

"Are there trolls, Eaparius?" Jorah asked.

"There are indeed. Although much of what is known as common knowledge of trolls is misguided. They don't oft scout the roads for travelers to ambush. And it is a rare day indeed when they eat the wary passerby." Eaparius laughed.

"Eat?" Cali said.

"Oh yes, young Cali. Trolls are carnivorous you see. They are voracious meat eaters and are not particularly specific on the source of the meat. So, yes, they will eat people. But rest easy, as I said, they are not hunters of people, we tend to put up too much a fight, and most of us don't have enough meat on our bones to be worth the effort." He smiled at them.

Cali pulled a small flask from her cloak, took a sip and handed it to Jorah. "Warming concoction." She smiled at Eaparius.

"Fine idea, young Cali." He looked around at the steely clouds and pulled his cloak closer. "I fear we may see rain on our trek up the mountain."

"For our trip, the weather mayhaps is the biggest danger." He smiled at them again. "Apart from that, we will need to watch for animals, but I expect we need not worry about trolls. The road we follow does not pass close by their encampment. On the off chance that we see one, we shall neither tarry nor make extra haste. Oft they ignore us as we ignore them."

Breaking camp, Jorah hitched the larger horses and prepared the wagon for the next leg of their journey.

$$\infty \quad \infty \quad \infty$$

As Eaparius predicted, their trip up the mountain was largely uneventful. They spotted animals and heard what may have been a bear in the underbrush. A cold rain had started shortly after the road began to climb toward the first bend in the pass, but the overhang of the curved roof protected them from most of it. Chase had climbed into Cali's cloak and settled in for a nap.

As they stopped briefly to eat lunch and rest, the rain subsided. They were still in a heavily forested part of the mountains, but it felt as if they must be nearing the top.

"Eaparius, are we close to the top of the mountains?" Cali asked as they ate.

"Not yet, young Cali. These mountains are quite steep, you see, so the road must wind back and forth as it climbs toward the peak. This meandering is what makes the mountain pass slow to travel, and also makes it dangerous in foul weather. If the rain holds off, we may break through the tree line this evening."

"The forest does not cover the entire mountain pass?" Jorah asked.

"No, young Jorah. As you near the summit, the trees fall away and it is all mountainous terrain until you reach the other side. It is in those upper areas where the trolls make their homes. It is also where you can see for leagues in either direction."

"Can we see all of Edelaine from there?" Cali asked.

"I daresay on a clear day you can, young Cali. At our pace, we should make the summit tomorrow, and if a clear day is gifted to us, you shall see a view as you have not seen before."

They pressed on up the mountain. The rain held off, but the chill remained in the air. Cali was glad that Eaparius had taught her the warming concoction first, and that she had made a rather large batch of it.

As the sky began to darken, the made their way out of the forest. It was a surprisingly fast switch, at first Cali noticed more rocks and greater spaces between the trees and brush along the road, then, as if opening a door to a new place, they were out of the trees.

The road beyond them looked to be cut from the rock itself, and in the fading light, everything appeared in varied gray hues.

Beyond the tree line, they made camp for the night. Jorah had napped in the back of the wagon on this leg of the trip, determined to take the night watch.

Eaparius made another stew, and they passed around the flask again to take the chill off of the evening air.

"It looks so barren up here," Cali said.

"It would seem so to you, young Cali. You were born and raised in lush green farmlands, by lakes and rivers. You shall see in the light of morning though, the mountains are far from barren. Rocky, yes, and much less green. But they have their own beauty and are teaming with life if you know where to look."

"These aren't the Gelid Mountains you spoke of are they, Eaparius?" Cali looked at him.

"No, child. These are the Shattered Peaks. The Gelid Mountains are far away to the north across the Great Deep. It is a place where snow lays pristine and frozen year round."

"Gelid Mountains?" Jorah asked.

"Yes, where the first Watcher met Time," Cali said.

Jorah looked confused and curious. Eaparius poured them all more tea and told Jorah the lore of the first Watcher and how the bow and armor came to be.

Of all Cali had learned of the lore so far, the story of the first Watcher was her favorite. She could see how through time they had fallen into legends though, so far-flung as they seemed.

"Eaparius, why are these called Shattered Peaks?" Cali asked.

"Ah, yes, it does sound dramatic, does it not? But it is not so exciting as it sounds. These peaks, due to their height, location, and large quantities of ore throughout the stone, have been prone to bear the brunt of storms. Throughout time, this gave them their jagged, sharp, I daresay, shattered, appearance at the summit."

As night closed in around them, they warmed themselves by the fire, passing around the flask once more, then settled in for the night.

∞　∞　∞

The morning broke, cold but clear. Jorah had put the kettle on and was frying up some sausages and ham over the fire. Chase sat near the fire, watching the fate of the ham intently.

"A fine morning, we may yet see that mountain view, my young friends," Eaparius said.

"How long do you think it will take us to reach the pass summit?" Jorah asked.

"If this weather stays true, we shall make a good pace I expect. I would say by afternoon half past, mayhaps."

They ate in silence for a bit, and Cali looked around in the clear morning light. The mottled hues of gray that she saw last night had been hiding beautiful soft shades of purples, sage greens, and light browns. The trees were gone, in their place were bushes and thickets, covered with small leaves and berries.

The rocks were broken and jagged, laying in pieces ranging from small stones to large boulders. Some of the larger chunks glinted in the sun what appeared to be small lines of a darker slate gray metal.

"Slate iron, young Cali," Eaparius said, noticing her gaze.

"Many smiths discount its usefulness, it is quite brittle when mined, you see. But older, more learned smiths know that if tempered and worked correctly, it is as sturdy as dark iron, and holds an edge just as sharp. The Shattered Peaks are brimming with it." He continued.

"I imagine there are many useful plants here," Cali said, looking around.

"Oh yes, young Cali. I plan for us to make camp at the summit, we can switch the horses there, take rest, and I can replenish my stocks of fluxroot, and mayhaps enjoy the views."

They packed and set off toward the mountain pass summit.

∞　∞　∞

The horses kept a steady pace up the mountain, they could see the place where the peaks met the sky ahead of them. They paused to rest and have a light lunch.

Cali, stepping off the wagon, gasped.

"Oh!" she said.

Jorah jumping down from the wagon followed her gaze and also froze, staring.

Eaparius laughed. "Yes, my young friends, your lands of Edelaine. Of course, it is mostly treetops and blue waters beyond, but there lies your home."

"I hadn't realized how high we had climbed up the mountain!" Jorah said.

"Yes, young Jorah! It is deceptive with the winding road through the forest. You will enjoy when we make the summit. The summit pass is due east-west, and you can see in both directions until the land meets the sky."

"I wonder how everyone is doing back at home," Cali said.

As they sat by their small fire eating, Chase suddenly jumped up and let out a low growl.

The three of them jumped up, looking in the direction Chase was sniffing. The area ahead looked clear, although thick with the brush and bushes, it could be an animal, but certainly nothing so large as a troll.

Eaparius was standing stock, silent, listening to the wind and faint sounds.

Without warning, a black bear lunged out of the brambles at a full run toward them, teeth bared and a ferocious roar breaking the relative quiet.

Jorah unsheathed his swords, blinked, and the bear lay dead in front of them, pierced by two arrows.

He gaped at Cali, shaking his head.

"So… so, that's what a bow strung by Time can do?" he asked, shaken.

Cali smiled timidly at him.

"Yes, young Jorah. I take it that is the first you've seen it used?"

Jorah sat down hard, still piecing together in his mind what he had just experienced.

"Yes. I saw her hold the bow before, and the light, it seemed to have its own light, but, but nothing like, that was unbelievable," Jorah said.

"What did it look like to you, Jorah?" Cali asked. She hadn't considered until then what it looked like from someone else's perspective when she used her bow.

"There was the bear, he jumped out and was running, I went for my swords, and you seemed to… you looked blurred almost.

Before I had finished pulling my swords, it was laying there, dead." Jorah shook his head as if to clear it.

"I'd have missed it entirely if I weren't paying attention," Jorah added.

"Yes, and such is the power of the bow, and also how it has gone unnoticed by many through the ages," Eaparius said.

"See, young Jorah, people are, in a manner of speaking, full-minded. At any given point, they are distracted by the thoughts of their daily lives. Some even consumed by those thoughts, with little concern or notice for the world happening around them. As such, it is often easier to hide in plain sight than in forced stealth."

Chase climbed up on Jorah's lap, nudging his hand with his nose, seeming to pull Jorah back to himself.

Eaparius saw Cali eying the bear's carcass. "Sadly, young Cali, we cannot take it with us, the smell of the blood would surely draw animals and others alike."

Cali, catching his meaning, nodded. Although her curious mind wanted to see a troll, she thought it better if some things were left unseen.

∞ ∞ ∞

As Eaparius had foretold, the view from the summit pass was incredible. They could see almost the entirety of Edelaine, but what was more remarkable is they could not see the entirety of the regions beyond to the east.

For the first time, Cali began to understand her part of the world had been a very small one indeed.

Although early, they made camp at the summit, resting both themselves and the horses.

Cali and Jorah joined Eaparius as he combed through the plants near the path. Cali helped him gather fluxroot, tying them by the stems and hanging them from the overhang on the back of the wagon.

Jorah brushed down the horses, checking their hooves for any rocks or other injuries from the road.

As they gathered around the fire, thoughts turned to the east.

"Eaparius, is that break in the forest below a river?" Cali asked.

"No, young Cali, that is the main road heading east to the capital. It is known by another name though, Great Riston Road," Eaparius said with a disgusted snort.

"That sounds… well, what makes it great?" Jorah asked.

Eaparius chuckled. "Yes, young Jorah, great indeed. It is great because it was deemed to be great by Lord Riston himself, and so came to be named after him. Lord Riston is a proud man from an even prouder family which have ruled over these regions for several generations."

Cali studied Eaparius for a moment. "You don't regard him much, do you?" she asked.

"Ahh, young Cali, he would be regarded much more highly if his sense of pride and love of wealth and power were not his main motivations, you see. With so many years of quiet abundance and prosperity, he has divined his right to rule as a given, and that the regions exist to serve him and his family, rather than the other way around."

"Will he meet with us and listen?" Jorah asked.

"He can be a reasonable man, and quite resolute, especially in matters where he feels his power or authority are in danger, so yes, he will meet with us. He is also a surprisingly intelligent man... although I daresay, intelligence does not innately equal wisdom."

Eaparius leaned in close and laughed, "but again, young friends, do not tell the other scholars I say as much, it may tarnish their goodwill."

CHAPTER
24

The journey down the east side of the mountains seemed quicker than the trek up. From their vantage point, they could begin to make out the large city seeming to punctuate the Great Riston Road which lay below them.

"That looks to be a large place," Cali said.

It was hard to tell from this distance, but the city in the distance looked to be half as large as Edelaine itself.

"Yes, there sits the capital city of Edrym. Standing ruler, Lord Riston, governor of the continent of Lufal." Eaparius said.

Eaparius looked at them thoughtfully.

"Neither of you has ventured outside of Edelaine, I daresay?" he asked.

Both Cali and Jorah shook their heads.

"Ah, then let us use this time to acquaint you with Edrym for our visit, young friends."

"Edrym is the central hub of trade and commerce on Lufal. As such, you will find it to be more than only large, on any day there are enough people to fill Edelaine three times over."

Lighting his pipe, as they approached the tree line ahead, he continued.

"While Edrym is a city of men, I daresay you will encounter others on our visit as well. You will do well to observe and learn on this first visit to such a place."

"Wait, others? Who else might we meet?" Jorah asked.

"You and young Cali have not met the likes of Elf-kind, Dwarves, or Gnomes. And I daresay you mayhaps have not even heard tell of the Tevici people."

"Tevici? They are real?" Cali asked, her eyes wide.

"Real? Why yes, young Cali, as real as you or I, and quite often misunderstood and outcast simply based on who they are," Eaparius said with a heavy sigh.

"Hold on, what is a Tevici?" Jorah asked.

"Cat people," Cali said.

"What!" Jorah looked from Cali to Eaparius and back again.

"Cat people! As in, cat, and, people?" Jorah looked stunned.

"Oh quite so, young Jorah! Although be wary, most do not care to be called cat people, even if it is an adequate description. Always remember, the other races of Idoramin are much the same as you or I. While we differ in stature, color, appearance, and even goals and aspirations, at the core we are all as the same. That is to say, deserving of respect and kindness."

Cali and Jorah sat quietly watching the view of the city ahead fall behind the curtains of the forest as they entered.

"The city itself is divided into parts, as most cities of this size are." Eaparius continued.

"In most large places each race will tend to congregate into sections, taking comfort from being with their brethren. Further, Edrym is divided into areas such as a merchant district, craftsmen district, royal district, residential, and the like."

They stopped to make camp for the night, relaxing around the fire as they ate and continuing to talk about their upcoming visit to the capital.

$$\infty \quad \infty \quad \infty$$

After they left the mountain and were again on flat land, they passed through the forest quickly. Still one day out from Edrym, they stopped at a small inn at a crossroad. Thankful to have real beds to rest in that night they ate heartily in front of a large hearth fire. Cali sharing bits of roast and bread to Chase under the table.

"How long do you suppose we will be in Edrym?" Cali asked.

"I cannot say with surety, young Cali. A few days, mayhaps a bit longer, though I believe we can keep this visit short. I can get a meet with Lord Riston quite soon, or at least the general of the Guard."

He paused a moment, the smoke from his pipe swirling between them.

"There are a few other necessary tasks we must do while we are here. Whilst I have my own notion as to your given weapon talent, we must be certain. And so, I will have you meet with one of my friends, a blademaster of great skill and reputation."

Jorah looked excited at the prospect.

"A blademaster?"

"Quite so, young Jorah. He is one of the leaders of the Guildhall of Champions. They are a group of warriors of differing skills. Any who wish to be part of the Guard must first gain entry and train until they receive approval from the leaders of the Champions. My friend, Mac, is one of the best blademasters in all Idoramin, and has trained countless warriors."

"Do you think, maybe he would talk to me? Maybe give me some pointers?" Jorah asked.

"I imagine he would, young Jorah. I hear you are skilled in wielding two swords, I daresay he would be interested to meet you. Young master Mac is one like you will not find in Edelaine. He is Dwarven, you see. A more stout folk you will not find in Idoramin."

"Eaparius, you said you have your own notion of my talent. What do you think it is?"

"Young Cali, I would say my notion is much the same as yours." He smiled at her. "You've practiced with young Bethal's throwing knives I've seen, but you have not felt the same pull to them I think?"

Cali shook her head. "No, I haven't. Not like with the bow."

"Just so, young Cali. I think your skill lies with the bow, and with some of your other talents, I have another young master for you to meet in Edrym. Master Holt is a bowman of skill unmatched by all but a few. I suspect he will be most excited to meet you."

∞ ∞ ∞

As they drew closer to the gates of Edrym the Great Riston Road began to earn its name, at least in size if nothing else. The road had widened to where four wagons could have traveled abreast without being crowded. Tended flowers and benches were placed along the road. And at places, there were smaller roads to the left and right which seemed to wind off into what looked like residential areas.

On the high walls were more patrolling guards and flags with the emblem of a shield surrounded by what looked like ivy vines.

Edrym guardsmen patrolled on horseback along the road, and more guards lined each side of the gated entrance to the city. Large banners hung on the walls behind the guardsmen bearing the same emblem as the flags above.

The road as it approached the gate changed from the worn, hardened path, to cobbled stone, smoothed from constant wear and time.

Cali and Jorah tried to look everywhere at once. Neither of them had ever seen a city such as this. The towering stone walls looked intimidating, making them feel quite small and out of place.

Eaparius guided the wagon through the entrance, the closest guard giving him a brief nod, and waved them through the gate.

There are so many people, Cali thought.

There were people on foot, some carrying packs of goods to the markets. There were many others in wagons of all sizes and conditions, she imagined also merchants heading for the commerce district.

There were men and women, some very short, shorter than Cali had ever seen except as children, but these were certainly not children. Stout men stood inside the gate talking. Cali thought she caught a glimpse of a Tevici, but the crowd of people closed in before she could be certain.

Inside the gate, to the left, there was a large stable house. They could see inside many horses and smaller ponies. Jorah pointed out what appeared to be two mountain rams saddled as horses would be. On the other side of the road was an inn, larger than Cali had ever seen.

The road split into three, Eaparius guided the wagon with care toward the road curving to the right. This appeared to be entering a commerce district. There were small shops, vendor stalls, and tents in all directions. Items ranging from brass candlesticks to rugs, from fish to barrels of dried pipe-herbs. Still, Eaparius eased the wagon through the crowded street.

"Mayhaps if we have time, you two would like to visit the commerce district. There is much to be found here that can be found nowhere else," Eaparius said.

The road again split, one to the right, and one straight ahead leading through another gate.

As they passed through the gate, the guard greeted Eaparius with a wave and nod. Cali and Jorah looked at each other, overwhelmed by the sheer size and variety of the city they had seen so far.

Another smaller set of stables sat beyond this gate, and Eaparius slowed, waving at the stablehand.

"Aye, Eaparius! To your house then?" the man shouted.

"Just so, young Tomas, can you send the boys to get these four horses and see to them?" Eaparius replied.

"Certainly, I'll send them up in a blink," Tomas said, waving as Eaparius urged the horses on.

The horses cantered their way up the road. They made a sharp turn to the left up a small hill to a house situated above, overlooking the stables, road, and gate below.

It was the strangest house Cali had ever seen. It was two floors, the first floor seemed to be set down part of the way into the ground. It was wide, and at one end there was a small round stone tower which was at least one floor taller than the rest. On the other side, a fenced-in garden and a well.

A large orange cat lay sleeping on the porch near the front door. The entire house and half of the garden were set in shade from massive evergreen trees. The sounds of the commerce district seemed distant, muted by the gated stone wall and the large, full trees. The smells of many cooking foods and untold other aromas mingled with the fresh tree smell surrounding his house.

Eaparius stood, stretching before stepping down from the wagon.

"Welcome to my home, and yours, my young friends."

CHAPTER 25

E aparius, sir! You have returned!"

Turning toward the house, Cali saw a very short woman with odd spiky hair, standing in the doorway.

"Ahh, young Midge. Yes, and we have much to discuss. Please call the others, we shall be in momentarily."

Giving a quick nod, the short woman turned back into the house.

Retrieving a chest from the wagon, Eaparius turned to them. "Midge is one of my pupils. Extraordinary intelligence for one so small."

"She looks quite young," Cali said.

"Quite so, young Cali! Mayhaps you'll be surprised to learn she is older than yourself. She is of Gnomish descent, you see."

They walked into the house, which was quite large, and as she suspected, the first floor was inset into the ground. The steps lead into a dark wood room with a massive stone hearth on the opposite wall.

A couch, along with several chairs and small desk tables were situated around the fire. There were several large pots around the room brimming with unusual plants.

Midge and two young men walked into the room.

"Ahh, very good, thank you, young Midge."

Eaparius turned, motioning to Cali and Jorah.

"My students, allow me to present Callera... Cali... Flynn, and Jorah Jenkins from Edelaine. My young friends, these are my pupils, Midge, Roland, and Thraeston." Each student nodding to Cali and Jorah in turn.

"Young friends, this is not only my home, this is also my study and workshop. My pupils dwell here, upstairs so that we can focus on their studies."

Thraeson's golden eyes took in Jorah, and then Cali, coming to rest on her bracers. "Magnificent. Your bracers."

Jorah stepped forward his hand out, to shake their hands, starting with Thraeston.

"Nice to meet you," Jorah said.

Midge coughed. "Can I show you your rooms then? This way." She smiled and turned.

Cali and Jorah followed Midge into a large open room which was the kitchen and dining area, a long table dominated the center of the room. Then past the table and up the stairs.

"It is good to meet you both." She smiled back at them as they went upstairs. "Roland is quiet with those he doesn't know at first, and Thraeston, well, he may talk a bit too much." She gave them a quick wink and laughed.

She motioned to the first room on right.

"This is me, then Thraeston, and Roland on the end. Your rooms are here on the left, Jorah, you can take the room on the far end, Callera, you can take the room there in the middle. This room here across from me became a bit of a catch-all and isn't well suited for guests." She grinned, opening the door onto a room filled with stacks of boxes, bottles, and several small barrels.

"If you want, drop your things in your rooms, and come back down when you are ready. And let one of us know if you need anything." Midge gave them a small nod and smile, going back down the stairs.

Cali instantly liked Midge. She wondered if it would be impolite to ask her about her Gnomish descent, her curiosity getting the better of her.

Shrugging at Jorah, they went and deposited their things into the rooms down the hall. Chase sniffed around her room, jumping up on the bed and laying down.

"Comfy then, are you?" Cali scratched his ears. "You can stay here boy, I'll be just downstairs."

Downstairs, cheese, bread, smoked ham and a large pitcher had been set out on the table, and a kettle was steaming over the hearth fire. Eaparius was at the end of the table, his students situated on the bench down one side. Jorah and Cali sat on the bench opposite them.

"Young Midge, how goes your studies?" Eaparius asked, lighting his pipe.

"Very good, sir. I was able to imbue the scrolls, they are not potent as I want, but it was successful." Midge looked perplexed.

"Very good, young Midge. Do not fret, keep at it until you reach the result you want. Roland, you?"

"A success, sir." He said in a quiet voice. "Summons worked as expected."

Eaparius nodded. "Quite so, young Roland. And Thraeston?"

"Perfectly, sir! The tome is imbued and ready, a heavy leather piece with excellent parchments. I am excited to put my quill to work on it, sir." Thraeston said. His unusual golden eyes coming to rest on Cali.

"Most satisfactory, young Thraeston. We shall have a need to use it quite soon. Please, all, eat, help yourselves."

Eaparius brought the tea kettle from the fire, setting it in the middle of the table for all to reach, as they ate in companionable silence.

"I will step out after a spell, I need to see to arranging a meet with Lord Riston as soon as possible. Mayhaps the meet shall be tomorrow if it can be managed."

Pouring himself a cup of tea, Eaparius continued. "Roland, can you get the message to Master Mac at the Champion's Hall that I will be visiting with him on the morrow?"

"Of course, sir. I will go now." He stood, leaving quietly.

"Thraeston, will you do the same for Master Holt?"

"I'd be happy to, sir. I won't be long," He replied, also standing to leave, nodding to them.

"Very good, very good. I am going to head to Riston's offices. Cali, if you and Jorah would like to visit the Commerce area, do so. Young Midge can accompany you and show you around if you like." Eaparius smiled at them, rising to also leave.

"I would love to, that is if you two would like to, and aren't too tired. You've had a long journey, I'm sure you're tired too," Midge said.

Cali, having brought all her coins, was excited at the idea of visiting the merchants. "Jorah, what do you think?"

"Count me in, I'd like to see the city," Jorah said. He seemed as excited by the idea as Cali.

$$\infty \quad \infty \quad \infty$$

Roland arrived at the Champion's Hall, past the gates into the Craftsmen District. He always liked coming to this part of the city. Wizards in their robes, and the cloaks which denoted their school, mingling with warriors with their shining steel forms. And the sneaks, as he liked to think of them, those who wandered the world, never settling in only one place.

Even though the Wizard's towers were at the far end of the district, he enjoyed catching glimpses of the occultists and elementalists practicing. Most especially the occultists. The very notion of their hidden knowledge and secretive lore had always appealed to him.

Roland hurried through the heavy oaken doors of the

Champion's Hall, heading left toward the armory. Master Mac, as the guild's foremost blademaster, would likely be either in the armory or on the practice yard.

The boisterous, armored warriors tended to look at him, and others who studied the magical arts, as weak. It was only the older, more experienced fighters who gained respect for the power ones like himself could wield.

He passed by a group of laughing young men, bulwarks, judging by the heavy shields leaning against their stools. He reminded himself he would one day wield powers greater than even theirs. No longer feeling somehow weaker or less necessary or capable.

"Oye! Ya idjit! I'll rank ya back to training blades if ya don't take care!"

Unmistakably Master Mac's voice, Roland continued into the armory in time to see the stout Dwarven warrior scolding a young student.

Catching Mac's eye, Roland waited until he was finished.

"Here, lad. You are one of Eaparius's, aye? What can I do for ye?" Mac looked at Roland.

"Sir, Master Eaparius wanted you to know he would be visiting you on the morrow. He is bringing a young, student."

"Hmm, right, right. Thanks, laddie. Let him know I'll be here, aye?"

"Certainly, sir. Thank you." Roland turned to leave.

He knew Eaparius wouldn't be back yet, so he headed toward the towers to watch the occultists before returning home.

∞   ∞   ∞

Looking up into golden eyes, the older man, known around the city only as Holt, stood up from his writing.

"I still don't know why you didn't train in our hall." He said smiling at the young man with the golden eyes.

"You move too quietly to be a student of old Eaparius."

Walking around the desk, he clapped the young man on the shoulder, motioning for him to sit.

"Thank you sir, but I'm much better with a quill and staff than I would ever be with a bow." Thraeston laughed.

"Maybe so, maybe so, but we could use another set of pointy-ears around here." Holt laughed.

"I would say that everyone could use more of us pointy-ears around."

"Just so, Thraeston! Now, what can I do for you this day?" Holt asked.

"Master Eaparius wanted you to know he's coming to see you on the morrow. He's bringing a… a young lady along with him," Thraeston said, a serious look on his face.

"A young lady, eh? She must be special then, I'd wager." Holt said, rubbing his scruffy chin.

"Oh yes, sir, she is. Red hair like I've not seen and —"

Holt laughed. "Red hair, you say? And that makes her special, eh?"

Not one for blushing, Thraeston simply shrugged, smiling.

"Just so, Thraeston. Let old Eaparius know I'm at his service."

Holt stood, shaking Thraeston's hand.

"And if you ever get bored with your books, come see me." He grinned at the young man.

Thraeston left the shadowy Hall of the Wanderers. He wanted to catch up with Cali as Midge showed her and Jorah around the Commerce District.

∞   ∞   ∞

Eaparius walked up the white stone steps to the castle in the Royal District. A tall, stern man in dark gray armor stepped from the heavy iron and wooden doors.

"Eaparius, sir! I have not seen you here for some time. People may think you don't like coming to the Royal District." The man grinned at Eaparius.

"Ahh General Trillan! Fortuitous to meet you here, I was on my way to set a meeting for the morrow with Lord Riston," Eaparius replied.

The General motioned to a nearby stone bench. "I was heading over to the Champion's Hall, but what serious matter brings this about?"

"Aegil Imps, Doyle. They attacked the steads in Edelaine," Eaparius said to the General, his voice lowered.

Trillan's eyes narrowed. "Aegil Imps. Are you certain, old friend? This is a serious matter indeed."

"Quite so, I saw them with my own eyes. Doyle, they killed the Guardian." Eaparius shook his head with a long, low sigh.

"How can that be, Eaparius? The Guardian, but she —"

"She wasn't prepared, sadly. It seems generations of peace and abundance has dulled all our awareness."

Trillan nodded. "Riston is due back this night. Come to the offices early on the morrow, we will meet."

Eaparius stood, shaking the General's hand. "I hope he recognizes the threat, Doyle."

"Aye. As do I." Doyle stood. "I am to visit the Champion's Hall, would you like to walk with me?"

"Most certainly! I have need to speak with Caronas."

"What need do you have for the master crafter?"

Eaparius smiled. "I have a young friend who is quite skilled in leather herself, I thought Caronas may like to meet her."

"Then let us be off, friend." Doyle clapped Eaparius on the shoulder as they set off down the steps.

CHAPTER
26

Cali had never seen so many different things for sale. Merchants selling finished wares all the way down to individual components. She was excited to visit the small shop which looked to carry furs, hides, and fabrics, but it was still a piece up the road.

Stepping into the fragrant herb shop, Cali spotted a small barrel labeled cooking spices. Sarah would love this, she thought, examining the small wooden container.

"It's quite good, that. Are you a chef, then?" Midge asked.

"Oh no, not me!" Cali laughed. "My friend, Sarah, handles all the food on the farm. I wanted to get some gifts for my people back home."

"We use that spice, if she likes to cook, she would like that, then." Midge smiled.

Midge looked around to spot Jorah on the other side of the shop.

"What about him?" she nodded in Jorah's direction.

"Who, Jorah? I was wanting to make him a bear fur cloak, but we couldn't bring the bear I killed with us on the journey down the mountain."

"Ahh, a leatherworker, then? I would love to see how you make pieces if you would show me? I fancy myself a bit of a tailor, I work with cloth." Smiling, she spun around.

"You made your robes? That's brilliant!" Cali smiled.

Midge looked pleased. "Oh yes, and some of the ones for Eaparius and the boys too."

Midge leaned in, lowering her voice. "You'll be sure to find bear, and many other furs, down at Furs and Fines. We can stop there next."

As the trio walked further down the lane, Thraeston walked up behind them, putting his arm around Midge and Cali as they walked.

"I had hoped to find you here!" Thraeston smiled at them and nodded to Jorah. "Where are we off to, then?"

"Midge told us of a shop, Furs and Fines. Cali can't wait to get there. She's incredible with leather." Jorah smiled, motioning toward his belt and sheaths. "See, she made this belt and sheaths for my swords." He said, looking at Thraeston.

"Quite so, those are fine looking sheaths, Cali. Well, let's not keep her in anticipation, eh?" Thraeston smiled, walking toward the shop.

Midge coughed quietly and rolled her eyes at Cali, smiling.

"There's so much to look at and buy here. I could take back a whole wagon of things for the farm," Cali said.

"I was thinking the same, Cali. Maybe we should, there's a lot here that would look great in the house back home," Jorah said.

Cali's eyes widened as they stepped into Furs and Fines. Piles upon piles of furs and leathers filled most of the room. The rest was filled with rolls of different cloth in colors and textures Cali hadn't seen before.

"Oh, we would need to make that two wagons!" Cali looked around, smiling, her eyes wide.

The shopkeep walked from behind a long wooden counter, smiling.

"Midge, my girl! How are you? I've some new cloth in a lavender hue that you would swoon over," he said.

"Hi, no, I'm not here for me today, this is my friend Cali, she works leather," Midge said.

"As a second thought, maybe I will look at that cloth! But first, leather." Midge laughed.

The keep showed them piles of furs and leathers. Cali chose large bear pelts in black and brown and several rabbit pelts. She thought if she had time before they left for Edelaine, she would make gloves for Midge, Roland, and Thraeston.

Jorah was looking through a table of leather boots, as Midge went to look at the cloth. Thraeston had wandered off to look at some thick small hides, with a leather-bound book displayed on the table.

Midge looked ecstatic talking to the shopkeep holding a large bundle of lavender cloth as Cali brought the pelts to the counter. She handed the coins to the man for the pelts, as Jorah walked up.

"Here, Cali, I'll carry those for you," he said, picking up the rolled pelts.

Midge looked around. "Thraeston, you coming? We need to start heading back."

Standing near the other side of the shop, he replied, "no, no, Midge, I am picking up some new book leathers, you go on ahead and I'll catch up."

As they left the shop, darkness had started to settle onto Edrym. The merchants had lit torches in their tents and stalls, the street still busy with shoppers.

"There's still so much we haven't seen. If we have time, would you mind showing us more, Midge?" Jorah asked.

"I'd love to, Jorah! Let us get back, Eaparius will probably be back already, we can find out his plans for you for tomorrow." Midge said.

∞　∞　∞

Eaparius had made it back before them and was stirring a large pot of stew on the kitchen fire as they came in, carrying their goods. Chase had joined Eaparius in the kitchen, laying close by the fire.

"Ah, there you are, young ones. I thought I may need Roland here to summon you." Eaparius laughed.

"Sorry, Eaparius, it was my fault, I could have stayed in Furs and Fines for hours more!" Cali grinned.

"No cause for apology, young Cali. I had hoped you would happen upon that shop. I see you found a few pelts that caught your eye."

"Oh yes! And twice as many more that I didn't buy. There's so much here, Eaparius, I was telling Midge that I could take at least a wagon or two of items back to the farm."

They went upstairs, putting their things in their rooms, and headed back downstairs, settling in at the table, as Eaparius began to set out bread and cheese and lifted the large pot onto the table.

Thraeston came in while they were upstairs, and was also sitting at the table with Roland.

"Planning to make more tomes, Thraeston?" Midge asked.

"Why yes, of course. I am sure we will have need of them." He smiled, pouring tea for all of them as they ate.

Eaparius settled back in his chair after finishing his stew, lighting his pipe.

"Young Cali, you, Jorah, and I will be meeting with Lord Riston and General Trillan in the morning at Riston's offices," Eaparius said.

"Eaparius, sir, do you think we may have time to visit the shops again? I would like to show Cali and Jorah around Edrym more." Midge asked.

"I expect so, young Midge. Mayhaps in the evening, as we also are visiting Masters Mac and Holt after leaving the castle."

Midge smiled and nodded to Cali.

∞ ∞ ∞

Cali, Jorah, and Eaparius walked through Edrym in the morning fog, heading toward the Royal District. Cali was surprised to see the streets were busy, even this early. Merchants were setting out their wares. Aromas of food floating past the tents and shops.

Guards nodded to Eaparius as they passed through the gate, walking up the wide road leading to the castle.

A tall, serious-looking knight in armor walked down the steps, raising a hand to wave at Eaparius.

"Good to see you, Eaparius," he called out.

"And you. General Trillan, these are my young friends, Cali Flynn, and Jorah Jenkins. Cali, Jorah, this is General Doyle Trillan, General of the Guard."

Jorah and Cali both nodded at the General.

"Good to meet you both. Come, Lord Riston is in his office," Trillan said.

The castle was beautifully decorated. Long, red rugs led from the entry down a long hall lined with doors on both sides. Intricate lanterns hung from the walls, casting a warm light through the hallway.

Entering a massive room at the end of the hall, Lord Riston sat at a large wooden table, covered with maps and other papers.

"Ahh, old Eaparius! Good to see you, Master Wizard." Lord Riston stood to shake Eaparius's hand.

Looking too soft to have been a knight, Lord Riston's thinning hair was tied back at the nape of his neck by a dark red ribbon. His royal light armor not hiding the paunch of this stomach over his belt.

Jorah glanced quickly at Cali smiling, they both knew Eaparius didn't seem to prefer being called a wizard.

"My thanks for meeting with us, Lord Riston." Eaparius bowed his head slightly.

"My friends, Cali Flynn and Jorah Jenkins, from Edelaine." He continued.

Riston gestured for them to all take a seat at the table, as a young woman brought in a rolling cart which had bread, cheese, and a steaming kettle. She poured a mug of tea for each of them, leaving as quietly as she entered.

"Now. Trillan here tells me there is a matter of some urgency that we must investigate immediately. What crisis have the wizards uncovered this time?" Riston smiled.

"Allow me to speak right to the matter, Lord Riston. Aegil Imps attacked the steads of Edelaine in force. They killed many, destroyed homes, and even caught the Guardian unawares."

"Imps! On Lufal? Surely you are mistaken, Eaparius," Riston replied.

"Sadly, no, Lord Riston. They moved through the area killing and burning as they went," Eaparius said.

Riston stood, pacing along the long edge of the table.

"Trillan. What reports do you have of this?" Riston asked.

"None, sir. This is the first report of it, but it bears further —"

"As I thought. There have been no reports of this at all, Eaparius."

"Yes, this may be true, Lord Riston. I saw the wake of the attack with my own eyes. The Guard should be readied. The other regions made aware." Eaparius looked determined.

"You said you saw the wake of the attack, eh? The imps moved on?"

"Quite so, my'lord."

"Then the danger has passed, and is no longer relevant it would seem. The threat no longer present in Edelaine," Riston said as if the matter were resolved.

Cali and Jorah looked at each other, then at Riston.

"Mayhaps the creatures have left Edelaine, but that does not lessen the urgency of making ready the Guard here and elsewhere," Eaparius said.

With a pinched expression, Riston took a deep breath.

"As you well know, Master Eaparius, the cities are well-protected. All have the ability to protect their citizens. Even up to the extent of taking cover to wait out any attack that could be launched from such ignorant creatures as imps," Riston said, folding his arms across his chest.

Cali could not believe what she was hearing. It appeared this Riston was planning on doing nothing!

"Sir, my Lord, forgive me for interrupting. But families in our land were slaughtered, along with their livelihood and homes. We are from a farming region, we don't have our own guard, shouldn't the Guard be sent to at least see for themselves?" Cali said, anger beginning to well up in her.

They all looked from Cali to Riston.

Trillan spoke up in the heavy silence. "Lord Riston, the girl is young and naive I am sure, but she makes a valid point. I can ready a small contingent to investigate the matter on your command."

At this, Eaparius bumped his staff against Cali's foot, she saw him give a slight shake of his head.

"Let us look at what we know," Riston said, forcing his voice to sound friendly.

"We have one single report of imps attacking a few little farms. Imps, in force, which is known to not be typical behavior for an imp, crude and brutish as they are. We have only the word of a child and a wizard."

He began pacing again.

"It is known through the lands that wizards are prone to predicting the doom of all on more than one occasion," He said with a cold smile.

"Further, even by your own reports, the imps are gone and are no more."

Riston, continuing to pace, looked at each of them in turn.

"If I took this at nothing more than your word, if, I were to consider this an actual threat, then as Lord of Edrym, and Governor of all of Lufal, the priority for my guard is to protect its resources. Its cities."

Cali looked over at Jorah, who looked as angry as she felt, his knuckles white as he gripped the arms of his chair.

Riston looked thoughtfully into the fire for a long moment, the silence hanging heavy in the room.

"Yes. Just so. I will ready the Guard. I will send a message to the other cities to ready their Guard to protect their cities as well."

"Protect their cities, sir?" Cali was fuming.

Riston looked at her smugly. "Yes, child. It is my duty to protect this." He made a grand sweeping motion with his hand.

"Is that your decision then?" Eaparius asked. "You shall not send the Guard to Edelaine?"

"Correct. Eaparius, the danger is past, you said as —"

"No, my'lord, I stated only that the imps had moved on from the steads. The danger has not —"

"My decision is made, Eaparius. There is no further danger in Edelaine. I will heed the warning and protect what must be protected. I daresay that we'll not hear any more of imps," Riston said dismissively.

"My Lord Riston? What of a small contingent to Edelaine to investigate? I can go myself, by your leave," Trillan said.

"No, Trillan. I will not have the General of my Guard, tromping around the countryside looking for imps that are no longer there. Nor will I have my Guard weakened by splitting the forces."

Eaparius stood. Cali and Jorah standing with him.

"General Trillan. Lord… Riston. We'll not take any more of

your time." Eaparius nodded to them as he turned to leave.

"That useless, doughy, mongrel!" Cali fumed as they walked down the wide street from the castle.

"How dare he! Who does he think supplies his lands with goods? Has he forgotten who he is supposed to be protecting?" Jorah said.

"My young friends." Eaparius stopped with a long look at them.

"I, too, feel your anger, your frustration, and I agree with it. Riston will not pursue any ends that are not his own. Nor will he spare any Guard if he has even the smallest notion that they will be needed to protect him and his wealth."

He put a hand on Jorah's shoulder and then on Cali's.

"We will find our own way forward, my young friends."

∞ ∞ ∞

CHAPTER
27

"What do we do now, Eaparius?" Jorah asked.

They walked for several minutes in silence.

"Young Jorah, we will continue on with our original plan for the day. Even with Riston's ignorance, we must still forge on, and so, on we will forge. We are going to meet with Master Mac at the Champion's Hall first."

As they made their way through the streets of Edrym toward the Craftsmen District, the crowds grew, everyone starting their days. Cali felt disconnected, somehow separate from these people going about their normal routines, unaware a danger that hadn't been seen for an age, was here in the world.

Past the gate to the district, a large stone building sat to the left. Cali could hear the rhythmic clank of swords coming from behind the building. Weapons training, she thought.

Jorah was excited to meet Mac. He knew the main purpose was for Cali, but he was hopeful to get some pointers on ways to improve his own skills.

Eaparius pushed open the heavy doors and they were greeted by the sight of armored warriors in a three-column formation in the large, open entryway.

"Oye, you lot will be in patrol formation. Ye'll do well not to step out of formation, and I don't want to see ye's back until lunch! Now git!" The short, burly man sent the trainees out through a door on the back side of the hall.

"Young Master Mac!" Eaparius called.

"Eaparius, my friend!" Mac walked up giving Eaparius a strong clap on the shoulder.

"Yer boy Roland came yesterday to let me know ye'd be here today."

"Just so, Mac, just so. Let me introduce my young friends, Cali Flynn, and Jorah Jenkins. Cali, Jorah, this is Master Mac, Blademaster of the Hall of Champions."

"Great to meet you, Master Mac, sir," Jorah said, unable to hide his enthusiasm.

"Good morning, Master Mac, nice to meet you," Cali also said.

"Aye, young'uns, you may simply call me Mac. A friend of Eaparius here is a friend of mine." Mac smiled and clapped Jorah on the shoulder.

"Miss Cali, I hear we need to test out your blade skills?" Mac looked her over.

"Yes, I've never used any blades but daggers though. And if it's okay, I know Jorah would like to test his too," Cali said.

Jorah looked a bit flustered. "I, I would be honored, yes! But

Cali first of course, sir."

Mac nodded. "I see ye have two swords, laddie. I'd like to see what ye can do with them. This way, the side yard is free."

They followed Mac through the Hall and out into the side yard.

Mac explained the basics of dueling and what was expected, then he handed her a training sword. As they dueled, Cali was concentrating hard, worried she would make a fool of herself.

Eaparius and Jorah were sitting on a bench, watching.

"Hmm, ye've never used a sword, lass?"

"No, sir. Only daggers or a bow." Cali handed the sword back to him.

"Ye've got good instincts with a sword, I'll give ye that. A bit of training and ye'd be good."

Mac nodded at Eaparius.

"Now, daggers ye say."

Cali unsheathed her daggers.

"Lass, those are fine looking blades, let me see those. Is that a tooth? And this one is antler, I recognize that." Mac looked over her daggers.

"Use these will ye, I don't fancy a cut right now." Mac grinned, handing Cali two training daggers.

Cali liked Mac, he was good-natured and had a sparkle in his eye. She imagined he would be fierce in a fight.

As they dueled, Cali hadn't noticed a small audience watching.

Several of the warrior trainees from the other training yard, and standing near the stone wall, Midge, Thraeston, and Roland.

"Now that's more like it, lass! You have some skills with daggers to be sure." Mac took the daggers from her.

They repeated the exercise with small axes, then a single larger training axe.

"Aye, lassie, see if you can manage that target over there with yer throwing knives if ye please."

Cali, nervous now that she realized she had an audience, managed to land three of her knives within the red circle.

Jorah cheered from the bench. And as she looked over, she saw Eaparius smiling. Several of the trainees were talking amongst themselves and nodding appreciatively.

"Jorah, laddie! Get ye over here." Mac called to Jorah as Cali went to sit on the bench.

Mac handed him two training swords, and they dueled. It was the first time Cali had seen Jorah fight, and Rowan was right, his brother was very good.

Throughout their duel Mac would pause, showing Jorah different ways to block or parry. Cali wasn't sure who was having more fun, Jorah or Mac.

"Jorah, lad, ye are good enough to be admitted the Hall of Champions, I say!" Mac said.

Jorah looked happy enough that he could have floated back to the bench.

"Eaparius, ye've got two talented young folks here. I'd be happy to train with them anytime." Mac smiled.

"Thank you, Master Mac, I always appreciate your expertise. I expect we'll see you soon. We are off to see Master Holt," Eaparius said, standing.

"Aye, Holt will like meeting these two. Jorah, lad, if you ever want to join the Hall, you come find me!" Mac clapped Jorah on the shoulder.

∞　∞　∞

"This, my young friends, is the Hall of Wanderers. Here, we will meet Master Arrol Holt," Eaparius said.

Cali was nervous, she wasn't sure what to expect, and while comfortable with the blades, none of them seemed particularly special.

As they entered the hall, it was remarkably darker than the gray day outside. At the far end of the entry hall, a group of trainees was sitting at tables filling small vials, while an older woman walked around overseeing their work.

Eaparius led them up the stairs at the far end of the hall, to a large open area with several doorways scattered around the room. Several men and a stout looking Dwarven woman sat at a table near one of the doorways.

As they approached, one of the men stood, raising a hand to them.

"Good to see you, old friend!" The man called out.

"And you, young Master Holt. This is Cali Flynn and Jorah Jenkins, from Edelaine."

"Good to meet you both." Holt held out his hand to shake theirs.

"So, young Cali, let's see what you can do with a few of my ranged weapons, what do you say?" he said, smiling.

"Thank you, Master Holt." Cali pinpointed what was putting her on edge. Everyone seemed to move quickly and almost completely without sound here.

"And manners, too? Eaparius found a good one in you, I see!" Holt gave them a quick wink, laughing.

"Let's head out to the practice yard, and we can see how you fare."

Holt was tall, his dark hair graying at the temples and cut brutally short. Dressed in simple brown leathers, he wore fingerless gloves and heavy bracers.

He led them through one of the doorways, which was little more than a narrow hallway with stairs leading down to a small weapons room. He picked up several different bows. Crossing through the other door in the room, they stepped out into the practice yard.

Holt let out a low whistle and a young man came running over to them carrying a small barrel.

"We don't want to have to waste time chasing down arrows now, do we." He grinned, motioning at the barrel filled with arrows.

"You remind me a bit of Bethal, you know. Here, let's see what you can do with this." Holt handed Cali a large crossbow.

It felt heavy and cumbersome in her hands, she'd never used one before. Holt pointed to a target about 40 yards away toward the tall stone wall surrounding the District.

Cali took several shots with the crossbow, and while they all hit their mark easily, she had no great love for the unwieldy bow.

"Hmm, quite so, Cali. Excellent aim, and you handle it well. But let's see how you do with this." He handed her a short bow.

It felt light and comfortable in her grip, much like the one Bodric had made for her years back. She loosed 3 arrows in quick succession, each landing within the small red center of the target.

Holt nodded approvingly and handed her a small version of the crossbow. "You may like this one better, these are meant to be used either alone, but many who use them use two at a time."

Manageable in her hand, Cali liked the weight and feel of the smaller weapon. Easier to load with the smaller bolts, she landed three in the center of the next target. Switching hands, Cali shot another two bolts with the same ease.

"Remarkable, Cali. Most of our students have to practice before they are able to manage their offhand. You're well-suited to these." Holt took the weapon from her, handing her the last bow.

The long, curved bow felt powerful in her grip. As long as she was tall, it curved back on either end, like her own bow.

Without any effort, Cali loosed several arrows into the next target at 40 yards. Then again hitting the target at 60 yards, 80 yards, and two more at the 100-yard target.

As she turned to hand the bow back to Holt, she noticed that not only were Midge, Roland, and Thraeston there watching again, but several people had come out of the Hall and were leaning against the wall watching. A few spectators from the Hall shook their heads, clapping.

Holt and most of the others watching looked surprised. Eaparius and Jorah simply smiled.

"Well, now. That is something I've not seen but a few of our Rangers manage. These training bows barely manage the 60-yard targets, they just aren't designed for it. I daresay you have a gift, Cali."

Eaparius and Jorah walked over.

"That was incredible, Cali! I think you may have some fans." Jorah laughed, nodding toward the group from the Hall.

Midge, Roland, and Thraeston ran over to join them.

Roland gave Cali a small smile. "That was most impressive, Cali."

"Thanks, Roland." Cali smiled back at him.

"That was... I've not seen anyone shoot like that since I left home. Simply magnificent! Just magnificent! I am at a loss for words," Thraeston said, his golden eyes twinkling.

Midge rolled her eyes, smiling.

"That made me wish I could shoot a bow, Cali. Though I daresay it would have to be a short bow!" Midge laughed.

"Just so, young Cali, just so! I would say we have our answer, yes?" Eaparius nodded at her.

"Why don't you all take the rest of the day and enjoy Edrym? I shall see you at the house this evening." Eaparius smiled at them all.

For the first time since they entered Lord Riston's office, Cali felt happy and unworried.

CHAPTER
28

Cali woke with a start, Bethal's voice ringing in her ears, "Trust yourself. You know what you need to do next, honey."

Chase snuggled closer to her as she shivered under the blankets. The fire in the small hearth in her bedroom was down to embers. She got up to add more wood, then splashed cold water on her face from the basin near the window.

It was still dark as pitch outside her window. She could hear the animals in the stables below Eaparius's house and save for the guards on the night watch, the city was quiet.

She sat by the fire, recalling her mother's face, and the face of her grandmother. It was as Eaparius had said, some of her other ancestors may reach out to her.

Her grandmother looked like an older version of herself, the same red hair, the same nose. It was strange to see someone so familiar that she had never met before.

I know what I need to do next, she thought to herself. Knowing she would get no more sleep tonight, she pulled from the table the rabbit pelts to work on.

∞ ∞ ∞

By the time the sun broke over Edrym, Cali had completed three pairs of rabbit-fur gloves. Fingerless, like her own, but with a flap that could cover the fingers when needed. Using her dagger, she cut the paper the shopkeep had wrapped the furs in to use to wrap the gloves.

Hearing movement downstairs, she went to investigate.

Midge and Roland were in the kitchen preparing breakfast, and Thraeston sat at the table, his quill scratching at a page in the heavy, leather-bound book in front of him.

"You three are up early." Cali tried to put on a smile.

"Our studies start early. Master Eaparius said he had to go to the Craftsmen District this morning, but charged us with getting breakfast ready and then to work." Midge smiled, setting bread and cheese on the table.

"Work?" Cali asked.

"Yes. Master Eaparius gives us assignments, which are part of our studies. We learn as we work. There is much to learn of a Watcher's path," Roland said as he set plates and mugs on the table.

That was the most Cali had ever heard him speak. It seemed he was becoming more comfortable with them. Oddly, Thraeston hadn't spoken yet at all, only nodding as she came into the kitchen.

Jorah came down the steps, stretching and rubbing his eyes.

"Smells good down here. What can I do to help? I'm famished,"

Jorah said.

They sat at the table eating breakfast. Thraeston finally closed the large tome to eat after Midge playfully smacked his head.

"Roland, you said there was much to learn of Watchers. So, you all know about…"

"Watchers and Guardians?" Roland smiled.

He continued, "yes when we were chosen by Master Eaparius to study, we first studied the history of the prophecy."

"So then there are those who know about it, beyond the Watcher and Guardian themselves," Jorah said.

"Yes, but only a select few. The highest levels of those who govern, though I daresay they don't put much faith in it, viewing it as myth, so Eaparius says." Midge shook her head.

"Those who were chosen as Watcher students also know, those who still live," Roland added.

As they neared the end of breakfast, Thraeston's hand kept reaching for his book.

"What are you studying today, Thraeston? It seems to have captured your attention," Cali asked.

"Oh. Oh yes, it certainly has!" Thraeston seemed to be finding his words again.

"You see, Cali, this is the tome I made. I am using it to record all the current Guardian lore, your lore," Thraeston said, his chin raised.

"You made this?" Cali asked.

"Thraeston here is a gifted scribe. Mayhaps that's why he has so many words at his disposal." Midge grinned.

Jorah laughed from behind his mug of tea. Even Roland let out a cough to hide his laugh.

"The book is beautiful, Thraeston. How you bound and embossed the leather is impressive," Cali said.

"I... thank you," Thraeston said simply.

Cali looked lost in thought.

"What is it, Cali? Everything okay?" Jorah placed a hand on her arm.

All their eyes turned to Cali.

"Yes, thanks, Jorah. It's just..." Cali sighed.

"It's just I can't help think about Riston yesterday. His ignorance changes things." Cali continued, shaking her head. She suddenly felt much older again.

"If you can, what happened? I heard Eaparius talking with Master Holt yesterday. He mentioned something about them talking about Riston today," Roland said quietly.

Everyone looked at Roland, surprised.

He looked back at them. "It does pay to talk less and listen more sometimes, you see." He smiled timidly again.

"It's no great secret that Master Eaparius doesn't hold much regard for Lord Riston, or Riston for Master Eaparius, as I've heard," Midge said.

"In this case, I have to agree with Eaparius," Jorah said, shaking his head.

"Jorah's right. We met with Riston to tell him to ready the Guard after what happened at home. He dismissed our reports, plans to simply shut the city gates if… and he made a point to say if… there was an actual threat. He tried to slyly slip in several times how 'wizards liked to start trouble', that they report the doom of all, and frequently." Cali clenched her hands.

"That imbecile wouldn't acknowledge a threat unless it came knocking on his family vault's door," Thraeston said.

He sounded and looked more serious than Cali had heard him.

"That was my impression as well, Thraeston," Jorah said. Jorah felt a bit more amicable toward Thraeston.

Roland looked over at Midge. "I think my studies can wait a bit longer today."

Midge and Thraeston both nodded.

Looking from Jorah to Cali, Roland continued, "what do we do next?"

∞　∞　∞

They talked long into the day, only noticing the time when Eaparius returned later in the afternoon. Midge and Roland busied themselves with preparing a large dinner, and Thraeston had returned to writing in the Guardian tome.

As they ate dinner, Eaparius told Cali about a master

leatherworker in the Craftsmen District named Caronas. People came from all over Lufal to buy her wares, and some even on the hopes of being taken in as an apprentice.

"Caronas is the only leather worker in all of Idoramin that the Rangers trust for their leathers, or so the stories say," Thraeston said.

"She is from Adreath," Roland said.

"What? Is that true, Eaparius?" Midge asked, wide-eyed.

"It is true, young Midge, though she does not make that a well-known fact," Eaparius said, looking at Roland.

"What is so special about this place, Adreath?" Jorah asked.

"It is the ancestral home of Elven-kind. The original elves, so it is told. Access to that city is forbidden except by those who have been granted leave to enter. They are regal, considered royalty among Elven-kind. Though they do tend to frown upon the other Elven races," Thraeston said.

"Caronas would like to meet you, young Cali. Now that we have divined your true weapon gift, we will need assistance, which Caronas has graciously granted."

"What!" they all said in unison.

"Caronas wants to meet with Cali? That's quite a thing," Roland said.

"Yes, I daresay it is, young Roland. We will meet with her on the morrow," Eaparius said.

Cali nodded at Midge, who stood, retrieving a bottle of mulled wine and setting it on the table.

"Now, my young students, tell me of your studies today," Eaparius said.

"Eaparius, they didn't complete their studies today, but it was my doing, so if there is any punishment for it, I will take it," Cali said.

She reached for the wine, pouring each of them a glass.

"Eaparius, I need to go back to Edelaine soon. I am going to begin training everyone for fighting skills, testing them, as best I can, to see what weapons they may be able to use. Much like we did for me." Cali added, smiling.

"Riston and his lot won't help us, that much is clear. Which means I must help us. And the first step for me to do that is to make sure my people are prepared to help themselves."

Cali straightened on her seat looking directly at Eaparius, waiting for his disagreement. Instead, he lit his pipe, then took a drink of the wine.

"This must be young Midge's idea, I would presume?" Eaparius raised his glass slightly, smiling.

Cali relaxed a bit. "Mum always told me to soften up someone before you hit them with hard news." Cali smiled at the memory.

"Just so, young Cali, just so." Eaparius was quiet for what seemed like a long time.

"Very well, young Cali. I sense you expected some dissent, but this notion has also been in my mind since our meeting with Lord Riston. After speaking again with Doyle, General Trillan, I must agree with this course," Eaparius said, nodding.

It was obvious that Eaparius was deep in thought, even as he spoke his agreement. His pipe smoke swirled around them as they sat in silence, sipping the wine.

"So be it. Young Cali, on the morrow you and I will meet with Caronas. Jorah, I would ask that you assist me in some errands, I will have need of some letters of great importance to be delivered, and I trust that you will see them safe."

Jorah nodded. "Of course, Eaparius. I will do whatever you need."

"As for you, my young students, I have some rather large tasks for you to undertake which will need to be completed with both care and haste."

Their eyes were on Eaparius as he continued.

"Firstly, young Thraeston, you shall begin collecting and preparing our library to be moved. Cartons, barrels and all else you will need shall be delivered here."

They all looked at Eaparius with matching surprised expressions.

"Secondly, young Roland. You shall begin preparing all our supplies, including the scrolls, legals, and governance parchments to be moved. I also leave to you to begin preparing all our sundries and mundane belongings for shipment."

They were all speechless, even Thraeston. Roland nodded.

"Lastly, young Midge. I wish for you to prepare all our alchemical supplies, herbs, stones, and all other ingredients for safe transportation. Whilst you do this, prepare an inventory of all items."

Midge nodded. They were all dumbstruck at this sudden,

shocking turn of events.

"Master Eaparius? What are we doing?" Midge asked.

"My young friends, your studies shall continue, worry not. We are simply relocating to young Cali's stead in Edelaine. Cali, am I safe to assume that we would be welcome?" Eaparius's eyes twinkled through his pipe-smoke.

"I think this calls for more wine," Roland said in his quiet way, smiling.

"Just so, young Roland," Midge said, everyone laughing.

CHAPTER
29

The morning broke, gray and cold, as they all met in the kitchen, feeling determined. Everyone helped with breakfast, which turned out to be quite a feast as they talked about what needed to be done that day.

"Young Cali, you and I will be going to meet Caronas after breakfast, she is expecting us. Young Jorah, if you have any difficulties locating those," Eaparius motioned at the stack of letters he had given Jorah, "simply ask one of the Guard. They are quite happy to assist. Now, let's enjoy this hearty breakfast, I feel certain we shall need it today." Eaparius smiled.

"Before we go, I have something for you." Cali jumped up, running up to her room and back to the kitchen. She handed each of them a small brown wrapped package.

"Thank you, Cali! I can still work in the tomes and keep my hands from freezing now." Thraeston said as he put on his new gloves.

"With the hard winter coming, I thought you all may need them." Cali smiled.

Jorah hurried up the street and stopped at the stables below Eaparius's house. His first delivery was for Tomas the stable master. He broke the seal and quickly scanned the letter.

"Tell Eaparius they will be ready as soon as he is ready to leave, and I will procure as many extra wagons as he needs," Tomas said.

Jorah nodded, heading off to his next stop, the Commerce District.

Jorah stepped into the fragrant shop where barrels of dried herbs, bottles of liquids and bags lined the shelves. The shopkeep read the letter, scrawled a hasty reply handing the parchment back to Jorah, who nodded and set off.

He delivered letters to the merchant who sold containers of every imaginable shape and size, as well as one to the owner of the Inn by the Edrym main gate.

Heading into the Royal District, he found the large building with the sign by the door, Offices of Governance. Entering, he delivered the letter to the clerk of contracts.

The letters delivered, he headed back to the house to see if he could help the others, glad they had eaten a large breakfast as it was nearing midday already.

A large wagon stopped in front of Eaparius's house. Two young men knocked on the door.

"Hello, Miss. We have a delivery of wooden crates. Where would you like them set?"

Midge saw the wagon full of crates that they would need for packing.

"You can line them here on the porch." Midge signed their parchment and went back inside the house.

"Roland, Thraeston, we shall soon have plenty of wooden crates on the porch. Help yourselves as needed!" she called through the house.

Returning to the inventory of supplies, there was another knock on the door.

"I am not going to get this inventory done if we have constant knocks at the door today!" Midge said, through clenched teeth.

"Madam. Per Eaparius's order, we are delivering lunch." A large, burly man bowed slightly to Midge.

"Lunch? Okay, very well. You can set it on the table." She stepped aside allowing him to set the large crate on the table.

Just then, Jorah came back in the door.

"Good timing, lunch was just brought," Midge said as she pulled the cloth back from the crate revealing several plates of cheeses, bread, and roast.

"Brought?" Roland asked as he also came in the room.

"Yes, apparently, that was one of Master Eaparius's letters. Sensible. It leaves us more time to ready to leave if we aren't cooking." Midge shrugged.

"And it smells wonderful, let's not let this go to waste!" Thraeston said as they sat at the table.

∞ ∞ ∞

Cali and Eaparius arrived in the Craftsmen District as the city was beginning to awaken for the day.

"Eaparius, I'm excited to meet Caronas, but what does this have to do with the prophecy and me?" Cali asked as they walked.

"Ahh, young Cali, remember that your mother crafted her own throwing knives after we divined her gift? Such is the same with all Guardians. Each Guardian crafts a weapon aligned with their innate gift, and it is enhanced and imbued by their Watcher."

"But if a bow is my innate skill, then I already have that, what else is there to craft?"

"So it would seem, but every archer needs a quiver, do they not? And while I know you have one, a fine one you crafted yourself, you will find this is a different matter altogether."

"Caronas is quite old, but being of Elven-kind, one could not tell from looking. I feel you and Caronas will get on quite well. And do not be timid to ask her wisdom on other leatherworking matters, young Cali, she would love to impart her knowledge to you, I am sure."

They walked past several small buildings where craftsmen gathered and trained their apprentices.

"I shall take my leave of you once you and Caronas are acquainted, I have people to see before we make our journey. Once you are done, I shall see you at home after."

"Ah, here we are. Come, let's meet Caronas."

∞ ∞ ∞

Jorah didn't know Eaparius had a library and was astounded.

The tower room was three levels, with a curved narrow staircase leading to each level. The shelved walls full of books and parchments, boxes, bags, large barrels, small barrel-like containers, bottles and more. But mostly books.

As Jorah volunteered as the muscle of their group, he carried the carefully packed crates to the front room and stacked them against the wall.

With his help, they made great progress, as they each packed boxes, Jorah cleared them out of the tower.

"I wonder how Cali is doing with Caronas," Threaston said as he handed Jorah his next box.

"I was just wondering the same," Jorah replied.

"I'm not a leatherworker, not really, just book bindings, but it would be a real honor for someone to work with Caronas," Threaston said.

"If Cali wants, I'll show her how I do the embossing on my books, maybe she would like to use the technique on items she makes," Threaston continued.

"Jorah, an odd question mayhaps, but is there space for us and all this in Edelaine?" Roland asked gesturing around.

"There is more here than I would have expected, but yes it will be fine. We built an addition on the house after the attack. And there's another addition being built while we are gone."

Jorah thought for a moment, running his hand through his hair.

"Funny, now I see why Cali had us build this latest addition, even though we didn't understand it when she first told us."

They all stopped, looking at Jorah curiously.

"How so?" Midge asked.

"She came to us and told us what she wanted. Most of it was practical. A larger storehouse, a separate laundry room, building onto the barn and stables. Then she told us she wanted a massive addition to the house, a training area with separate rooms on the floor above."

Jorah shook his head at the memory. It seemed like an age ago rather than a fortnight.

"It made no sense at the time, but it works out perfectly now. So yes, there is more than enough room." Jorah smiled.

∞　∞　∞

Caronas was a tall woman with silvery-blond hair and pale gray eyes. She had her long hair in an intricate braid, and Cali couldn't help notice her ears were pointed.

Edelaine was such a small piece of the world, Cali thought to herself yet again.

She examined some of Cali's leather pieces, showing her ways to strengthen the stitching, hide the seams, and even gave Cali a stack of parchments which were some of her own patterns.

Caronas had arranged with Holt for them to have private access to the practice yard for a brief time. She wanted to see how Cali handled her bow and how she reached for her quiver. She seemed satisfied with what she saw, and they headed back to Caronas's shop.

Pulling a sheet of parchment, Caronas made a quick sketch of the quiver she thought Cali would like. It was exquisite. A long quiver, with wide comfortable-looking straps which could also hold the shorter crossbow bolts, and a place for her daggers.

"What are these two spots for?" Cali asked pointing at a spot on the hip strap.

"Those are for the handheld crossbows if you choose to carry them, dear. Holt told me the ease at which you used them." She smiled at Cali.

The quiver design also had a small pouch which could be used for whatever she liked. Since she had an affinity for herb lore and healing, they designed the pouch interior to hold bottles safely.

"What do you think, dear?"

"Caronas, it is beautiful, I love it," Cali said, excited to get started.

"Very well, then you shall have it. Come to me on the morrow, I shall have the materials you need," Caronas said.

"And take this, you will find a use for it, or I suspect, know a scribe who would." Caronas handed her a beautiful leather book satchel with all of the design parchments.

"I have several pelts, I could go get them now," Cali said, not wanting to wait until the next day to get started.

Caronas laughed, putting her arm around Cali's shoulders.

"Patience, young one. This quiver can only be made with a very specific hide, one, I am quite sure, that has never before been seen at Furs and Fines."

∞ ∞ ∞

Cali walked back to the house, hardly able to contain her excitement to start work on the quiver the next day. She already had a quiver, but nothing like the one Caronas designed.

As Cali arrived back at the house, two men pulled up in a wagon. A large burly man and his helper brought two crates from the back of their wagon to the door. Dinner, delivered from the Inn.

They settled in at the table, a relative feast set out before them and wanted to hear all about Cali's day with Caronas.

"She is unbelievable!" Cali said ecstatically.

"She designed a custom quiver just for me. We are going to start making it tomorrow."

Cali didn't realize how hungry she was, she took a few bites then continued.

"And designs! She gave me a stack of her designs," Cali said holding up the satchel.

"She is incredibly gracious, I can't believe I get to work with her tomorrow again," Cali said, her excitement bubbling over.

Thraeston gasped. "That is a beautiful satchel."

"Funny you mention it, Thraeston. It was made by Caronas herself, and it is for you." Cali smiled.

CHAPTER

30

Breakfast was an easy affair the next morning with the remnants from the meals delivered the day before. As they ate, they discussed their plans for the day again. Cali was to spend the day with Caronas, while Jorah and the rest worked on preparing for the upcoming move.

"My young friends, we all have much to do today, on the morrow we will be having guests for dinner. Master Mac and Master Holt will be joining us, as we have some matters to discuss. We may have others, but it shall be at least these two friends."

And with that, they were off. Cali walked with Eaparius to the Craftsmen District, as he had business to attend to. Jorah, Midge, Roland, and Thraeston continued packing for the journey with Chase sniffing around the crates or sleeping by the fire.

"I've seen this before," Cali said.

"I would think so, dear. Although you are one of the few of this world who has," Caronas replied.

The hide was thick and heavy, yet soft to the touch. It was a dark blue, but it didn't have the feeling of a fine soft fur on its surface.

"This can't be the same hide as my bracers, but it has the same feeling about it," Cali said, feeling the hide.

"Why can't it be the same?"

"The color is all wrong, see?" Cali held out one of her bracers.

"Yes, dear, but it is the same hide. Eaparius can explain it all. This hide works up much the same as other heavy leathers you may have worked with. The only difference is the thread we'll be using," Caronas said.

Caronas oversaw Cali's work with the hide for the rest of the day. She helped Cali with hiding the stitches, and they made padded slots for the interior of the pouch.

They paused only to have a small lunch, which they had on the porch, watching the busy people in the Craftsmen District. Eaparius joined them to check on the progress of the quiver.

"Ah, young Master Caronas, it appears you are a bit more along than I thought," Eaparius said.

"Yes, Eaparius. Cali is quite gifted with leather, and a fast learner. A natural talent. In another life, I would have been honored to take her as an apprentice myself," Caronas said.

Cali was at once both ecstatic and saddened. It hadn't occurred to her that the life of a Guardian would prevent all else that may have been in a normal life. She wondered how much else would be given up.

"Quite so. Young Cali is one of the more gifted people I have encountered in my years," Eaparius said.

"Well, coming from you that is truly saying something, my old friend." Caronas smiled.

"Shall we do the finishing in the morning then?

"That will be wise, Eaparius, we shall easily finish this work today."

∞　∞　∞

Cali and Eaparius walked through the clear morning light to the Craftsmen District.

"Eaparius? What is this finishing of my quiver you and Caronas were talking about yesterday?" Cali asked.

"Ah yes, young Cali. That is where we will enhance your quiver to serve you, it will be imbued with some of the energy you know as magick, helping you when you have a need. I daresay you will never have worry about your belts or quiver being damaged."

"Why are my bracers this color, if the hide is blue?"

"Your bracers, along with your bow, have been colored over the ages by the blood of your ancestors, you see. It is their blood which was used on the stones, it is their blood which has become part of those."

"Wait, Eaparius. The hide is blue. Is it, this isn't the hide from the spirit beast that attacked the first Watcher, is it? I mean, how could that be?"

"Indeed it is, young Cali. That is the only leather which can truly serve a Guardian."

They entered Caronas's shop, she led them to a small room in the back. On a round table covered with a green silken cloth, the quiver lay in the middle. There were symbols on the cloth which formed a circle around it.

"Young Master Caronas, will you also lend your power?" Eaparius asked.

"I would be honored, Eaparius. Shall we begin?"

Eaparius nodded, motioning for Cali to come stand at the table.

"Cali dear, don't worry, this is a simple matter of magick, but you play the key role. It is your blood we will need for the finishing. A small cut and you will place your hand face up on ours."

Cali nodded as they began.

They stood around the table, Cali wide-eyed and unsure what to expect. Eaparius and Caronas stood with their hands hovering palms up over the quiver, speaking in a language Cali had not heard before.

Eaparius nodded at Cali. Taking out her dagger, she made a small cut on the palm of her hand, then placed it in their upturned hands still hovering over her quiver. They turned her hand in theirs, placed it on the quiver, and covered it with their own hands.

Cali was worried, she didn't feel anything happening. She wasn't sure if she was supposed to feel something happening. Then it was done. They removed their hands and nodded.

"Was, was that it?" Cali asked.

"Yes, dear, as I said, a simple matter." Caronas smiled.

"But, I, well, nothing happened, I didn't feel anything," Cali said, biting her lip.

"Nothing indeed, young Cali. See for yourself," Eaparius said.

Although the quiver didn't have a stone like her bow or bracers, the blood on the quiver disappeared.

Then she heard it, a low, almost inaudible crackling sound. The blood absorbed into the leather and seemed to spread. Slowly the hide turned from the dark blue to the reddish brown of her bracers. An intricate design began to appear in the leather, embossed into the surface itself, the design retaining the blue color.

As the last of the color spread, a light began to glow from within the leather itself, engulfing it completely, and then was gone in a flash.

"Your quiver, young Cali." Eaparius nodded to her.

∞   ∞   ∞

Returning to the house, they found all but the necessities had been crated and stacked in the front rooms. Jorah and the others sat at the table talking as Cali and Eaparius came in.

Jorah let out a low whistle. "That is quite a piece of work, this is what Caronas was helping you make?"

"She truly is as good as the stories say, then," Midge said.

Even Roland looked impressed.

"Magnificent, Cali, just magnificent! I am astounded by your skill in leather, and Caronas's design, of course. But it was you who did the crafting," Thraeston said.

"Thanks," Cali smiled.

"Eaparius, when do you expect we'll be leaving?" Jorah asked.

"Young Jorah, we still have some left to do here today, and will be meeting with our friends tomorrow. I daresay in a day or two of that meeting we shall depart."

Cali looked around at all the crates, barrels, and belongings. "How are we going to transport everything we need?"

"Ah yes, young Cali, do not worry yourself, we shall have all the wagons we need for our journey. After lunch, I have one last set of tasks for you all. Young Midge, do we have an inventory?"

"Yes, Master Eaparius." She handed him a long parchment.

"Very good, very good. I shall look over this and note on each item how much more we need. After lunch, you all can go visit the merchants, place the orders for these, and then enjoy the rest of the day." Eaparius smiled at them.

"And, I daresay, if there are wares that would serve the farm, young Cali, do purchase them, we can make space on the wagons," Eaparius said.

CHAPTER
31

Cali and Jorah were excited for another trip to the Commerce District. It was more than all the goods available, it was all the people. Cali enjoyed people watching, and couldn't wait to tell the others at home about meeting Master Mac and Caronas.

"If there's anything we would like to buy for ourselves, this will be the time. I expect Master Eaparius won't linger long after today," Thraeston said.

"We have time, we can go to all the shops each of us want to visit. I like seeing all the different wares." Cali smiled.

First, they went to the alchemist and herb merchant to place the order from Eaparius's notes. It was a large order, the shopkeep said he would have the items delivered the following day.

Leaving the herb shop, Cali stopped short. She poked Jorah in the arm, motioning up the street.

"Jorah, look!"

"Oh!" Jorah stared.

The others' gaze turned in the direction of Cali's attention.

"The first Tevici you've seen, I take it?" Roland asked.

"Oh my, yes. They are… well, they are quite beautiful, don't you think?" Cali couldn't take her eyes from the pair.

"They are an interesting race, Tevici. Secretive, secluded, highly skilled Wanderers, and quite intelligent. There was a time when they were hunted. Atrocious and unforgivable. Understandable why they are less trusting," Thraeston said.

"Hunted? How do you mean?" Cali said, turning to the others.

"Their fur," Midge said, shaking her head.

"What! They were hunted like animals?" Jorah said.

"Yes. There were those who saw them as nothing more than animals, even though that was far from true," Thraeston said.

They visited many of the shops that day. Stocking up on quills, parchments, and inks. Cali placed orders for several large kettles, utensils, and sets of mugs for the farm. Knowing that Cali, Midge, and Thraeston were likely to spend longer in Furs and Fines, that was the last shop they visited.

By the time they left the shop all of them helping carry piles of cloth, leather, and furs, the sky was darkening, and the breeze had a slight edge. Cali had placed a large order for several full spools of a heavy dark green cloth, which Midge insisted would be excellent for use around the farm, blankets, curtains, and the like.

With deliveries expected throughout the next day, the group

chose to stay at home. Eaparius left after breakfast, telling them he would be back in the afternoon.

"Cali? I was wondering about, about your quiver," Jorah said.

"Yes?" Cali said.

"Does it, you know, do anything? Like your bow, or your bracers?"

They all stopped to look at Cali.

"I must confess, I wondered the same," Midge said.

"You know what the bow can do?" Jorah asked, looking at Midge.

"Only from our studies, of course. We've not seen it ourselves."

"It's really something. Incredible and more than a little unsettling." Jorah smiled at Cali.

"I can feel the quiver. Not in the normal way, it feels oddly weightless in the normal sense. But it feels like a part of me somehow. Almost like it is protective. Beyond that, I don't know," Cali said.

They talked a while longer, then drifted off on their own. Roland sat in front of the fire at one of the small tables reading. Thraeston stayed at the long kitchen table, his quill scratching away in a leather-bound book. Midge was bringing in baskets of herbs and plants from the garden, hanging them to dry, or packing them in crates. Jorah was outside, using the scarecrow in the garden to practice the moves Mac had shown him.

Cali cut and stitched the largest of the bear pelts. It was a dark sable color and had been expertly prepared, the fur shiny and smooth. It would make a beautiful cloak. She hoped Jorah would like it, with the weather starting to cool, they may need their heavier cloaks on the journey back to Edelaine.

Taking stock of the pelts she had left, Cali started on another, much smaller, cloak from the piece she had left over from Jorah's. This one would be for Midge. From the other pelts, she would make one for Roland and Thraeston as well.

Jorah came back in from the garden, Cali stood handing him the rolled cloak.

"What's this, then?" he asked.

He unrolled the cloak, the shiny bear fur soft in his hands, and swung it around his shoulders.

"Cali, this is incredible, thank you!" Jorah said.

"Of course, Jorah. I think we'll all need one before the winter settles in. I am making one for you all, too. Midge, yours is almost finished," She said, holding up the smaller cloak.

"Thank you, Cali! These will come in useful," Midge said, smiling.

"Thraeston, what are you over there scratching on now?" Midge asked.

He looked up at them. He closed the leather book, then handed it to Cali.

"It's for you, Cali. I hope you don't mind, I began copying the designs that Caronas gave you. I thought you might like to have a book to keep all your design patterns in," Thraeston said.

Cali ran her hand over the cover of the leather-bound book. It was a dark brown, with lighter brown leather stitching along the edges and for the binding.

Opening the cover, she saw her name in a large fine script. On the pages following, she saw designs Caronas had given her.

"It's not finished, there are more designs I need to add from her stack of parchments. And of course, you can add your own designs to it as well," Thraeston said.

"It's lovely, Thraeston, thank you. Though I may have you put my designs in for me, your writing is superb compared to mine!" Cali laughed.

Thraeston smiled. "It would be my pleasure."

∞ ∞ ∞

Eaparius arrived shortly before the delivery from the Inn. Apparently, he had told them the dinner for tonight would need to be larger and grander. They set out the large ham, roast, a platter of boiled potatoes and carrots, cheeses and bread. Eaparius set out a large bottle of whiskey and a pitcher of ale.

Midge answered the knock on the door.

"Master Mac, Master Holt, please come in," She said, opening the door wide for them.

They all settled at the kitchen table talking jovially about nothing of importance when another knock came at the door.

Again, Midge answered the door.

"Ma... Master Cyrene! Please come in," Midge said excitedly.

Roland and Thraeston traded a quick glance as she entered the kitchen.

Master Cyrene was a tall woman, with long black hair and eyes that looked just as dark in the firelight of the kitchen.

As she walked to the table, the men stood, giving her a quick nod.

"Young Master Cyrene, thank you, thank you for joining us this evening," Eaparius said, motioning for her to sit.

"My young friends, this is Master Cyrene. She is an Elder at the school here, and also on the Council of Skye."

"Please, my friends, help yourselves, eat, enjoy. We shan't talk serious matters on empty bellies." Eaparius smiled, offering them drinks.

It was enjoyable, if not a bit odd company. Eaparius had not told Cali or the others the exact purpose of the dinner, but they suspected it was more than just a last meal with friends.

As they all settled in more comfortably after the huge meal, Eaparius lit his pipe, looking at them each in turn as they refilled their mugs.

"I daresay you know my purpose for our dinner, besides enjoying your company." Eaparius smiled.

"My young friends, as you know, there are a rare and small set of people that know the truth of the prophecy. Of those, even fewer were, in their time, students of the Watcher." Eaparius gestured around the table.

Midge, Roland, and Thraeston all had identical looks of surprise on their faces. Cali and Jorah must have as well because both

Eaparius and the others laughed.

"But, I thought the students were all wizard-types," Jorah said.

At that, both Holt and Mac laughed heartily.

"Aye, I could see why ye think so, lad, but nay, not just them," Mac said, pulling out his own pipe.

"Just so, young Master Mac. He speaks true, young Jorah, those selected from each age to be a student of the Watcher come from all walks. Those that go on to other paths still hold the oath of Watcher, in their silence, and in their assistance."

Eaparius nodded to Cyrene.

"I have spoken at length with these esteemed Masters, my friends. I have told them of your plan, young Cali. I trust these three beyond all others, and have asked for their expertise, and their help."

"What you do mean, Eaparius?" Cali asked.

"Young miss, your plan to arm your friends is wise, of this, we all agree," Cyrene spoke, her voice was both quiet, yet full of strength.

Holt rubbed his scruffy beard thoughtfully. "The problem lies with this, how do you plan to go about training all these people?"

"We have a training area. It was being built when we left to come to Edrym," Jorah said.

"Aye, laddie, and training dummies, and targets. But what of weapons and experience to teach others?" Mac asked.

Jorah nodded, looking at Cali.

"I will do what I can. You both have seen my skills with weapons." Cali looked at Mac and Holt.

"We have at that, there is no denying your skill. But do you plan to teach everyone, plus train yourself?" Holt looked at Cali.

"I will do what I must. And this must be done," Cali said.

"And she has me to help. And my brother. Bodric. Tom. And we have others too," Jorah said.

"Young Jorah, you both possess great skill. But there is more to be done. We have a question dangling over us like a looming storm cloud, why did the Aegil Imps attack?"

"And where did they go after?" Cali said, sighing.

"Quite so, young Cali," Eaparius said, his pipe smoke swirling around him.

"If I can be so bold as to say it, Cali, it is only the Guardian and the Watcher who are able to find those answers," Thraeston said.

"You are quite right, young sir," Cyrene said.

She turned her dark eyes to Cali. "So you see, miss, you have much work ahead of you with the mystery of this darkness, and learning your own strength."

Cali jumped up, pacing the length of the table.

"Then what would you have me do? I will not leave them undefended, nor will I have them unable to defend themselves. They've already lost too much. I will not have them lose more."

Coming to a stop near the hearth fire, she continued.

"Besides, we'll have Eaparius and my friends." She motioned to Midge and the others, who nodded their agreement.

Cali straightened her back. She knew she was right. As her Mum and grandmother had told her, she knew her next steps, and they were right and true. She needed only to trust her own instincts and make Edelaine safe again.

"Listen, lass, settle yerself. What we are saying is ye don't have to do it on yer own." Mac reached over and patted her hand.

"Right you are, Mackenzie." Cyrene smiled at Mac. "This is why we are here tonight, young miss."

Holt reached over and patted Jorah on the back. "Let's get ready to go to Edelaine."

CHAPTER 32

Cali was happy she'd had time to make cloaks for her friends, as the morning came for them to leave, the day broke clear, but cold. The grass and trees around Eaparius's house were frosted silver in the morning light.

The wagons secured by Eaparius had been packed with care the day before. Tomas and his stable hands brought their rested horses from the stable, hitching them to the wagon. To ward against the chill, each horse wore a quilted blanket for warmth.

They had three wagons, Eaparius's wagon and two others. Eaparius and Midge were first in their convoy on his wagon, followed by Roland and Thraeston. Next came Cali, Jorah, and Chase. They were meeting Mac, Holt, and Cyrene at the Inn for a hearty breakfast before departing.

Mac and Cyrene also had a large wagon laden with crates, barrels and other packages. Holt chose to ride his enormous black horse, adorned with leather saddlebags and a heavy quilted blanket as well.

Over breakfast, they talked about their plan for the journey. Stopping for lunch and for dinner, they would camp each night with a rotating guard for the wagons. They expected no trouble, but they wanted to reach Edelaine quick and safe. Holt would scout a small distance ahead of their convoy, Mac and Cyrene would bring up the rear in their wagon.

After breakfast as they prepared their wagons to leave. Several horses and mountain rams were brought from the large stables across the road and tethered to wagons. Cali was excited to be heading home, though she would miss the bustle and all the merchants and their wares in Edrym. With a last look around, she climbed on her wagon as they set off.

They left out of Edrym following the Great Riston Road west.

While the day remained cooler than usual, the skies were clear, and they made good time, stopping the first night at the Inn at the crossroads. Knowing this was the last night to sleep in a real bed for several days, they all relaxed and turned in early.

The following days were much the same, clear and cold. They had made camp at the base of the mountain pass, and again partway toward the summit. They had spent the time at camps getting to know each other better. Midge, Roland, and Thraeston still seemed awestruck by Master Cyrene.

An unusually large red hawk had joined Master Holt. It flew above when he scouted ahead of their group, and joined him landing lightly on Holt's leather padded shoulder when they were at camp.

The next day, as they neared the summit pass, Holt came galloping back to the group. They took a quick break as Holt reported in.

"Looks like the trolls are riled up about something. Several groups of them were out, even wandering close to the road. We'll need to take care at the summit," Holt said.

They looked around nervously.

"Very well, young Master Holt. The day is young, mayhaps we'll not break for camp until the other side of the summit pass," Eaparius replied. Mac and Cyrene both nodded their agreement.

"Good plan. The horses aren't overtired, and the weather has held. The farther beyond the summit pass we camp, the better." Holt had a serious look on his face as he stared at Eaparius.

Eaparius nodded and turned to the others.

"Worry not, young friends, these trolls aren't hunters of men, if you recall, not enough meat and too much trouble." Eaparius smiled at them, trying to lessen their worry.

"On the off chance we encounter one, do not engage, allow me to subdue it. We don't want to make enemies of the troll clans."

They set off toward the summit, Holt staying with the group, riding alongside Eaparius's wagon, his hawk perched on the roof.

They could hear far off noises and the occasional roar which must have been the trolls. None payed them any mind or came within close reach of the road.

Holt rode back through their convoy, riding with each wagon briefly to talk. Without warning, there came a crash that sounded like the boulders were being slammed together.

They stopped short, eying the jagged crevices around them.

Then a massive gray creature that could only be a troll came charging out from behind a ridge of rocks toward Eaparius's wagon.

Holt's hawk took flight, sounding her screeching alarm. The horses on Eaparius's wagon reared and tried bolt, threatening to wreck the wagon.

Everyone jumped from their wagons running wildly toward the front of the line.

Midge, with a courageousness far larger than her small size, jumped in front of the rushing troll, her staff held high. A whistling wind that looked to have physical form rushed past her toward the troll pushing it back several yards, furrowing the ground.

Eaparius pulled her back, and using his own staff, seemed to hit the troll with a blast of blue light.

The troll stopped, looking confused, then fell backward into a large heap beside the road.

Everyone was on alert, looking through the rocky terrain to see if any other trolls were nearby.

"What did you do to him?" Jorah asked.

"He is simply unconscious, young Jorah," Eaparius said, still scanning the nearby ridges.

"And will be for some time." Roland grinned. "Master Eaparius stunned it."

Holt let out a low whistle and his hawk landed on his arm. He appeared to whisper something to the bird which took flight immediately. It circled overhead returning a few moments later. Holt stroked it's head fondly.

"We are clear for now. None others close enough to be of concern. We should move on and get out of their ranging area," Holt said.

"Aye, let's get on then before the wee lassie and Eaparius start throwing any more light around." Mac laughed.

Eaparius and Holt calmed the horses and the group set off again their pace a little faster than before. They wanted to put as much distance between them and the summit as they could before dark.

∞   ∞   ∞

They doubled the guard at the camp but had no other encounters with trolls or anything more threatening than the rustling of brush from small wildlife. They awoke to steel gray skies and cold winds blowing around the camp as they made breakfast and prepared to set out.

"The winter has come, then," Midge said as they all sat around the fire eating.

"Quite so, young Midge, quite so. Mayhaps we'll reach the base of the mountain before it arrives," Eaparius replied, eying the sky.

"It's not due to settle in for a bit longer, I thought," Cali said.

"That's true, Cali, but the ice is on its way," Midge said, the ominous clouds pressing down on them.

"I fear you are right. This 15-year winter may arrive a touch early." Holt added, pulling his cloak more firmly around his shoulders.

"How can you tell?" Cali asked, as Chase curled up on her lap.

"I can feel the ice," Midge said.

Cali gave Jorah a quick glance who just shrugged.

Eaparius chuckled. "Young Midge is an Elementalist, much like myself, young Cali. We have a deep affinity with the elements in all their forms, you see, much like yourself with nature."

"Aye, the ice may talk to ye, but this cold talks to my bones. We'd be best off this mountain before it visits," Mac said.

"We'll watch the skies, and if the horses aren't overtired we may eat lunch as we travel rather than breaking for long," Holt said.

"Just so, young Master Holt. A fine idea. Let us be on our way then."

∞ ∞ ∞

With little less than a half-day's journey to the base of the mountain, they made camp for the night.

The winds were less biting in the thick, forested area of the mountain, but the constant rustling through the trees kept everyone alert. None of them rested as well that night.

Cali and Jorah sat talking for much of the evening, talking of Edelaine and happy to be this close to home. They told the group of the steads that had been there, and how each had specialized in one production area. They talked of the large lake, rivers, and the forests. Cali hadn't realized that she was homesick until they reminisced over the campfire.

They awoke to the sound of sausages sizzling on the fire, and a lightly falling snow. The wind still swirled through the trees blowing the feather-light flakes all around.

Thankful she had made the cloaks, and more thankful still that she had several bottles of warming concoction left, she sent a bottle with each wagon. They hurriedly ate and prepared the horses to leave.

As they set off on the last leg to the base of the mountain, the snow increased, coating the road and resting on the branches of the evergreen trees. A deep quiet settled around them, the only sounds were from their own passing.

Chase had curled up between Jorah and Cali, as Jorah handled the reins. Their line of wagons slowed to take extra care on the winding road as the snow continued to fall around them.

"Do you remember the last 15-year winter?" Jorah asked.

"Not much. I remember snow, and Da and Bodric had made a path to the barns and storehouse. And I remember a lot of hot drinks by the fire, but not much else," Cali said.

It was getting a little easier to think about her parents, but she didn't think that ache would ever fully go away. She would be glad to be home and close to them.

"Rowan remembers it more than me. Of course, we were kids then, so I'm sure it seemed like an adventure to us."

They rode along in silence for a bit.

"Do you think we're prepared?" he asked, worried.

"I do. I think we are more ready than we realize, it may be a hard winter, but it will be okay," Cali said.

"It was a good idea to bring everyone to winter over together. Strength in numbers and all that." Jorah smiled.

"Yes. I just hope we don't need that strength for anything but keeping the fires going." Cali smiled back.

CHAPTER 33

"Did you look over the new addition?" Rowan asked.

"Yes. A fine job Dorin and the men did on it. I expect Cali will like it too," Bodric replied.

"Flora and her mom were talking about finding someone to start doing proper classes for the children. I think it's a good idea. I told her we'd work on it," Sarah said.

"I had all the supplies from the last trip to the other farms put away in the storehouse. There were a lot of hides and pelts too, I had those put in the small barn for Cali."

"Sarah, I think that's a great idea, I'm sure we can figure something out. Rowan, that's good. I know she'd want to have some to work on after the winter starts in earnest," Bodric said.

They sat in silence, fiddling with their mugs, and watching the others come and go from the dining hall.

"Bodric, I don't like it. They should be back, and the winter is settling in early," Rowan said.

"Can we have someone ride out toward Edrym?" Sarah asked.

"No, we can't do that. If the winter is here early…" Bodric shook his head. "The mountain pass is no place to be in the winter."

They sat, looking grave, while the others finished their lunches and headed out to attend to chores.

"If the snow is here in Edelaine now, then it started on the pass at least a day or two ago. Which means if they were already crossing, they would be making a slow time of it. All we can do is wait and ask the —"

Tom came running in the dining hall. "Bodric! You all come on, wagons!" He smiled, running back out the door as quick as he came in.

∞ ∞ ∞

They instantly recognized Eaparius's wagon, even through the falling snow. The other wagons, plus a man on a large black horse were unexpected.

"Looks like Cali and Jorah brought back some friends," Sarah said, bouncing on her feet excitedly.

"It does, at that, Sarah," Bodric said, letting out a huge breath as they made their way out to meet the wagons.

Eaparius raised his hand in greeting to Bodric and the others, standing to stretch before climbing down. A very short woman was on the wagon with him. Two more young men climbed down from the next wagon as Chase came running up to Bodric, excited and bouncing around. Cali and Jorah came walking up, with a stout, short man, and a tall, dark-haired woman.

Everyone had come out of the buildings to greet Cali, Jorah, and Eaparius. Excited that they had made it back safe and sound.

"Cali girl!" Bodric called out, his relief written all over his face.

Cali ran up and gave Bodric a hug, then Sarah, and Rowan.

"It's so good to be home and see you all! You all know Eaparius, of course. Let me introduce you to our friends," Cali said to everyone.

"This is Midge. She is brilliant, and is one of Eaparius's students, as are Thraeston, and Roland." Cali gestured to each of them as they gave the group a nod.

"This is Master Holt. He is a Ranger from the Hall of Wanderers in Edrym."

"This is Master Mac. He is a Blademaster with the Hall of Champions. And this is Master Cyrene, from the Hall of Magicks."

Cali continued on, introducing their new friends.

Rowan came up and gave Jorah a clap on the shoulder and pulled him into a brief hug.

"We'll get your wagons over to the big barn and your horses stabled and fed," Rowan said, smiling and motioning for a few of his stable hands to come help.

"I'll come along with you," Holt said, shaking hands with Rowan.

"Come on, you all must be freezing, let's get you into the dining hall and get warmed up," Sarah said.

Word of their arrival spread fast and everyone took a break from work to come to the dining hall. Sarah and some of the others brought out kettles of tea, bread, and cheese as everyone settled in.

"Cali, this is amazing," Midge said her eyes wide as she looked around the dining hall.

"Thanks, Midge. I just told people what I wanted to do, they are the ones that did the hard part." Cali smiled.

Cali told them about the new additions that they'd built. The dining hall, expanding the barns, storehouse, making a new room for the laundry, and finally the newest addition, the training hall on the other side of the house.

Roland shook his head. "Most impressive, Cali. And with the winter here, very smart."

"It is brilliant, truly! You have a beautiful farm, and the work they must have put in, magnificent!" Thraeston added.

Rowan and Holt came in to join them.

"Your stables are remarkable, Cali. Better than those in Edrym, I'd say," Holt said, smiling. "Firan even approved, she settled in for a sleep."

They looked at Holt curiously.

"My hawk. Her name is Firan. She's been my friend and companion for many years. You've not to worry about her, she's accustomed to humans, and I venture she'll keep your barns and storehouses clear of rodents." He smiled at them.

∞ ∞ ∞

Slowly people went back to their work until it was only them left in the hall.

"Let me get another kettle, I want to hear all about Edrym!" Sarah said as she stood to get another kettle of tea.

"I see the new addition looks finished," Jorah said.

"Dorin and the men did a great job on it, you'll have to come see it once you all are settled in," Rowan said.

"Everyone has settled into their jobs and like keeping busy. We still have logging and stone crews gathering wood and stone. Especially since it seems the winter is going to drop on us earlier than we thought, it will be good to have the extra wood drying," Bodric said.

"Tom and the men made trips back out to each stead to gather what supplies and personal items were left, and the storehouse and barns are well stocked," He continued.

Sarah poured them all fresh cups of tea and set down a plate of fresh bread and jam.

"Flora and her mom thought it would be nice to have a proper teacher for the children too since the winter is settling in," Sarah added.

"That's a great idea, Sarah. I am sure we can do something for that," Cali said.

"So, your turn. Tell us about Edrym. What did you learn…" Bodric looked around at Eaparius's students and the newcomers.

"It's okay, Bodric. They are well-versed in the prophecy, more than I was even." Cali smiled.

"Sarah, you would love Edrym! There are so many merchants with goods that you couldn't even imagine! I may even have a few gifts that I brought back. Anything you need can be found in the Commerce District, or if it isn't, they can find it for you," Cali said, shaking her head, smiling.

"Gifts! Cali, you didn't have to do that, there were more important things that you needed to worry about," Sarah said, but Cali could tell she was happy.

"I brought back items that I thought we could use around the farm. New items for the kitchens and laundry, and a huge amount of cloth that we can use around here, curtains, blankets, anything we need. And Midge here is a great tailor, I think she could make anything with cloth." Cali smiled.

"There was one shop, called Furs and Fines, they had every type of leather, pelt, fur, or cloth you could dream of! I brought back quite a few pelts and hides to work on too," Cali looked around sheepishly.

"I would imagine that was your favorite merchant in the entire city, Cali girl," Bodric smiled.

"We'll have to put them in the small barn with all the others. Turns out many people were saving their hides and pelts for you, Cali. You'll have plenty of leather to work over the winter if you want it." Rowan smiled.

"And what of the Guard, are they sending them out?" Sarah asked.

The newcomers sighed, almost in unison.

Cali shook her head, telling them about their meeting with Riston and his insistence that there was no danger remaining. Further, that if there were any danger, he would certainly call the guard to protect the cities.

"The cities!" Bodric said.

"Young master Bodric, we were all as frustrated and angered as you." Eaparius shook his head.

"So, we are on our own?" Sarah said, sounding scared.

"No, Sarah. We are not on our own. We have friends more powerful than the Guard of Edrym. And with us all pulling together, I daresay Riston would come to us for help." Cali smiled.

∞ ∞ ∞

Cali and Jorah showed Midge, Roland, and Thraeston to Eaparius's room. Then leading them upstairs, got them settled into rooms on the second floor. Holt took one of the rooms above the stables with Tad and the other stable hands. Mac and Cyrene were given rooms next to Eaparius.

Retrieving only what necessities they needed, they decided to unpack the wagons and supplies the next day, they took the remainder of the day to rest from the journey, and get comfortable in their new rooms.

Cali was pleased to see Dorin and the other builders had built more furniture for the rooms. The empty rooms now had proper beds, tables, chairs, and even small shelves. She would have to remember to thank him and his men for all their hard work.

"If you need anything, just ask. Take some rest after you get settled in if you like, and we can meet for dinner in the hall later," Cali said.

Returning to the dining hall, Jorah and Cali rejoined Bodric at the table.

"I can't thank you enough for keeping everything running around here, Bodric," Cali said, smiling.

"Was nothing, Cali girl. Happy to be able to help while my leg mends." Bodric smiled.

Bodric poured them all more tea.

"Now, Cali girl, tell me your plan."

"Bodric, I thought surely Edrym would send the guard, but it seems the type of men who govern cities aren't much concerned with the rest of us," Cali said, frowning.

"Now I understand better why I knew I needed to build all this." She gestured around her.

"Sarah was right on one hand we are on our own. As far as those in charge care. But we are not alone, and we do have help."

They sat quietly for several moments.

"We are going to train everyone to defend themselves. We must, Bodric. We've all lost too much, I won't let them suffer more loss if I can change it."

"What of Eaparius's students? How does that fit in?" Bodric asked.

"They are potential Watchers."

Bodric looked surprised. "What?"

"Yes, in each age a few individuals are chosen because of their skills to study with the current Watcher. Apparently, through their studies and work, the next Watcher shows themselves, through deed or knowledge, or both, I'm not sure."

Bodric ran his hand through his hair.

"Well, that makes sense as to why we can speak freely with them. I admit I was surprised when you showed up with not only the others but a Gnome and Forest Elf as well."

"What? Forest Elf?" Both Cali and Jorah stared at him, wide-eyed.

Bodric laughed. "Wait, you two hadn't noticed your friend Thraeston was an elf? How could you miss that?"

"Thraeston. An elf?" Cali said.

"I never saw pointy ears, but he always wears his hair tied back but covering them," Jorah said, thinking back.

"So, how did you know, Bodric?" Cali asked.

"I've met a few. They have a certain, quality, about them, plus those gold-colored eyes. Now, tell me more about the plan. People are going to want to know, Cali girl."

CHAPTER
34

The next morning dawned bright and clear, the sun glinting off the snow. Cali hoped that the 15-year winter would hold off before it settled in fully. Shaking her head, she knew she would have to talk to everyone soon to let them know about the training that was coming.

I don't think I'll ever get used to people looking to me to lead them, she thought.

She wanted to talk to Eaparius before making any announcements to everyone. She would need to work out all the specifics with him, Holt, and Mac as they would be doing a lot of the hands-on work.

Taking her hot mug of tea, she stepped out of the kitchen. Dorin, Tom, and several others were clearing paths through the snow to the barns, storehouse, and other areas.

"Dorin!" Cali called out, raising a hand in greeting.

"Good cold morning, Cali!" he called back, walking over.

"I wanted to thank you for all your work. I was helping the others get settled into their rooms yesterday and saw where you and the men made more furniture for each of the rooms. Thank you for thinking about that and getting it done."

"Sure, Cali, wasn't nothing. We love to build, and a few of these guys are really talented woodworkers!" Dorin smiled.

"Really? That's great, Dorin, I'm sure we'll be keeping them busy then! Pass along my thanks, will you? And come see me in the hall once you've finished your breakfast."

"Be happy to, Cali. See you at breakfast." Dorin waved, returning to clearing the paths.

∞ ∞ ∞

Sarah and the others in the kitchen outdid themselves, many breakfast pies had been set out on the table. There were cheeses, fresh warm bread, and it seemed like endless kettles of tea. Cali couldn't wait to give Sarah the spices and kitchen tools she brought back from Edrym.

Cali looked around the table at Eaparius, Mac, and the others as they ate.

"After breakfast, let's go to the training hall. We can take stock of what we have, and what we still need to get started," Cali said.

"Aye, lass, fine idea. I don't want to idle too long," Mac said, stabbing at the stack of sausages on his plate.

"Young Cali, you said there were multiple rooms in the training hall?" Eaparius asked.

"Oh yes, Eaparius. Three large rooms upstairs and the

downstairs is one long hall that we can use for training."

"Cali, you wanted to see me?" Dorin sat next to Bodric.

"Dorin, yes, thanks. After we eat, we are going to the new training hall. I'd like you to come, as we see what else we may need you'll know straightaway," Cali said.

"Good idea, Cali girl. We didn't build much furniture for it, we wanted to wait until you returned. And whatever we need, I know Dorin can see it done," Bodric said, clapping Dorin on the shoulder.

Walking through the kitchens, the group headed to the new training hall.

They had done a wonderful job on the hall. The main floor was long and open. Tables had been placed at one end, and weapon racks lined the walls. Differently shaped racks to hold different weapon types, each of them held one wooden weapon.

"We can get rid of the wood weapons. Bodric made those for us so we could use them to model the racks," Dorin said.

"Lad, ye did fine work here, and we'll keep the wooden weapons. In fact, ye can make more of them, it would help," Mac said.

"Yes sir, Master Mac, I'll have one of my men start making more of them," Dorin replied.

"Aye, lad, just Mac will do." Mac smiled at him.

"This far end will be a fine place to teach bows." Holt nodded approvingly.

"And this other end for blade practice," Mac added.

"Dorin, could your men also make training mannequins? And targets for Holt too?" Cyrene asked.

Cali noticed whenever Cyrene spoke people stopped to listen. It was a quality about her that spoke strength and power. Cali wondered if she had come to help continue the wizard training of Midge, Roland, and Thraeston.

"Yes, ma'am. I will have them made." Dorin nodded to Cyrene.

Upstairs, there was an open area, with three doors leading away.

The lockable room Cali had requested was large, taking up almost half of the upstairs area. The two smaller rooms using the remaining space. One of the rooms was long and narrow, the other square on the end of the upper hall.

"Eaparius, I thought we would use this room for all our herbs, books, and other supplies. With some of them being poisonous, I don't want any curious little ones accidentally getting in," Cali said.

"Just so, young Cali, just so! This will make a fine library and storeroom."

Eaparius looked around the room with a nod.

"Young master Dorin, I daresay we will need many shelves. Floor to ceiling. And mayhaps a ladder to reach the upper ones." Eaparius nodded to himself.

"Yes, sir, Eaparius. We have stacks of planks ready, I will get the men started on this today. And what of the other rooms?" Dorin said.

Eaparius looked at Cyrene.

"Tables with chairs. Both large for a group, and smaller ones for one or two people to sit with books," Cyrene said.

"Yes, ma'am. I'll bring the tables up from downstairs, and we'll start building more," Dorin said.

"Cali, you and Jorah said you had plenty of room for us, but this!" Midge looked around smiling.

"Midge is correct, Cali. What you have done here is truly magnificent! I can see us working by this fire here with all we need so close at hand. Yes, magnificent!" Thraeston said.

Cali smiled. "Thanks. And Dorin, thanks again for all your hard work. You let Bodric or me know if you need anything."

"Sure will, Cali. Let me go get the men busy on this. We'll start on the big storeroom for you." Dorin said as he turned to leave.

"What do you think, Bodric?" Cali asked.

"I think we have a lot of work to do, Cali girl." Bodric smiled, putting his arm around Cali's shoulders.

∞   ∞   ∞

The training hall came together quickly. As Dorin promised, the shelves all around the storeroom upstairs were completed first. Tables and chairs put in the other two rooms. Targets and training mannequins were situated downstairs, and more training weapons were made and placed in the racks.

Midge, Roland, and Thraeston were busy getting the storeroom library arranged. And they all worked on unpacking the goods they brought from Edrym. Holt and Mac had brought a small supply of basic weapons. And Cyrene had Dorin build additional shelves in the smaller room for the books and supplies she brought.

Jorah assisted Mac any chance he could, and Bodric had made fast friends with Holt.

As everyone began settling in for dinner in the hall, Cali stood, motioning for everyone's attention.

"I can't tell you how good it is to be home with you. I'm still just amazed by how much work you all have put into making this." Cali gestured around her.

"I'm sure some of you have heard this already. The quick version is, we met with Lord Riston in Edrym, and he decided to not send the guard to Edelaine."

Murmurs erupted around the tables.

"I agree. We were angry too. I'm not worried though. As we've always done here in Edelaine, we pull together and take care of what needs taking care of. I mean, just look at what we've accomplished here." Cali smiled at them all as many nodded their agreement.

"The hard winter is here. It must've gotten a bit impatient and decided to visit a bit early." Cali smiled as several in the hall laughed.

"But, again, I'm not worried. We've been preparing, and we are ready. We all still have work to do through the winter, though it will lessen a bit in some ways, and increase in other ways."

People looked around the room, not sure what Cali was going to say.

"As you know, we built a training hall. And for those who don't know, we have the best bowman and blademaster in Idoramin. I have vowed to do everything I can to make sure you are all safe. And that is what I'm doing."

Cali looked around at each face in the room.

"We've all lost too much. We can rebuild houses. We can regrow crops. We can breed new livestock. But some things lost we can't save, except for in our hearts."

Cali held the pendants around her neck as she said this, trying to will herself to keep going and not cry.

"So much was lost. But they would not have us cower and give up. And we can no longer hope to depend on others for protection. We will defend ourselves."

She was nervous, unsure how they would react to this news. Looking around at their faces, she saw Bodric and the others nod encouragement.

"I can't and won't force anyone to do what they don't want to do. But I will ask every single one of you to be trained to defend and fight. Don't do this for me. Don't even do it for Edelaine. We have to do this for those we lost, and for those still here."

Cali's voice broke a little. People around the room were nodding, other dabbing at their eyes.

"I won't let us lose any more than we already have. We are going to start training immediately. Each person will meet with Masters Mac and Holt to see what weapon feels most natural, and we will train."

She looked around at them all, seeing the determination in their eyes.

"Also, we are working out details to begin schooling the children. We have the room, the means, and the resources, and this long winter will be a great time to start. We'll let everyone know when we have it worked out. Now, let's eat!"

Several people let out cheers and claps as Cali returned to the table.

Sarah reached over and squeezed Cali's hand, her eyes bright.

Rowan leaned forward from Sarah's other side, "See, I knew you'd be good at all this."

CHAPTER 35

S ilence surrounded and permeated the house.

Nothing mutes out the sounds of the world like snow, she thought, as she waited for the kettle to boil and watched the falling snow.

It started again sometime in the night before Cali woke with a start, the large fluffy flakes already covering the cleared paths outside.

It was well before dawn, the stead still fast asleep. Cali came down to her kitchen and put a kettle on for tea, she knew she'd not get back to sleep tonight. Chase laid on the bench beside her.

There had been more this time. Her mom and grandmother, and another, older woman Cali sensed was her great-grandmother twice removed. They had shown her things she'd already done, like building the additions and the training hall.

They showed her how the Aegil imps had come silently over the Shattered Peaks, upsetting the trolls, and then attacking the steads.

And then the hardest part to see. They showed her images of

the imps attacking her farm, and how Bethal had stood fast and held the line as they charged. How she dropped many of the imps before they ever came close. How she advanced toward them as she took them out, retrieving her knives from their dead bodies to fell another until finally she was overrun.

The larger, boar-riding imp brought a fresh surge of imps from the tree line, and though Bethal slew many, they were too numerous.

Then the cryptic conclusion of the dream which caused her to wake with such a start, Bethal and her ancestors echoing back the words Eaparius had said.

The one fact about imps I can speak to beyond their brutality and lack of cunning, is they are not oft known to act in cooperation except from the orders of a superior.

∞　∞　∞

Alarmed from her thoughts, Cali pulled her daggers at the unexpected sound in the quiet. Walking silently to the kitchen door, she threw it open, daggers ready to attack.

"Oh!" Thraeston jumped back into the snow.

"Thraeston! What are you doing out here? It's the middle of the night and it's snowing! Come in where it's warm, I was just waiting for the kettle to boil."

"Th…thanks, Cali. I'm sorry if I startled you, I think you startled me more." Thraeston grinned.

"I couldn't rest, so came out and was going to the library. I saw the light in your kitchen and was going to say hello."

"I couldn't rest either. You are welcome to join me for some tea if you like," Cali said returning to the table.

"Thanks, I would like to. I'm glad it was you awake here in the middle of the night, I actually have something for you," Thraeston said, reaching into his cloak and pulling out a flat box.

"I thought you may enjoy these." He pushed the box across the table to Cali as she poured them tea.

Cali smiled. It was a flat wooden box, with a brass hook closure on the front lid.

"Thraeston! This, you didn't have to do this! I would have made you the cloak regardless, and the gloves too!" Cali said.

Inside the box was a shining new set of brass leatherworking tools. Awls, needles of various sizes and shapes, and a set of small embossing stamps.

"Do you like it though?"

"Like it, it's wonderful! I've been wanting to start working on some new pieces, and this is just the thing," Cali said, smiling.

"But really, Thraeston, you didn't have to get me anything. Thank you though, this is, well, magnificent!" She smiled at him.

Thraeston smiled. "I'm glad you like it. It's not payment for your gift, I got this for you when we all went to Furs and Fines that first trip into the Commerce District. I meant to give it to you before leaving Edrym, but of course, we all got busy."

"Oh. Good. I didn't want you to think you had to give me anything in return. But if you ever want anything made, just ask."

Cali laughed.

They sat in silence for a bit, drinking their tea, and listening to the quiet.

"There isn't a more potent silence than fresh snow, is there?" Thraeston said, looking thoughtful.

"I was thinking the same thing earlier. Do you remember the last 15-year winter?"

"Oh yes, quite well, though it's much different in a city than in a place like Edelaine. You never get to experience actual silence in the cities," Thraeston said.

"Coming to Edrym was my first time out of Edelaine."

"Is that so? That explains why you were fascinated by it. We will have to cross the Great Deep and visit Ansivald sometime. That is a true city."

"Ansivald? The seat of Idoramin? You've been there?" Cali asked, her eyes wide.

"Yes, long ago. Every race can be found in Ansivald. Even those in dispute. The rule is firm in that city, and all coexist, bringing goods from all parts of the world. The scope of it makes Edrym little more than a roadside village."

"Thraeston, can I ask you a question? If you choose not to answer, I will understand."

"Of course, Cali. You may ask me anything you like, and I will answer if I can."

"Are… are you Elven? I hope that is okay to ask," Cali said.

Thraeston grinned, pushing his tied back hair up over his elongated ears.

"Why didn't you tell us?"

"It would make for an awkward introduction, would it not? Hello, I'm Thraeston, Elf of the forests?" He laughed.

Cali laughed with him. "I suppose that is true, but it seems as if you, I don't want to pry, but it seems as if you didn't want people to know?"

"I'm sorry if that's an unmannerly question," Cali added.

"No, it's not unmannerly." He smiled. "In a city like Edrym, people treat those of Elven, or even Gnomish, decent differently, you see. The Dwarven-kind like Mac, not as much. And I am sure you noticed there were only the two Tevici that we saw while you were there."

Cali nodded.

"Most people don't concern themselves with things like that, especially people like you, Roland, Midge, Eaparius. But there are those, especially in a city like Edrym, that hold themselves, above."

"Like Riston and his ilk," Cali said.

"Just so, young Cali." Thraeston did his best impersonation of Eaparius.

Thraeston looked thoughtfully into his tea.

"I am a bit of an anomaly within the Elven-kind of the forests also."

"How so?"

"My eyes. You see, of the different lines of Elves, the golden eyes are usually only seen among what people call the 'pure Elves', what is considered the royal Elven line. So, one of the Forest, usually having the darker colors, you can imagine how this would stand out."

"I can see that and how that could cause a young person some trouble or grief," Cali said.

Thraeston nodded. "It did, at that."

"Well, you've no need to hide anything here," Cali said, smiling.

Thraeston grinned. "It does help keep the ears warm to cover them too."

Cali laughed. "I'll have to make you fur ear warmers! Come on, let's take our tea and head over to the library."

$$\infty \quad \infty \quad \infty$$

"Cali, I wonder if I may have a moment?" Cyrene asked as they finished breakfast.

Most had already left the dining hall for their morning work, and only Cyrene, Roland, and Jorah remained at the table.

"Of course, Master Cyrene."

"Roland here told me of a young girl, one of your friends, I believe her name is Flora?"

"Yes, she was hurt during the attack, but her family survived. She's a bit younger than me, with twin sisters who are still quite young."

"It is they that I wish to speak to you about."

"The twins?" Cali was puzzled.

"Yes. You see, one of the skills we must develop as mentors to those up-and-coming, whether wizard, wanderer or champion, is to divine what spark of talent may lay within them. And, whether that spark is sufficiently strong enough to warrant teaching."

"Wait, you think the twins are wizards?" Cali looked shocked.

"Yes, I do. It was Roland here who brought my attention to it, it seems our young mister Roland is quite extraordinarily gifted himself. I've not seen one so young have the ability to sense it as naturally as he can. He picked up on it when he was speaking with Flora."

Roland blushed, looking both shocked and extremely proud.

"I have observed the girls over the past few days. There is no doubt they both warrant teaching. I wanted to speak to you about it first before I approach their parents. I thought you may join me when I go to speak to them."

"Of course, Master Cyrene. I would be honored to join you. Her parents are very nice, I've no thought on how they'll react to this news." Cali smiled.

"It can be a bit of a surprise. But if I am correct, and I've never not been in these cases," Cyrene smiled, "their parents will already know."

CHAPTER
36

Midge, Cali, and Jorah left the side door of the training hall talking amongst themselves, headed to the dining hall.

"Did you hear what Master Mac said to me?" Jorah said, the excitement barely contained in his voice.

"What?" Midge and Cali asked.

"He said he wants me to help him train others with swords! Me! Helping Master Mac!" Jorah said, walking a little taller.

"That's great, Jorah! You are good with the swords, I'm not surprised he wanted you to help," Cali said.

"Swords were never my thing. I've always preferred my staff," Midge said.

Cali and Jorah both stopped.

"You trained swords?" Jorah asked.

"Don't look so shocked! They were small ones." They all laughed and continued walking.

"I still can't get over the twins being wizards. I mean, Flora, and her little sisters, they have always been so, I don't know, sweet!" Jorah said.

Midge poked him in the ribs. "Am I not sweet, then?" she smiled.

"I don't mean anything by it, it's just… I've never known anyone from Edelaine having magick. Bit of a surprise is all," Jorah said.

Midge laughed, feigning a mean look.

"Their parents were relieved, I think," Cali said. "When Master Cyrene and I went to talk to them, they had said that some odd things had happened, bowls had fallen and broke, or doors had opened. I think they thought they were crazy." She laughed.

"Yes, that is the way of it for parents who aren't familiar with any wizards. They don't have any reference," Midge said, nodding.

"I think it's great," Jorah said as Midge gave him a sideways glance.

"No, I really do! I think you wizard types are incredible. And if I can say so, a lot stronger than you let on. I saw that bit of light-flinging you did back on the mountain," Jorah said, pretending to shy away from Midge.

"I have to agree with Jorah on this, Midge. That was incredible. It looked like air, but what air would look like if you could see it," Cali said shaking her head.

Halfway to the kitchen garden fence, Cali and Chase both stopped suddenly, the smile gone from her face.

"Cali? What is it?" Jorah asked.

Cali looked at the forest on the other side of the small barn and snow-covered fields. There were no tracks, nothing looked out of place or different.

"Cali?" Midge said, laying her hand on Cali's arm.

"Something is wrong," Cali said, still searching the trees.

Following her gaze, Jorah had his hands on the hilt of his swords. Midge already had her staff, tensed and readied herself.

They stood silently for several long minutes. Nothing moved or made any sound from the direction of the forest.

"Cali, are you sure? I don't see anything out there," Jorah said in a low voice.

"Yes. I can feel it. Something is wrong. Chase, go to the house, now."

Chase circled Cali's legs, then ran toward the house.

"Jorah, you're fastest, go, quick as you can. Anyone you pass, tell them to get everyone to the dining hall and stay there. Find Bodric, Tom, and any others, tell them to stand guard at the doors."

Cali nodded her head in the direction of the house. "Go, now."

"I'll be right back, Cali." Jorah took off running to the house, telling the hands he passed to get to the dining hall.

"Bodric!" Jorah ran full speed into Cali's kitchen.

"Bodric, find Tom and anyone else, get everyone into the dining hall and guard the doors."

"Slow down there, Jorah. What's going on?"

"Cali says there's something in the forest. She's sure of it, she wants everyone in the hall, and you all guarding the doors in case it gets past us."

Bodric looked alarmed. "I'll take care of it, get back out there."

People headed past Jorah to the dining hall as he came back out and began running back to Cali.

Just then, Firan, Holt's large red hawk soared overhead, screeching her alarm sound. Within moments, Holt and Mac both ran out of the training hall toward them.

Suddenly, an arrow came from the shadows of the trees coursing toward Firan.

Without thinking, Cali drew her bow, shooting the other arrow from the sky as the hawk turned a wide arc back toward them.

Then it happened, the line of imps charged from the trees.

"Jorah, stay close in case they get past me!"

Cali drew her bow shooting the imps as they emerged from the trees. There was no sound, she felt calm, the warmth of the bow flowing through her.

She knew the others had run out to join her, she knew this without looking, she could feel their presence and strength around her.

Another line of imps stepped from the trees, letting loose a volley of arrows before charging at them.

Midge blew the arrows off their course, sending them out into the open field. Roland, holding his staff and muttering, slowed the oncoming imps, a shadowy mist forming around them.

Cali saw the imp emerge from the trees on the back of a massive boar.

Just like the one Mum showed me, she thought.

"Focus on the small imps!" she yelled.

Both Mac and Jorah had stepped up and were fighting the imps which had closed in on them.

Eaparius shot forward a line of tall flames which curved in front of their group like a shield.

She could see her friends in their slowed-down battles, none of them seemed in immediate danger.

The small imps were down, as Cali focused her fire on the boar-riding imp who didn't want to cross the fire.

Then, she saw him.

A large figure stepped out of the forest. Taller than any man she had seen, with more muscle and brawn than five Dwarves put together. His skin was a dark mottled gray, dark as slate in most spots. He appeared to have cracks in his skin from which a dark purple seemed to radiate, almost as if it were lit from within.

It didn't look like the pictures of the Dranoxi, but Cali felt certain it was.

Worse… he wasn't moving slowly.

∞ ∞ ∞

"Cali!"

She heard Eaparius shout from behind her, and Bodric shouting from farther away.

The large figure moved impossibly fast, turning into a thick, blackish-purple smoke, and appearing next to Mac and Jorah in his original form.

"No!" Cali heard herself scream.

Eaparius pushed both Mac and Jorah back with a gust of wind, at the same time the figure leaped as smoke toward Midge.

Cali's arrows sailed cleanly through the smoke and into the ground. She waited until he took solid form and continued shooting.

Midge met his leap with a massive gust of wind, just as he had reached out to strike her.

His fist grazed her as the wind pushed him back, knocking her small form back several yards.

Cali felt a heat pass over and around her, could see a shimmer in the air as if an invisible shield were surrounding her. Midge stood, and they all felt strength course through their bodies. Thraeston knelt behind them, one hand on the ground, the other holding his staff high.

Cali continued to shoot, her arrows lodged in its cracked skin.

Bolts of light as Eaparius sent his stuns, and a sickly dark green mist that she thought was being sent by Cyrene and Roland. It seemed to slow him down, but that was all.

His arm, thick and heavy as a tree trunk hit Cali across the chest, knocking her airborne and back several yards.

She felt fiery anger surge through her as she landed. She nocked two arrows, the bow glowing brightly from within, and landed them solidly. The first arrow in one of his pitch-black eyes, the other in the darkly glowing purple crack over where she thought his heart would be.

He paused his advance, and with a furious screech, fell heavily to the ground as everything returned to normal speed.

∞ ∞ ∞

"Cali! Cali, are you all right?" Jorah had run to her side. Bodric wasn't far behind.

"I think so." She stood, a sharp pain tearing through her chest and side. She pulled her bow and slowly began to advance on the figure. They all joined her, tense and ready.

It was dead.

"Cali girl." Bodric came up and pulled her into a hug. He backed away, his hands on her shoulders looking at her.

"Are you hurt at all?" Bodric asked.

"Is everyone else okay?" Cali asked, looking around.

Everyone nodded.

"Thank you, young Thraeston. That could have been much worse," Eaparius said.

They all looked at Thraeston who just nodded, then Eaparius.

"He cast a protective barrier around us, you see. Else, those hits would have been more severe," Eaparius said.

"That wasn't severe?" Midge said.

Cali almost laughed, grabbing her side as she did.

"Ouch. Yes, if that was a weak blow, thank you Thraeston, truly, I wouldn't want to feel one at full strength. I think he cracked my ribs." Cali winced.

Cali pulled her dagger.

"He's dead, lass," Mac said as he kicked the large lump.

"Thankfully, yes. But I need to be my full strength." She smiled as she cut the palm of her hand, then cupping her bracer.

She knew she would be sore, but she felt better and more able to move.

"Let's go to the hall, I'm sure everyone is scared," Cali said.

"We can guard for a bit to watch for more."

"No, Jorah, we don't need to. They're gone, that was the lot of them," Cali said, swaying a bit from the exhaustion setting in.

CHAPTER

37

As they made their way to the dining hall, Cali saw many faces watching them from the windows.

Rowan, Tom, Dorin, and the other men had been guarding the doors walked out to watch them approach. Sarah came running out, hugging Cali and making her wince again.

"Sorry, Cali! Are you okay? Are they gone?" She asked.

"We are all right, Sarah. They are gone." Cali smiled.

They made room for them, a mixture of gratefulness and awe in their faces as Cali and the others sat at their usual table. Sarah brought them a steaming kettle of tea and a bottle of whiskey. Then went to the kitchen.

No one wanted to leave, and the chores and work were mostly abandoned for the day.

"Cali?"

Cali turned to see Flora's dad.

"Mr. Nomarr. Thank you for helping guard the doors." Cali

smiled.

"I was not enthusiastic about my little girls falling in with this wizard stuff. But I don't know what that was. I don't know that I want to know. But if Master Cyrene and Roland can teach my girls to defend themselves, then I thank you for having her here."

Cali smiled. "Your girls are in expert hands, Mr. Nomarr."

"Thank you, Cali. And all of you." He nodded to them and turned to leave.

Turning back to the table, Cali poured a large swig of whiskey in her tea. As people started to wander off sitting at other tables or heading to their rooms.

∞ ∞ ∞

"I am sorry, Cali," Thraeston said. His voice uncharacteristically morose.

"What? Why?"

"I tried to shield you. All of you. He broke your ribs, Cali."

"Thraeston, yes, he broke my ribs, and he would have broken much more if it hadn't been for your shield. You may well have saved us all, you know." Cali smiled at him.

"Thank you." He sounded unconvinced.

"But, Thraeston, if you are concerned about it, then do something for me. Practice that and make it stronger. I know you can do that if you want to."

He looked up at her. "You are right, Cali. I will work on it."

"And hopefully we won't need it again," Jorah added, smiling.

"Midge, you took a hit too, are you sure you're okay?" Cali asked.

"Just a bruise. That thing wasn't big enough to hurt me much." Midge grinned.

As the hall cleared out more, Cali looked to Eaparius.

"I know that wasn't a Dranoxi, but it certainly felt like it could be. What were we dealing with?" Cali asked.

"That, young Cali, was a Blackguard," Eaparius said, lighting his pipe.

"A what? It looked like a giant. I've never seen muscles like that. What was wrong with its skin?" Jorah asked.

"Quite so, young Jorah. Ages ago, there was a war. A war between Cali's ancestors and a race known as the Dranoxi. Vicious, demon creatures, who sought to rule this world. After generations, and great sacrifice, the Dranoxi were banished to the Undying Night realm."

Eaparius refilled his mug, his pipe smoke circling over the table.

"Much is lost through the history. But the legends say some Dranoxi managed to escape the banishing. They somehow remained here in Idoramin and went into exile."

"The legends also said that being separated and cut off from the source of their evil power, they changed, weakened, withered even. They evolved into a more humanistic form but retained a portion of their former strength."

Eaparius was quiet for several moments.

"Eaparius, you said, 'the legends say' that some managed to remain. But we know that much of the early history of the prophecy was thought to be only legend by those who didn't know the truth," Cali said.

"Just so, young Cali. But the accounts of the Blackguard were believed to be an actual legend. Fae-tales used to scare children into their chores. There was never any evidence found that led the scholars to believe in their existence."

"Until now," Cali said.

"It would seem, my young friends, that the generations of peace which led to the folly of Watcher and scholars alike became Edelaine's folly, for we foolishly did not see this. But I vow, on my oath as Watcher, we shall not fall complacent again," Eaparius said, his brow furrowed and jaw set.

"Wait. So, if the Blackguard are real, and they are a withered, weak, human-like version of one of those demon creatures, then what is a real Dranoxi capable of?" Jorah asked.

He's right. Some Guardian I am, that thing could have killed us all. Where's all this power I'm supposed to have? Cali thought to herself.

The weight of what she was settled in the pit of her stomach like a stone.

They sat in silence for several long moments.

"There is good news here," Cali said, forcing a smile.

They all looked at Cali, puzzled.

"We have evidence they are real. More importantly, we know

who was in charge of the imps."

"That is true, young Cali. That puzzle piece is no longer missing." Eaparius nodded.

"And they've been defeated." Jorah smiled.

As the shock of what happened faded, a more celebratory mood settled over the stead. Cali was grateful she'd been able to defeat the Blackguard with their help, but knew she had a lot of work ahead of her.

The Idoramin Chronicles

http://www.moriganshaw.com/books/

- Edelaine's Folly: Book One of the Idoramin Chronicles

- Edelaine's Fall: Book Two of the Idoramin Chronicles

- Rise of Ruith: Book Three of the Idoramin Chronicles

- Ruith Unbound: Book Four of the Idoramin Chronicles

The Idoramin Novellas: A Companion Series

http://www.moriganshaw.com/books/

- Eaparius and the Forgotten Scrolls

- The Cormac Journals: Tales From the Deck
  Coming Soon!

Hey there… just a quick thanks from me to you for picking up this installment of the Idoramin Chronicles.

Did you know that reviews are the lifeblood for writers like me?

If you enjoyed reading this, please take a moment to leave your review:

https://tinyurl.com/FollyReview

I read them all, and I am grateful for your review!

Until we return to Idoramin, be well, my friend.

~~ Morigan ~~

Pssst… hey… yeah, you… interested in getting your hands on future books before everyone else? Then after you leave your review, check this out – when spots open on my ARC team, subscribers have the first shot:

http://www.moriganshaw.com/join-the-resistance/

ABOUT MORIGAN

Long-time computer geek and lover of all things fantasy, Morigan loves to read, is a not-so-secret addict of MMORPG games, and wanna-be artist and illustrator.

Her biggest goal with her writing is to try to bring the same experience people have loved from authors like John Flanagan, J.R.R. Tolkien, or R.A. Salvatore into her own stories.

After a successful career in web development with multiple Fotune-500 companies, governmental agencies, and local non-profits across the U.S., she currently lives with her son and cats in West Virginia, where she continues to feed her love of MMORPGs when she's not writing.

Made in the USA
Monee, IL
31 January 2021